WHITE SHOES

A NOVEL

EDWARD S. LOUIS

ANAPHORA LITERARY PRESS

BROWNSVILLE, TEXAS

Aɴᴀᴘʜᴏʀᴀ Lɪᴛᴇʀᴀʀʏ Pʀᴇss
1898 Athens Street
Brownsville, TX 78520
https://anaphoraliterary.com

Book design by Anna Faktorovich, Ph.D.

Chapters 1 and 2 appeared as short stories in *Aethlon: The Journal of Sport Literature*.
Characters and events in this book are fictional. Resemblances to anyone living or dead are purely coincidental.
Thanks to Will Paplham for help with proofreading and to Anna Faktorovich for preparing the text for publication. Any remaining errors are my own.

Published in 2017 by Anaphora Literary Press

White Shoes: A Novel
Edward S. Louis—1st edition.

Library of Congress Control Number: 2017937215

Library Cataloging Information
Louis, Edward S., author.
 White shoes: A novel / Edward S. Louis
 220 p. ; 9 in.
 ISBN 978-1-68114-326-2 (softcover : alk. paper)
 ISBN 978-1-68114-327-9 (hardcover : alk. paper)
 ISBN 978-1-68114-328-6 (e-book)
1. Fiction—Sports. 2. Fiction—Humorous.
3. Fiction—Thrillers—Psychological. I. Title.
PS370-380: American Literature: Prose fiction
813: American fiction in English

WHITE SHOES

A NOVEL

EDWARD S. LOUIS

CONTENTS

1 White Shoes

The Hill pours down from the baseball field and the cemetery into Harmon Falls.

I like to run up The Hill from school before we play. It makes me too tired to hit, but the legs get pumped up, and I look mean and muscly for the game.

The Hill is long, a mile up, and so steep I almost scrape my face on the road as I run up it. The spikes on my shiny White Shoes clatter on the road, so when I go fast it sounds like I'm riding a charger into battle.

I like knights. I read about them at the library. In the movies they always look lame. They look better when I imagine them.

I stop at the spring over the hill to wash off my shoes. I go behind some bushes for relief, get distracted by a butterfly, and the yellow drops stain my right shoe. I scrape it in the grass, trade the yellow stain for a green one, then try to wash that off in the spring, but it stays on. I wish the shoes were perfect white again. The butterfly wobbles off. I sprint up to batting practice.

The sun sits right on the hill and shines in the pitcher's eyes. Coach throws batting practice, squints to see the plate, spits, and scratches. He looks like Popeye with his thick, bare forearms. I stretch, straighten my socks, put my hat on backwards for fun, and take my swings from the back corner of the box. Coach knocks me down twice, and I wonder if it's cause of the sun. I brush some lime from the foul line onto the stain on my right shoe to try to make it white again. I don't like stains on the shoes.

I do two handsprings and run to the dugout to get my glove. Doke hits me in the head with a rosin bag. My hat falls off in a cloud of white smoke. I pour a cup of water in his hat, which he does see, and rub some pine tar on the place on the bench where he always sits, which he doesn't see. Boy will he look funny when he goes to the mound, but only the infielders and outfielders will be able to see. I see Mook whittling something in the side of the dugout and wonder what it is. He likes to carve things with his Swiss Army knife.

Coach Luke yanks my hat on straight, I spit in my glove and rub it in to keep the pocket soft, and Lenny the scorekeeper rubs some lamp-black under my eyes to cut the glare. As I run for center field, I turn and watch Coach sit down where Doke always sits, and I nearly shit. I swear. Then I do another handspring anyway.

Coach Luke hits us flyballs. I do the basket catch like Mays, and Coach Luke glares at me. He knows I can catch and throw, though, and I chuck it to the plate on the fly. The ball hits Samula's mitt square in the center, cracks like a 12-gauge. Samula shakes his glove hand like he just burned it on a hot engine. Coach sits tight on the bench, chattering at Doke as he warms up.

Doke takes the mound for the first inning, and I get serious now. I cuss at Slick in right field to fire him up like I'm fired up. I can cuss at him, cause he's only a sophomore, though I'm only a freshman. We don't cuss at the upperclassman, but they cuss at us.

Pudge yells at Doke from third base, "Faha, Doke, faha." That's how he says it, just like that: "Faha, Doke, faha," over and over again. The crickets sound like they're sawing dead logs out in the weeds beyond the fences.

When it rains hard, or when a train goes by down in the valley loud as a storm, I sing as loud as I can while I stand in center field. No one can hear, cause the air's heavy with fog, and I'm way the hell out there anyway. At least nobody's complained yet. The sun's warm today, though, and the air's light as goosedown. I start to hum a little Sinatra just for kicks, none of these guys knows Sinatra anyway, till Slick yells at me that the inning's over so get the hell in the dugout. Sometimes I get caught up in the song.

I sprint to the dugout and pass Coach Luke going to first. He whispers at me to wake the hell up. Coach jogs down to third kinda like a three-legged dog. He has a large, round black stain across the seat of his pants. I try not to notice out loud.

Samula's up first. I don't know why Coach bats him first, cause he's slow as a '52 Ford on bald tires. I'm fast as a mad dog that smells fear. Sometimes I think Coach doesn't know anything about baseball. But Samula is a good hitter, maybe better than me.

Samula's a freshman like me, and when he's in the on-deck circle, two of the seniors get him to take a huge chaw of tobacco like they do. I know he's never done it before, but he doesn't say anything, just takes it and puts the chaw in his mouth like he knows what he's doing, like he's done it before. I ain't done it before. I don't think he's ever kissed a girl before, either, but I have. Yeah, right.

So Samula steps up with his right cheek sticking out like a tumor from the chaw, takes a ball and two strikes and then hits one down between short and third. It takes a hop into left and damned if he doesn't have himself a hit. Coach Luke just shakes his head when he sees the plug in Samula's cheek, but Coach kinda squints at him from third like the sun's still in his eyes.

So Coach keeps staring and then gives Samula the steal sign on the first pitch. Samula stares back.

The stretch. The pitch.

Samula heads for second with his knees and elbows pumping, his face turned straight up toward the sky. He kicks up dust like a tractor on a dirt road. The throw bounces twice. Samula slides. The umpire yells something and signals safe. He can't see very well. That same guy does most of our games, and one time he called me out.

Samula gets up, and when the dust clears, he's standing on second base looking kinda sick. The lump in his cheek's gone, and I know he didn't spit it out. So where do you think it went?

So Samula takes a very short lead off second and stands perfectly still while the next three guys go three and two, hit a few foul balls, and then make outs. Burger hits this pop-up that seems to float like a hawk, hanging forever before it comes down for the third out.

Then Samula starts to run. Wild-eyed, he sprints past the mound, past the line, past the dugout, over the fence and over the hill. He looks green as he goes by. He comes back five innings later, looking thin and white in the face. It's true. I swear. My hero.

I re-tie my shoes, adjust my cap, and sprint back to centerfield, my white shoes gleaming in the sun, cool as March wind. Mook's still whittling in the corner.

I'm just about finishing the chorus of "Polka Dots and Moonbeams" when their guy rips one over Stud's head in left. I go to back up, but it's too late. The ball slips under the fence like a scared rabbit, and he gets a double.

I go back to center, yell to Slick, anything between us you help me with the fence. You help me; I'll help you. Let me know where I am, okay? He yells okay, lefty coming up.

Well I don't get one verse done before this guy rips one over my left shoulder. I sprint to deep right-center like an eagle after a hawk. I listen for Slick, hear nothing, hit high gear, stretch full out for that diving bird, watch, feet pounding, as the ball hits into the tip of the webbing of my glove just as...

You know how they say this black curtain goes down in front of your eyes just as you die? I hit the top bar of that cold, thick-metal fence with my ribs, flying and skying, and that old curtain falls. I mean, I'm in the dark: no sight, no sound, no smell, not even the fresh-cut grass.

Then the curtain goes up. I'm standing, facing the infield. The ball sits half-in, half-out of my glove. More in than out, thank you. It looks bright white white, new and shining, kinda magical, sitting in there. Then I hear guys yelling, throw the ball, throw the ball! A baserunner rises out of the shadows—you know? I let fly a rainbow. I mean, it looks like a kid throws it. The ball bloops over the shortstop's head into third on a bounce. But the guy's already on third. The runner tagged and ran, and he's not only on third, but thinking about heading for home. How embarrassing, I think, if he scores from second on a fly ball. But he stops to think, so he's too late. He stays at third. You shouldn't stop to think. Guys yell all right and great catch, but none of it makes much sense to me yet, as I'm still not back in my brain. But I'm breathing now.

We get them out and my head's starting to clear. As I sprint in, I yell at Slick, why didn't you yell I was getting close to the fence? He says, you got there so damn fast there wasn't time. I never thought you'd catch it. I say, I just told you. He says, sorry. My ribs are really starting to ache now that the juice is gone. Sorry my ass.

So I get to the dugout and guys pat me on the back.

Doke slaps me hard on the rear end, and it really stings, but I don't mind cause it makes me forget the pain in my ribs for a minute. Coach squints at me, but doesn't say anything. I mean, he says nothing at all.

Pudge pops up, so I'm on deck. I try to swing the bat, but my ribs burn like hell. I notice that the sky seems darker, and I wonder if it's because my head's not clear, or if there's really a storm coming up. You can't trust this spring weather. I straighten my socks and re-tie my shoes.

Coach Luke yells at me, and I realize that low rumble I've been hearing is the umpire yelling, batter-up!

Coach squints at me and crosses his arms Indian-style, from the movies. It hurts to hold the bat high like I like to, so I hold the bat low like Coach likes me to. I hope the pitcher walks me, even though

I hate walks. I'm not sure I can swing the bat. But I want to.

I love to hit a baseball like nothing else. Better'n cheeseburgers or monster movies or girls with long blonde hair.

I take a strike. Coach always likes me to take a strike. He says I'm too anxious, got no discipline. I say I'm aggressive. He says I got no concentration. I say it's my passionate nature. He looks like he's going to say something foul, stops, says something like *shithead* under his breath and walks away. That's how it always goes. But he knows I can play.

I remember where I am and notice that I've just taken a second strike. Coach Luke shakes his head. Coach is still squinting.

I take a ball off the outside corner. I knew it was going to be a ball. I could tell by the spin and the arc. I don't know why the umpire hesitated. I think he wanted to call it a strike. Umpires want to do things like that. In our league they wear black shirts and hats, and the plate umpire wears a mask so thick you can't see his face, even to be sure he has one.

Coach calls me from the third-base box. I almost don't recognize his voice, because he hardly ever says anything to me except grumbling something foul. I go down to third. You're letting your arm drop, he says real civil. Lift it more, like you like to. Show me you can do it, so I let you stay in the game. So I see he understands, and I smile and lift up arm and hold the bat up. That's it boy, he says, and pats me real nice on the ribs. I had forgotten the pain for a minute, concentrating on hitting and all, but now it comes back in waves, right where he patted. Coach doesn't smile. He just squints at me, and I stagger back to the plate.

I take two more balls. This pitcher's faster than he looks, but he's got no curveball. Every time he starts to throw it, he pokes his head out twice like a rooster strutting after a chicken, then the ball floats in like a rainbow. I swear.

So now I know the fastball's coming, so I tell my ribs to shut the hell up, and I finally think about maybe bunting, but there's already two strikes, so maybe I'll just kinda throw the bat out with my good arm, or maybe I'll dip my knee into the pitch and let it hit me like Reggie Jackson, or just take the pitch and what the hell, but dammit it's coming right down the middle and I can't stop myself so I swing like a lunatic with all my strength and feel the contact and hear the beautiful wood-on-leather lookout-Sinatra Elizabeth-I'm-comin-ta-join-ya-honey sound to beat all sounds and the lights flash and I black out from pain but the pain's gone as I'm sprinting for first and the ball shoots like a Big Bertha 88-shell and the second baseman makes the play of his life in the hole on the short hop and comes up throwing in a cloud of dust and the white shoes are flying and I'm stretching and I beat it by half a step but the damn umpire calls me out anyway and I can't believe it. I swear.

So I turn around back down the line to get my bat and there's the first baseman smiling. He's the guy who hit the ball I caught over the fence. He's tall and lanky, but he's got no neck, like someone shot him just in the side of the head with steroids. Kick your ass, he says. See you try, says I. Got thirty-five inches you'll have to get through first, I say, shaking my bat at him. Bet you do, he says, and smiles again and goes off.

So I go to get my glove. Stud says, good stick; you'll get him next time. I say thanks and notice that Mook is still whittling.

I go to dust off my shoes with my glove, which is sitting on the bench, and out of the glove onto my clean white shoes spills a slop of used tobacco juice. It had to be Doke, cause he won't look at me on my way out. And I don't have a handkerchief. But I'll get even. Please, God, please let someone hit me a flyball. I'll catch it right in the juiced-up pocket and then shoot Doke a ninety-mile-an-hour person-to-person message, and if he's lucky enough to catch it before it hits him, let him try to explain to the umpire who doctored the ball.

But nobody hits me one this inning. It starts to rain. That's spring for you. So I clean my glove and my shoes on the damp grass between hitters, and my shoes glisten again. I hear this steady metallic coo, coo, and Slick yells over to me that it's a rain dove over in the woods. I think he really thinks that's what it is, so I don't know how to tell him it's a bulldozer backing up down by the quarry.

It's a long inning. Doke is having his troubles, and he walks two guys. The wind kicks up, and it's getting chilly. Maybe I'll dump some rosin in his shorts when he's in the shower after the game.

I get bored. A coal train goes by, down below the hill, and with the wind hissing and shooing nobody can hear a thing, so I start to sing "My Way" at the top of my lungs.

They load up the bases on an infield hit, and the rain falls harder. The next guy hits a short pop to left, and we circle the wagons trying to get a bead on it. Pudge ambles out like John Wayne, kinda sideways, but Stud calls everybody off finally and catches it. I fall in beside him and we head in. He's whistling "Jeremiah was a bullfrog." I smell the wet grass, which smells sharp and sweet and green.

Damn good singing, he says to me. You heard me? Thought you were singing to me, he says. You wish. Shit, he says. Good whistling yourself, I say. I pass Coach on the way. He says nothing. By now I can't hold it in anymore, so I stop him and say, I can't believe you didn't even say good play. He squints at me.

Last inning, I say. Then he says, "If you'd a throwed the guy out at third, I'd a said good play." Then he spits tobacco juice on my left shoe. Then he walks away. Now I got two stained shoes.

I check the bench for pine tar, then sit down in my usual place. Lenny sits by me. Great catch, man, he says again. Thanks, I say. Lenny and I been on the same team since little league. He's not too good a baseball player, so now he mostly keeps score. He sticks with it, though. You got to admire that. He's a freshman like me. He really looks up to me.

Flap sidles over, too. Good hands, good hands, he says. I don't talk to Flap much. When Samula and Lenny and me made the team, we had to run the gauntlet. Right after we found out we made it after practice, we ran to the showers so we could get hot water before it ran out. When we come out, the upperclassmen were standing there in two rows. No other way to get out but right between. And I mean, we didn't even have towels. Somebody took them. I stopped wondering why nobody else hurried to the showers. So this gauntlet, see, they can hit you, but if you bust somebody, Coach kicks you right off the team. So I pound my chest and let out this wild Tarzan yell, like the movies, kinda scare them off, you know, and then I sprint right through the middle. Only a few of them hit me, they were so surprised. I got through so fast I couldn't stop, and I cut my knee on a bench sliding into the lockers. That got my blood up, so I just kept running, out the door and up the stairs and one lap around the gym for good measure, naked as Sunday morning. Nobody was there till Coach walked in just before I made it back to the stairs. He started after me in that limpy run of his, and I think he would have caught me, he was so angry, except his asthma set in, and he'd have kicked me off the team for sure.

When I got back they all gave me a cheer, all but Samula and Lenny, who were looking pretty scuffed up from the gauntlet. After I got out so easy, the seniors closed in on them, especially Flap, Samula told me later. He seemed to enjoy it too much. Maybe that's how he got the name Flap. Anyway, I don't especially trust him, so that's why I don't say much to him.

So now I look over in the corner of the dugout and Mook is still working, but he's put away his knife and is using a round file. There's an almost perfectly round, eye-sized hole in the wall. What you doin', Stud asks Mook, and I get up to look. Making a hole to look at girls in the stands, Mook says. Look.

I look out. The stands are completely empty.

Ain't nobody out there, Stud says. Don't no girls come to our games. How do you know, Mook says. Never is, Stud says, even when it doesn't rain. You never know, Mook says. Somebody might come. Only people ever come is Stud's dad and Smoke's wife, when he pitches, Slick says. She's not my wife, Smoke says. She will be if you keep it up, Slick says. Might be a little Smoke 'fore long, Stud says. Maybe more than one, I say. Whole pack of Smoke's, somebody says, and everybody laughs.

Coach Luke comes into the dugout to find out what the hell's going on. He tells Smoke to get his ass up and go pinch-hit for Bud, who took Samula's place after his intestinal disaster. It turns out while we were looking through the peep hole, Bud got his index finger caught in the backstop where he was leaning, waiting to hit. He cut his finger on a loose wire and fainted at the sight of his own blood. Now he's sitting in the other corner of the dugout with his head between his knees. We spare him the nasty jokes, because at six-three and two hundred twenty pounds, shaven-headed and pale and barfy looking, Bud does not look like a happy young man who would enjoy a friendly barf joke.

You guys must have shit for brains, says Coach Luke. I swear. He says "I swear" just like I do. Maybe that's where he got it from, from me. Coach just squints at us. He mumbles something to Coach Luke, then waddles back to third.

Well, Smoke can swing a bat, but he's slow as a toad in the June sun. He's also less graceful than a camel on ice. The rain doesn't help, either. What the hell, you know what I mean? So on the first pitch Smoke hits a rocket down the left field line, down where we got no fence, and the ball hits the slick grass and runs nearly to the woods. Smoke slogs down to first in these funny stiff-legged strides, looking at the ball, admiring his work, when he gets his steps crossed. He rounds first, catches the bag with his left big toe, and falls flat on his face with a splat. He's flailing in the dust and the mud, and the left fielder still hasn't got the ball. Smoke finally gets up, mud all down his front, but he's too embarrassed to go on, so he just kinda stands about ten feet from first base with his head hanging.

The left fielder finally gets the ball, and after two relays it gets to second base. Coach Luke is screaming by now for Smoke to move his ass before they throw him out. He mopes back into first a step ahead of the throw.

Stud says it must be the longest single on record. Counting the roll on the wet grass, I guess it at about five hundred fifty feet.

Slick comes up next and smacks a two-and-one pitch into deep deep right, but the rain and the heavy air hold it up, and their right fielder gets it right in front of the fence.

End of three and no score. Two guys out injured, my ribs killing me. It's cold. It's raining. Nobody's here to watch: no girls, no parents, no friends. And now Coach Luke tells me I have to catch, since Samula and Bud are out and nobody else wants to do it. And you can't even sing behind the plate, cause everyone will hear and think you're nuts. Damn, I love baseball.

Coach Luke helps me hook on the equipment. The tools of ignorance, Stud says as he goes toward left field. Willie doesn't need any tools, Coach Luke says. He's ignorant enough already. Stud don't understand, Doke says. He's always out in left field. You and the horse you rode in on, says Stud.

Wille: that's me. They call me Willie. Call me Willie, too, if you want.

In pre-season Stud sees me do the basket catch and says, say-hey, Willie. Will 'e catch it, Slick says, and the name stuck. And then Willie White Shoes. Then Fast Willie White Shoes. Now I got more nicknames than I got names. Even my mother calls me Willie now. I think she thinks she named me that. I swear.

So coach found out I can run and throw, and so he puts me in center field, and that's not so bad, with the band and Sinatra out there tuning up and waiting for me and all. But now it's behind the plate for the rest of the day. At least I get to tell Doke what to do. Just let him try to shake me off. But no more white shoes, and no more wet grass, and no more Sinatra.

And we're only through three innings, and my ribs ache when I have to chase Doke's curveballs. And I gotta do this for four more innings. Hell, four more years. Four more years, four more years: who'd want that?

I would. No complaints. After all, what could be better: I'm alive, and I'm playing baseball. And this is the American game. My game.

2 Willie Redux

I was thinking: baseball is like America. It's a team game, but when you're up to bat, you have to pull your load yourself. And while it used to be about working together, it's become about money. And sometimes drugs. Except when you're still a kid: then it's about learning and growing up and playing the greatest sport that ever was.

At least that's what they tell us.

In that way, baseball is about life, too. You may not like the pitcher, or having to sacrifice and move the runner around, or having to play away games, but you can't choose those things: you step up to the plate and take your swings and hope for the best and try like hell.

So like I was saying it's the fourth inning. Yup, we play seven in high school. The rain is falling, and I'm scared the ump will call the game. I'm crouching in the mud behind the plate, rain dripping from my mask into my eyes, my ribs singing "Taps," and my white shoes turning soggy and brown.

In case you forgot: I'm Fast Willie White Shoes. We're talking 'bout a baseball game—what else is there to talk about, 'cept maybe girls? But I don't know much about girls. Notice

I didn't say *nothing*.

So it's the third inning, and Doke's gotta face this Frankensteroid guy again, the one who bounced me off the fence the first time. Chin music, I say—anything but a fastball down the hole so he can spread his picnic over yonder fence when I'm not there to bail out ol' Doke. He takes two balls—we're being cautious—and then Doke hangs a curve a little too close to the plate and Mr. Neck tattoos this comet almost to the left-center field fence. Slick, who took center for me, lives up to his name by hitting a puddle and catching up to the rabbit on the seat of his pants—two bags for the Steroid Neck.

So with two strikes on the next guy, and with the rain and all Doke chucks one over the backstop, and the runner gets third, but the batter gets a pantsload on the next pitch as Doke's curveball muds him and then drops straight over the center of the plate for strike three. They bring in the run on a grounder, and the Neck says, "Yo, thirty-five, lotta jive," as he crosses the plate, but I'll get even. A pop-up to Burger and we're out of the inning, and I'm praying the ump won't call the game because I want to hit so bad I'd sell my sister's left eye to get up again. Not really that bad. I was kidding.

When we get to the dugout, Coach is hopping mad at Slick for not catching Mr. Steroidneck's double. You know how when you go to the outfield you grab a few blades of grass and toss them in the air to see which way the wind's blowing? Well, Coach hauls Slick outside the dugout and says "What's wrong 'ith you? Don't you check the wind?" And he picks up a handful of gravel, not grass, and tosses it in the air, and of course it all comes right back down on his head. We and Slick try not to die, more from embarrassment than laughter. We could hear the fans say, "Like, get a coach, Man," but there aren't any fans to say it.

So now we've really got to think about getting some runs, and ol' Stud doesn't wait long. We call him Stud because one of the prettiest girls in school follows him around all the time. Almost all the time: she doesn't come to games. I swear. Coach yells to Stud, "You're due, Kid, you're due," which sounds really stupid since Stud has hit in every game we've played this year. I swear I wonder about Coach.

Well, Stud steps up and wets the end of his bat like Sgt. York with his rifle—like, why does he need to in the rain?—then shoots a pool ball right between the legs of the pitcher right over the bag into center. Stud, of course, being a leg man, steals second, doesn't even bother to slide. Why get his pants dirty? He's that cool. Burger steps up next and hits one cloud high to deep deep center, but it gets caught, Stud easing into third. Then Pudge waddles up to the plate. Coach loves Pudge, I think because he looks just like him, right down to the beer belly, except of course Pudge has a—what do they call it?—page boy haircut, my ma says, and Coach is nearly bald. Ma knows a lot of shit most people don't know, except about baseball.

Pudge windmills his bat a few times and sends a fly ball to right, which hangs up in the heavy air. It's not too deep, but the right fielder skids as he catches it, and Stud comes flying home like a successful bomber pilot, and we've tied it up, like I knew we would, and only one more guy till I get up. And I'm not too worried about the game now, because the rain has turned to mist and is starting to look like snow, which means the field will stay hard so there's no need to quit, even though the sky is turning from slate to charcoal. I love springtime.

Pecks steps to the plate and strikes a pose, and the pitcher puts a strike right down the drainpipe. I haven't told you yet about Pecks, our shortstop, who bats before me, or about Mange, who plays second and bats after me. Pecks' real name is Gregory, and he lifts weights and plays football in the off-season, but the real reason for his nickname is the same reason Coach has him play shortstop: he charges every ground ball, no matter how hard they hit it, and takes about every other one off his chest. Coach doesn't care if he makes errors, as long as he charges every ball. He could make every play like a wizard, but if he didn't charge every ball, Coach would yank him. He goes home with bruised pecks every night, but Coach loves him, and that's the important thing, along with the fact that he plays every inning of every game, so he never misses an at-bat. I want to take every at-bat. Hell, I'd take all the other guys', too, if they didn't want them. I love to hit more than even Ted Williams did, and that's saying something.

Mange is a different character entirely. His real name is Runner, which is name enough, since all through school he's snored through every single class of every single day, until the bell rings at the end of the day, and then he starts awake, his eyes wide as softballs, and sprints out of the classroom, down the hall, out the door and home. No one really knows how he gets to class; we just find him there, and he's always asleep. Even the teachers don't wake him up. Mangiest lookin' critter you've ever seen, too.

I don't think a word has ever passed from his lips. At least I've never heard one. But he plays a mean second base, even though I think he plays with his eyes shut. He never gets in front of a ball, and I don't think he's ever seen one enter his glove, but he never misses a grounder, so for some reason Coach doesn't care. I guess a second baseman doesn't have to be as macho as a shortstop. Why do we call him Mange? He lives down by the river, his hair looks like a bird's nest, and he wears infield dust on his face every day of his life. What dedication. My hero.

So I don't know if Pecks even swings at a pitch, but he looks damn tough at the plate with his chest and his jaw pushed out, so he takes three and two, then walks on a ball two foot outside.

And guess what? Now it's Willie time, Willie to the plate, gonna eat this pitch whole, gonna take it picnickin' out yonder, yes, and now I'm at the plate, pose cooler than Pecks does, taking my swings, and I'm almost ready when the pitcher slips in a lucky strike, no smoke at all, dangerous with Willie up, and in comes another, and there's no way it's a strike, but the frickin' ump calls it anyway, and now I'm mad, and I spit on my own left shoe to make it shine, and he winds up, and I wind up, and in it comes, and I swing like Hercules, and the crowd roars amazed, if there was a crowd, and I don't feel nothing, but I look around to see where the ball went, cause it must have went somewhere, but everybody's coming off the field, and the catcher rolls the ball out to the mound and laughs at me, and I can't believe it, like I really can't believe it, because I never, never strike out, especially against a weener of a pitcher like this guy, and I'm so embarrassed I could shit right here if it weren't a baseball field. I swear. And worse yet, I'm the last out, so I won't get to bat again for nine guys, maybe not at all if we clobber them and the ump calls the game after five, but at least the score's tied, and maybe it'll stay that way and we'll have to play forever. I hope so. Long as we win finally.

So I try not to look at Coach as I put the catcher's stuff on, but I know he's boring a hole in my back and would like to break a bat over my head, but I'm only a freshman and by the time I'm done I'll hit more homers than he's got hairs on his head, which now that I think of it may not be too hard to do.

Doke takes his warm-ups, and I shoot one just over his right ear to second, and the batter's up, and I notice a fog is settling over the field, kinda like you see in old horror movies. Well I can't believe it, but Doke walks their ninth batter, and the only one madder than me is Coach and maybe Doke himself. Their leadoff guy is tough and quick, and he slips a single tween Pudge and Pecks into left and things are looking bad in mudville, as the rain continues to fall and I may not get to bat again if the ump calls the game.

Nobody's stealing now, probably because my arm's so good, but maybe because the basepaths look slick as snot with rain and snow.

The next guy pops to short, and Pecks finally gets it, though he ends up on the seat of his pants in the wet outfield grass. And then what does Doke do but walk the next guy on four pitches. So we got bases loaded and number four coming up and then Frankensteroid.

Number four, now, he don't look so friendly himself, more like a linebacker than a ballwhacker—maybe Frank's been sharing his steroids—and I swear he's growling. First pitch Doke don't want no more walks, so he puts it down the center, and Linebacker hits a rocket to left, but God bless ol' Stud who looks like a major leaguer to me and who barely has to move to catch it, then sends it right back in, and the runner on third skids when he tries to score so holds up, but things are not looking better cause here's the steroid kid headed for the plate.

He doesn't even look at me, just says "First pitch, center field fence," like he's Babe Ruth or something. I wonder if we should play him some chin music, but a wild pitch might score the run, or maybe just pitch him in or out and make him strain for one, but I got to make him think we're not scared of him, and, what the hell, every man deserves the chance to embarrass himself.

So I give Doke the ol' number one down the pike, and he looks surprised, but I think he's getting cold so he sends it anyway, and Mr. Neck pumps one toward center and the stratosphere.

The air's heavy but the fog not too thick yet, and Slick goes back smoothly but cautiously. He glides clear back against the fence and has time to wait until the ball nestles firmly into his glove. Third out, no runs.

Mr. Neck goes by with this surprised look on his face, and I say "That's right, Boy, center field fence, right on it," but he don't look like laughing, so I head for the dugout.

Back in the dugout Mook looks dedicatedly through the hole in the side wall. The stands are still empty. Big surprise. Mange leads off and grounds to second, as he always does. I think Mange is dedicated to second base, like that's his life. Everything in Mange's life takes place right where the second baseman stands on a baseball field. I think if there was no baseball field here, maybe if no one had ever invented baseball, Mange would be out in the middle of this here field just standing, watching, waiting for something to happen, right where second base sits.

Then Doke's up hitting about a dozen foul balls, getting all the balls dirty so none of the rest of us can hit right, then all of a sudden Mook lets out a holler.

"What is it?" Stud says.

"Girls, twelve o'clock high."

We all run to the hole to look.

Up the road beyond the stands I see two waterlogged girls walking toward the field. They look like they're about eleven years old. They walk into the woods outside of rightfield and disappear.

"They look like they're about eleven years old," Burger says.

"It's a start," Mook says. "More'll come. To see us play."

"Nobody ever comes," Stud says.

Then we hear a crack, and damned if Doke hasn't poked one into left for a hit. The ball skips to the leftfielder like a flat rock over waves, and Doke ambles down to first and stops directly on the bag. Coach Luke pats him on the fanny. I wonder why we do that, anyway, pat each other on the fanny? I hope there's not more Flaps around. Maybe it's just part of the game, you know, the history, like chewing tobacco and tossing rosin bags and cussing and the smell of the wet, cool grass.

We're at the top of the order, and Smoke steps in again, looking awkward as an ostrich, but he can hit. He takes two and then just like the first time sizzles one down the left field line. Smoke knows what he can do, and I think he waits for one pitch, just one pitch that he wants, and damn the rest. If he don't get it, then, hell, he'll go ahead and strike out, but if he gets it, it's boom down the line and bases.

So Doke is rounding second and heading for third, but I'm watching Smoke and Smoke is watching the ball and—I know you won't believe me, but it's true—damned if he doesn't trip over first base just like he did the last time. 'Cept this time he doesn't quite fall, but he looks like he's on roller skates, all stretched out and about to fall, arms and legs flailing, trying to catch up with his body. He does that for two-thirds of the way to second, almost slow-motion, but can't quite get his feet caught up and finally goes face first into the mud about twenty-five feet from the bag.

He just lies there. The second baseman gets the throw, notices that Doke is standing on third looking at Smoke, and walks over and tags him out. Coach Luke helps Smoke up and off the field, shaking his head the whole time (that is, Coach Luke was shaking his own head, not Smoke's, though shaking Smoke's might have done more good). Smoke doesn't even clean the mud off his uniform. He just looks out on the field like he's never seen this game before.

Slick's up next, and he hits a grounder in the hole between second and first. The second baseman bobbles the ball, then throws it into the ground at the first baseman's feet. Slick is safe, Doke crosses the plate, and we all jump up and down and scream like a bunch of ten-year-old fools.

Stud hits a screaming liner to short for the third out, but as I suit up to go back out I notice on Lenny's scorebook that we're now ahead two to one.

Now we're ahead and I still don't want the ump to call the game, because who wants to finish the day on a strikeout? So I'll catch a little more and hope Doke's arm holds out and we terrorize their pitcher in the sixth when I can get one more chance. Just one good hit, that's all I want, and I can go home happy and come back confident tomorrow. Not that I lack confidence, you understand, only that it's a kinda good luck thing, superstition if you will, like always making your last basket before you leave the basketball court or catching your last pass before leaving the football field. Some guys always put their socks on the same way or never step on the foul line or the pitcher's mound or leave one button unbuttoned on their shirt. Me, I like to hit one last good one before I go home.

So the pitch is coming and their batter hits one past Doke toward the bag at second, and Mange somehow gets there without anyone really seeing him do it, and he picks it up without really seeing it and loops it over to first, but the guy beats it by a step. Tough play, I say. And what does Doke do but get upset and walk the next guy, then throw the first pitch to number eight to the backstop so both runners move up. Doke doesn't really like Mange, but, like most guys, he's afraid to tell him, because Mange has never said a word to anybody in his life, and he's one of those guys you're afraid will just all of a sudden blow up and pull a knife out of his sock and slit your throat as soon as you're the first dummy to say something to him.

Well Doke settles down and throws a strike, and then I see that I've gotta have a talk with him, so I call time and go to the mound.

"Whatta you want?" Doke says, kinda surly.

"Zip up your zipper," says I, and goes back to the plate. We do important things in these catcher-pitcher conferences, you know.

So on the next pitch the batter tries to bunt, but as I had called the high fastball, knowing what I know. The guy pops it up, right back to Doke, who almost doubles the runner at third, if only he was a little quicker. Number nine is easier: Doke sends him to the mud with an inside curveball, then pops him up to Burger on an outside fastball. But here's number one, and he's fast, and he's a problem, with ducks at second and third and two out.

To make a long story short, this guy hits about two dozen foul balls while going to three and two, but Doke, you gotta give him credit, hangs in there. My hero. Then a really strange thing happens. Doke throws in a knee-high fastball, Number One fouls it back hard right at my face, and I'm blind for a second, till I realize the ball has stuck in my mask. Everybody is looking around for the ball, till the umpire yells strike three, and Number One is about to get angry, but then thinks quick and starts to run for first base as if I had dropped the ball. He spins his wheels in the mud, and I'm tugging on the ball trying to get it out, but it's stuck for good, so I can't throw him out, so I take off after him. Now I'm sure the guy on third is heading for home with the tying run, so I've got to catch this guy, and I'm right on his heels, but I know I won't get him, so I take a dive at his heels to tackle him, and on the way down I hit his heel with the ball, which is still stuck in my mask, and the umpire yells "Out!" and I'm still a little shaky, but I trot for the dugout, at least to where I think it is, and the guys are running up to me and yelling and patting me on the back, and their guys are screaming at the umpire that I can't do that and the batter should get first base or at least another strike, but I don't hear much of it partly because my head is hurting now more than my ribs and especially because Coach actually says to me, "Good play, Willie." Now I can't verify that exactly, because I was a bit shook, but I truly believe he said it. If he didn't, he should have, and at least we're still up a run. That's the upshot, though they go on only under protest, and it takes the ump five minutes to pry the ball outta my mask.

So it's the bottom of the sixth, and Burger shoots one straight over the pitcher's head into center for a single, and there's joy in willieville because that means that unless somebody hits into a double play, I'll be sticking this inning. And Pudge and Pecks come up and I'm thinking, no double play, please no double play, and Pudge flies out to left and Pecks pops up to second, and I notice the fog is getting thick as your blood in January and now I'm praying don't call the game, please don't call the game, cause I'd give Pudge's left nut to get another shot at this guy, and I listen, and I pray, but the ump doesn't say anything but *batter*, so I'm ready to strut my stuff, and if only Sinatra could see me now he'd have something to sing about.

This time I'm really mad, and no messing around, so after the first strike I really settle in and almost can't stop myself from swinging at one that almost sails over the catcher's head, but I'm ready, I'm angry, I'm dirty, and the pitch comes, this roundhouse curveball, and I give it Henry Aaron's best swing, and I almost fall over, but I feel contact, but not too good, and I look up and see the ball floating out toward right and the firstbaseman going out and the rightfielder coming in and the secondbaseman damn it anyway racing out like a fighter pilot and they're all converging and I hear Coach Luke yelling run, run, and I run and I'm running and the white shoes are flying and I see the ball plop right into the wet grass with a splash, and I'm on first, yes! and I feel like a wimp cause it wasn't a home run but at least it's a hit and you know they ain't going to strike out Willie twice, oh no.

So Burger's on third and I'm on first and I'm ready to steal second, but Mange pops the first pitch to left for the third out.

Only a single. If I could only get one more at-bat, just let me get one good pitch, one good one, but then Coach grabs me by the arm and says not to put on the catching gear, to get my own glove and go to right, and I say why right? and Coach says cause Pizza'a gonna catch the last inning and I'm going to right for defensive purposes, and I say why right, why not center as that is my place and let Slick play right? and Coach says just do what I say, and I'm feeling dumb after only a wimpy single so I just do what he says and go to right.

Now Pizza doesn't usually play much because he can't run, I mean he can't run *at all*, and he's round as a new baseball, but Coach will pinch hit him or put him in at catcher for an inning because his dad's a lawyer downtown, I think, or an insurance man or something like that, and Coach likes to keep the town happy, and Pizza does catch okay. Flap's in for Burger at first, and I'm in right, and the band's starting up, and we're still ahead by a run, and three outs and we win.

I love baseball. Even though I think Mr. Steroidneck is coming to bat this inning.

I'm just starting into "The Lady Is a Tramp" when their leadoff hits a grounder to short which of course bounces off of Pecks' chest, but fortunately right to Doke, who turns and fires to first and gets the guy by a step. My heroes.

Slick turns to me and says, "Man, it's getting dark out here," and he's right. A silver fog has made a thick cloud that hangs over us, outfield and infield both, like we're playing under a dome, and the rain feels more like sleet now than mist. And things are looking even worse when their next batter grounds a single to center, and the next guy rips a double down the left field line. If not for Stud's arm, they tie the score, and maybe I get to bat again.

So it's one out, second and third occupied, you know, and who steps to the plate but the monster himself, and he's left-handed and already smashed my ribs and here I am in right field. I swear. And what I'll do if he hits it I'll never know, because the sky is eating everything in sight, which isn't much anymore. The dugouts are nearly gone from view, and anything beyond them is already digested.

On the first pitch Mr. Neck hits one way foul right that passes into nothing. I don't even hear it fall. He takes two balls, and Doke is laboring, then he fouls back a curveball, then takes a curveball outside. And what do you suppose happens next?

Well, my head is spinning and my ribs are aching and I realize I'm not nearly deep enough in right field when Frank hits one way up into the clouds in right. The air is so heavy I can't even hear the crack of the bat, and the ball just disappears into a cloud, so I have no idea where it is, so I just go to where I think it's going, and notice that the runner is tagging at third, and then I hear a quick *zip* and the ball comes down right at me and I put up my glove and the ball politely falls right in and I grab it and take it out to throw home and I'm so stiff with the rain and cold I can hardly throw and I let one go and it's a rainbow and it goes right back up into that some cloud it just come out of and it disappears again and everyone is standing around wondering what's going to happen except the runner at third who tagged and is heading for home and Pizza who is standing just exactly on home plate with his mask off and his glove up, and even I don't know what's about to happen and I'm thinking what a stupid throw, it's supposed to get to home low on a bounce when all of a sudden the ball falls out of the cloud and the ball and the runner get to Pizza at exactly the same time and he looks surprised, like it's one of those things the priest says about God, it's a mystery, but he holds onto the ball and the runner bounces off him and I see the ump raise his thumb and signal out. Who'da believed it?

Then Slick is running by me yelling "You did it, you did it, we win, we win," and I can't believe it's over and we did win but I wish I'd got to bat just one more time.

And there's old Steroid waiting for me at first base, and I slow down, and he says kinda deep and low "lucky bastard, we'll get you next time Thirty-five White Shoes," and I say good game you monster, and I wonder if I've got another nickname and what will my mother call me when I get home tonight.

I pass Coach, and he says, "Eejots. Be a man, ya dumbass," and I don't know what he means by that: be a man?

But it doesn't matter. We won, and we play again tomorrow, and I'll be back, too. Maybe sooner than tomorrow. But tomorrow, at least, for sure. I swear.

3 My Name

So Lenny and me are walking home after the game, down the hill and into town in Harmon Falls. The rain has stopped, but big drops are falling from the trees onto the cold sogging ground so they sound like footsteps following you.

"C'mon, Willie, you were great," Lenny says. "The catch over the centerfield fence, the guy you tackled going to first base—man, the Steelers should've seen you."

"Yeah, but this is baseball, not football. The tackle was an accident."

"But you got the guy out, and we won, and you got a hit."

"A wimpy single."

"A hit, man, and you'll get a thousand more," Lenny says. "Ten thousand more. Everybody knows Fast Willie White Shoes. You'll be a star someday."

"Yeah, a real star. They don't even know my name. I mean my real name. It's always some nickname or other."

"With a nickname like *Willie*, who needs a real name?"

"Maybe, but a name is yourself, your family, your mother and father, what they called you. For some people, anyway."

I thought about it for a minute. "A wimpy single."

Lenny didn't say any more, so we walked to the bottom of the hill, past tenth and ninth streets, and headed down Central. We passed the Perpetual Life Insurance office, then Nub's BBQ and Tuxedo Shop and Hopies' Bar. Hey, that's what the sign says. We turned down an alley past Tip-Top News, then onto Main: Kay Serat's Watch and Jewelry, Post Office, and by Speedy's Shake Shop, with a neon sign lit up in blue, "Hamburgs." We came to the tracks, and Lenny crossed north, and I crossed south.

"Good game, man—we won. You were great. Be cool. The fans went wild." Lenny is always the optimist.

"Yeah, the fans: all none of them." I couldn't exactly say "good game" to Lenny, since all he did was keep score. But he's a good guy, know what I mean? "Take it slow, Len. You be there early tomorrow for batting practice?"

"You know me, Willie; I always get there right after you do."

"Hope I can hit better tomorrow. You know, Lenny, what I really need is a dad to teach me how to hit. I feel like I'm almost there, but I just ain't quite got it, timing's not quite right, or stroke's not quite right—I don't know."

"You already know how to hit," Lenny says. "Your stroke is great. Man, you swing like the great Clemente. It just takes time. Besides, everybody's got problems. Look: take it easy, Willie."

"Yo, Lenny: thanks. See you tomorrow. How 'bout them Bucs?"

"Hey, man, how 'bout them *Cubs?*"

Lenny has always liked the Cubs.

I turned south past the railroad tracks. I could hear a train coming from up north, calling strikes on its way down. Probably a long one at this time of day, dozens of cars full of coal and oil. Dusk was settling in like a blanket. I passed the Quick Start gas station, the YooHoo donut shop, and Fleena McGee's Beauty Salon—that's what it says on the window in fancy printed letters.

I always wondered what that means, "Beauty Salon." What do they do in there? I thought beauty was like a fastball: either you got it or you ain't. Do they sell it in little boxes, or maybe, thinking of some of the women who go in there, big boxes? Maybe it comes in bottles and they drink it. That would make sense. Maybe *salon* is *saloon* spelled wrong, saloon like they have in the westerns. Like: "Hey, pardner, sling me a glass o' some beeoo-tee—and leave the bottle."

Then a couple short blocks, then turn, than another block, and there's my street, and then half a block and I'm home. Oh well. The maple leaves are starting to grow and shine like oiled leather.

When I go in Ma is cooking dinner, and she's got a Nat King Cole record playing. He's singing "Nature Boy." Like I know it's an old song, but Ma likes it, and I kinda like it too, and no older than Sinatra. It's like it comes from a different place and a different time. I guess it does, but sometimes it seems like a whole different planet, a place where things make some kind of sense and people play baseball all the time. I close the door quietly and I smell something that might be meatloaf.

Ma's head pokes around the door to the kitchen: "Star's home," she says. "How'd you do?"

"Fine, Ma. We won."

"You always do, Willie," she says, and her head disappears back into the kitchen. I follow, hoping the smell isn't really meatloaf, but afraid of what else it might be.

"Not always, Ma. In baseball, you win six outta ten, you're great and you win championships. You hit three times out of ten for your life, and you're in the hall of fame."

Ma doesn't even turn around, just points the spatula: "You play, you win. You go to school, you win. Every day you live, you win. When your grandfather was twelve, he went to work in the mines. Never got to finish school. But he grew up and built a house up on the hill and fed his family. He was a winner, too."

"I know. You told me a thousand times: till the black lung got him. And white lung got Grandma's father from stone masonry. We all lose someday."

"You live right, you win then, too. St. Peter opens the gate only for a winner," she says.

"You told me that, too."

"So you remember it. Get washed up and have your supper. Then you can do your homework."

"Ah, Ma."

"Don't you 'ah, Ma' me. You know what to do. Not one boy in a thousand makes the big leagues, no matter how good they are. So you'll do your homework anyway. Look at me: I never got an education. Now I can barely make enough to feed us and keep a roof over our heads."

"You shouldn't work so hard, Ma." I sit down, and she puts it in front of me: meatloaf. I don't know whether to be disgusted or relieved. Oh, yeah—and there's something else that looks like maybe potatoes, and maybe peas.

"What choice have I got?" she says, and I'm wondering the same thing. "So make the big leagues and I'll retire in grand style. If not, go to law school, and I'll retire in grand style anyway."

"You gotta have the gift of gab for that stuff, Ma. That's more like Lenny than like me."

"So you'll be an accountant, or you'll sell life insurance, or you can be a pharmacist like Mr. Filangelo, or you and Lenny can go to law school together—if I can afford it."

"Or just work in the coal mines like everybody else."

"No coal mines for you, boy, no sir."

"If they were good enough for Grandpa, they're good enough for me."

"You don't know just how bad the black lung is, do you? Well I do. I suffered with your grandfather through every bitter hour, alongside Grandma. Taking care of him killed her. Don't you remember?"

I couldn't remember. I was small then.

"I thought you were old enough to understand pain. You must have blocked it out. Wish I could. No, better to remember. I'm going to make sure it doesn't happen to you. Let's get this straight, Mr. Willie White Shoes: the mines are not good enough for you. You're going to make something of yourself. End of argument."

"Like my father. He left."

"Willie. That's not worthy of you." Ma got up and went outside. I tried to imagine the meatloaf was something else and that I was someone else eating it.

In case you haven't noticed, even my mother calls me "Willie." I finished the stuff that looked like potatoes, pushed the stuff that looked like peas under what was left of the stuff that looked like meatloaf, and went outside. Ma was sitting on the step.

"Ma, I got a question for you. What's my name?"

"What do you mean, 'what's my name?' Why, *Willie*, of course. Fast Willie White Shoes, isn't that what the other boys call you? Everybody in town knows that."

"Not that—I mean my real name, what you named me."

"Well, Willie, William, I guess."

"Uh uh. That's just part of the nickname. I mean my real name. Just tell me."

"Don't be silly, Willie. Willie White Shoes. Fast Willie White Shoes."

"You forgot, didn't you?"

"Willie, I think you're serious. How could you?" She gets up and goes inside. I'm thinking I ain't gonna get an answer, but I follow her anyway. She's in the kitchen cleaning up, and when she finds the hidden peas, she looks up at me.

"We were going to name you Henry after my father or Floyd after your father's father."

"Which one?"

"Neither. We named you John after John Wayne. Or Louis after Louis Armstrong, or Humphrey after Bogart, or Franklin after Roosevelt. What difference does it make? You know you have a good name."

"I want to hear you say the right name."

"You know we gave you a good name. And everybody calls you Willie, anyway. Willie is a good name."

"It's a good name, but it's not my real name."

"But a good name."

"A good name."

"A very good name."

"Yeah, it's a very good name, but what's *my* name?"

"Why do you want to know?"

"Just say it, please."

"Go do your homework." She set to cleaning again.

"Look, Ma, I know things didn't go so well for you and Pop...."

"That's it: we named you after your father." Then she goes outside again. I wish that woman would just stand still for a minute so I could get an answer out of her.

So I go out again and plop next to her, and nobody says anything for a while. I sit on the step feeling like a fool, which is not unusual for me. The streetlights look like fallen moons, and they're almost bright enough for baseball. Ma looks like she could sit there for years and not say a word, and just when I think she's about to, Stud appears out the darkness walking our way.

"Say hey, Willie," he says to me. "Evenin', Mizz Smith."

I say "Hey, Stud," and Ma says, "Hello, Wilbur."

"Nobody calls him "Wilbur," Ma. We call him *Stud*."

"But his name is Wilbur, Honey, and you not wanting to be called Willie."

"What's wrong with *Willie?*" Stud says.

"Nothing. Have a good one, Stud."

"Have a good one, man," Stud says, passes a wave to Ma, and disappears into the darkness.

"Why do they call him *Stud?*" Ma asks.

"Because he's the only one of us who has a girlfriend."

"Oh, well, you're still too young anyway. I hope Wilbur's not like your father—and you'd better never be, either."

"What does that mean?" I start to say, but she gets up and goes back inside again. The woman cannot sit still.

Now, I ask you, what am I supposed to do? Imagine, here I am at Yankee Stadium, a rookie, the lights are up, Sinatra has just sung the national anthem, and the announcer is giving the starting lineups, me in centerfield, of course, and no father to see me play and my mother leaves before I even get up to bat. The air swirls with mist—a night when magical things could happen: inside-the-park homers, pop-up triples, sliding catches on the slick green turf. What I need is a father to cheer for me and kick my butt when I lose. How am I supposed to grow up with nobody around to throw baseball when streetlights draw spring evenings into neverending summer? Where is that boy when I need him, anyway? Long gone, gone as a Mantle homer into the distant night. Never coming back. Long since going, going, gone. Not even a memory.

What would you do? You know, what I really need here is a "father figure." Somebody to talk and throw baseball with, somebody who loves the smell of a new leather glove soft with oil, someone who loves the smell of the grass and the wind turning its face up off the river, somebody who thinks God made every morning for summer and baseball. Somebody like you: that's right, you.

I'm not joking, now. I mean *you.* Come on now, Reader, you're not doing anything anyway, nothing but reading this silly book. Just step on in and play the part. It'll be just like a Woody Allen movie, but better, cause you can imagine it for yourself and the book will still be there when you're done. You can give it to friends, or better yet, suggest they buy one for themselves. Come on now; don't be shy.

READER: Who are you talking to? Are you talking to me?

WILLIE: Yes, you, De Niro, of course. Ain't nobody else here, unless there's still somebody reading over your shoulder.

READER: No, just me.

WILLIE: And me. You play the FATHER part, and I'll play the son. It'll be fun. We'll toss baseball under the streetlights and talk about old times.

READER: Look, I'm not even...

WILLIE: Just tough it out and play the part.

READER: But I'm not your father. I'm not even in the book.

WILLIE: You are now. Really, you always were.

READER: Now don't give me any of that metafictional stuff. I just wanted to relax and read a book. I didn't want to work this hard.

WILLIE: So play along and we'll finish this chapter in time for the Cubs game on TV

READER: Oh, God.

WILLIE: Don't blaspheme. Act like a father. No more complain-ing. I know this is tough for you. Life's been tough for me without you. And if I ain't had enough trouble, think about Ma. Remember Ma? Look at you: here you are, back to see us, and you didn't even bring her flowers. You just pick up the book and start to read. Fine father you are.

READER: If you don't think I'm doing well enough, I could just close the book and...

WILLIE: No, don't, please. And don't try using that ellipsis thing on me either. You got this far, so stick it out and finish. Nobody wants to be a quitter. And you may never get a chance to be a character in a book again.

READER: Maybe I'll just write my own book and make myself a character, something autobiographical. I'll call it...

WILLIE: When you do, don't forget me again, your son. Make me a character in it, too.

READER: Will you stop interrupting?

WILLIE: Sorry. So stop thinking about yourself and say some-thing fatherly.

READER: Like what? I don't know what to say.

WILLIE: Neither do I.

(Long silence.)

READER: You're putting all the pressure on me.

WILLIE: You're right. So think of something while I get a ball and a couple of gloves. We can throw and talk.

(Exits.)

READER: I can't think of anything. I'm not reading because I wanted to *say* anything. I'm reading because I want to *read* something. Now who am I talking to? Not the writer...

OVER-THE-SHOULDER-READER: I'm just glad it's you and not me. This is too weird for me.

(Very brief silence.)

WILLIE: (Returning.) Here's a glove. Ready?

READER: Back already? That was quick.

WILLIE: Things work that way in a book. You can catch, can't you?

READER: Well, yeah.

WILLIE: Mind if I call you "Pop"?

READER: I guess not. Just don't tell anyone. Hey: how do you know I'm not a woman, anyway? They say most novel readers are female anymore.

WILLIE: It doesn't matter. We're both fictional now, so just play the part.

READER: Okay. Hey, why don't I ever get to decide what I say?

WILLIE: You're right. Go ahead and help yourself.

(A short silence.)

READER: Thanks.

WILLIE: Glad to oblige. So what do you do for a living?

READER: For a living? What difference does that make?

WILLIE: I just want to know. I wanna know what sort of stock I come from. Who are you? What do you do? Am I like you? What do you do for fun? Why didn't you come home to Ma and me? By the way, good catch. And your arm ain't too bad, either.

READER: Now that I'm in the book, you can make me whatever you want, since it's from your perspective.

WILLIE: Not exactly. You're still whatever you were when you came here, plus whatever you decide you want to be when you're not here.

READER: Really? It doesn't always seem like that.

WILLIE: Give it a try.

READER: Okay. I'm a baseball player, a movie star, a master chef, and a part-time secret agent. A bit much?

WILLIE: I need somebody real and respectable. Just tell me you don't sell drugs.

READER: Willie!

WILLIE: Please tell me.

READER: I don't sell drugs.

WILLIE: And you don't kill anybody.

READER: I don't kill anybody.

WILLIE: But you do stichomythia well.

READER: Thanks, but that must be the author speaking for you. A kid your age wouldn't know a word like that.

WILLIE: So what do you *do*? You run guns in Africa. You drive trucks with nuclear waste and you didn't want to expose us. You're in the FBI. You were a draft dodger rather than an L.A. Dodger. You run the communist party.

READER: You've been watching too much TV

WILLIE: I got a good civics teacher. So out with it: what do you do? And by the way, do you mind if I call you FATHER instead of READER?

READER: Knock yourself out.

WILLIE: Now you're the real thing. So speak up.

FATHER: So, here it is straight: I work in the deep coal mines.

WILLIE: You could do that here.

FATHER: I work with explosives. Your mother never liked it. Too chancy.

WILLIE: She'd get used to it.

FATHER: And I got a woman and a kid in West Virginia, and a woman a kid, in Wyoming, and probably others somewhere else, too.

WILLIE: Bastard.

FATHER: Me or you? And don't curse.

WILLIE: It didn't bother you in the first two chapters.

FATHER: Well, I'm you father now. And besides, you don't understand what it's like out in the real world. You'll see when you get older.

WILLIE: No, I won't.

FATHER: Wait and see. Maybe you'll get a sequel. You'll learn a lot by then.

WILLIE: Why'd you come back here, anyway?

FATHER: To see what you're like. I wanted to meet you to see if you're like me. I wanted to know if you're any good.

WILLIE: Well, I ain't. And ain't you got one like me somewhere else?

FATHER: Not exactly. And look here: you're okay. You've got friends, you're good to your mother, you play baseball. You got a hit in chapter two.

WILLIE: A wimpy single.

FATHER: But a hit, and you'll get more, thousands more. And you made a great catch over the centerfield fence—boy, I could see that like it happened right before my eyes. And you came in at catcher. And you're going to have a girlfriend before long.

WILLIE: How do you know? Who's in charge of this story?

FATHER: Wouldn't you like to know. But I've got more to say, so listen up. You're going to take good care of your mother and be good to your girlfriend and, and do your schoolwork and practice your baseball and get good and do something interesting now and then to make the story exciting. Go make something of yourself. That's what we're here for, your readers.

WILLIE: And you'll do the same?

FATHER: I'll do my best. Here, catch.

WILLIE: Good curveball. Pop: thanks for checking in on me.

READER: That's okay. Send me some of your royalties.

WILLIE: This book won't make any. My glove is starting to wear out. You shoulda bought me one while you were still my father, before you became READER again.

READER: How about if I just read the rest of the book?

WILLIE: Fair enough. But before you go back to your easy chair—one more thing.

READER: What's that?

WILLIE: Tell me my name.

READER: What do you mean, your name? It's printed right there: *Willie.*

WILLIE: I mean my real name.

READER: Fast Willie White Shoes?

WILLIE: No, I mean the name you and Ma gave me, my real name.

READER: Is this a test? I didn't take notes.

WILLIE: No test, and notes wouldn't help. I just want to see if my father remembers his son's real name. You were my father once.

READER: I'm not FATHER anymore; I'm READER again, notice? Your father is just a ghost.

WILLIE: So give me a break and help me out. Ask not what the character can do for you, but what you...

READER: Civics teacher again?

WILLIE: My name: please.

READER: We named you John, after the prophet in the Bible.

WILLIE: Wouldn't want to put any pressure on me, would you. But you can't do that: there's a John Smith out there already. Better try again.

READER: You'd rather be Zebediah? Tough that out. All right: we named you Joe: that was *my* grandfather's name. So go live up to it. I want this book to be interesting. Besides, maybe that's why we call you Willie, so you can do things a baseball player named Willie should be able to do.

WILLIE: Thanks a lot. The least you can do now is stick around till the end to see how I turn out. Any final words of advice?

READER: Be a man.

WILLIE: What does that *mean?*

READER: Get on with it. I'm reading. So I'll put the ball and glove away and sit on the step. Someone is walking this way again, coming out of the mist....

* * *

It's Lana, Lenny's sister, coming out of the mist. She's pretty cool, but don't you go thinking nothing about her and me yet.

"Fast Willie White Shoes," Lana says, stopping by the step. "How ya doin'?"

"Peachy."

"Who was that you were talking to? Was that your dad?"

"Mine and anybody else's."

"What do you mean?"

"It's not like I had a real father to watch me play baseball and teach me how to hit and how to negotiate a signing bonus and all the important stuff."

"Don't think you're the only one in the world without a father, Mr. Fast Willie White Shoes Cool Stud."

Oh no, another nickname.

"And it's not like you're alone," Lana says. "You have your mother, and she's cool. You got baseball and your friends. Other people get along, like Lenny. And me."

"Lana, what happened to your father? Lenny never said. Did the mine get him?"

"No. He was in there when it blew, but he got out. A lot of dads didn't. But he was never the same after that. Mom says he started to drink, and one day he left. She never heard from him again."

"It does that to some guys. That's gotta be tough on Lenny. I know how it is, having nobody to play ball with you."

"What about me? Can't you see past hitting and catching and who comes to watch your precious baseball?"

"Lana. Wait. Don't go. You're right. I didn't think."

"So think. I wish I had a dad, too, Mr. Fast Willie White Shoes Bonehead. But the world goes on. And I got somebody who stands by me, and so do you, even though you haven't noticed. So don't feel sorry for yourself. Sometimes things drive people away, things they don't understand even inside their own head. So try to get outside your own for once and think of your mother, or Lenny, or me. We know what's it like to be alone, too. I gotta go."

"Lana."

"Yeah?"

"Thanks."

"See ya, Joe Willie."

People are idiots sometimes, and it looks like I'm an idiot, too. The streetlights are shining in my eyes like they're searching for something. I don't know what. The distant whistle of another train coming from the north sounds like a ghost out of the blackness of the night. The front door opens and Ma comes out and sits down beside me on the step. We sit quiet for a while.

"People are idiots, Ma."

"Sometimes they're just people, Willie."

"I didn't mean you, Ma."

"Neither did I. I've been an idiot in my time. And so have you. But you have to live with what you did and go on and do better. You have to grow up and learn how to be a good man."

"Are you sorry about me?"

"Never. Don't ever think it. I'm not even sorry about your father, because now I have you. I only wish I could give you something more, Willie."

"You don't have to give me more. But Ma: please call me *Joe*, at least sometimes, so I can remember who I am."

"You know who you are. You're Fast Willie White Shoes, the best son I've got, and you made yourself that."

We sit together under the streetlight. The train passes with its rhythmic beat and startled whistle. When it's gone, I feel the wind turn from the east, and I can hear the river gently in the distance. I get up to walk there. Even from a couple blocks away the water smells like fish. I hear steady, light footsteps, and Stud emerges from the shadows heading for home.

"Yo, Stud."

"Yo, Willie."

"You're lucky, man: a mother, a father, a brother, a sister, and a girlfriend. You know who you are."

"You're lucky too, Willie: cool ma, cool friends, baseball to play, and nobody else to hassle you."

"But how do you know what to become if you don't have people to show you?"

"You sleep through biology class? You already got the best of both your parents. Now you gotta make something of it yourself."

"The best and the worst."

"So make the best of the best and grow outta the rest."

"I'll try."

"So try. Later, man."

I walk on to the riverbank, where the moon shoots gold as lightning off black water, and the waves press steadier than a heartbeat.

I think about Ma, Lenny, Lana, Stud. Wind kicks up off the waves. Froth grows on the wash and dissolves as it strikes the bank. You can see it even in the dark. The smell of fish hits me strong, and I wonder if Ma has leftovers from dinner, hoping not.

My civics teacher told us this Chinese story about how you never step in the same river twice. No one with any sense would step in this river once, what with the runoff from the coal mines and the factories. But that Chinese river: a name is like that. Not the name you get when you're born, but the one you earn while you live. I ain't just Joe or Smith or Joe Smith; I'm Willie, Fast Willie White Shoes. I'm pretty sure I'm not Joe Smith, cause that's the guy I sit next to in home room at school. To Lana I'm Fast Willie White Shoes Cool Stud, or Bonehead. I'm what you name me and what I name me and what maybe someday what my wife and kids and grandkids and baseball fans all over the country will name me. From now on I'm what I decide to call me and what I can get the world to call me from my desire and from my—what's that word Coach Luke always uses: *tenacity*. Not a bad word. The waves striking the shore make a sound like applause. I'm like that river, *becoming*.

"Will."

I hear this voice say "will." I look around, and nobody's there. I mean nobody. I look up and the moon is sitting there round as a baseball. Is that looney or what? Will: like is that another name or is it supposed to mean something? Did I really hear that or is somebody pinch-hitting for my brain? Maybe don't tell nobody I told you.

I wonder.

Something.

I listen again.

Nothing else. I turn around and head for home. Harmon Falls is quiet as a cat sleeping.

Good time to stop thinking and sleep.

The sound of the water paws at memories, washes away thoughts, at least for one night.

Dreams will come, but they will fade into a darkness greater than night.

Same river twice. Same river twice.

4 A Fan

That's not exactly clear, is it? I'm not a baseball fan especially, but I am a fan of Willie's.

I hope you don't mind if I interrupt for a bit. I'm Willie's mother. I think the last chapter may have been a little tough for him, so while he's sleeping, since it's late anyway—oh my, it's nearly midnight, and the moonlight is pouring thick as milk in the livingroom window—I'd like to tell you a little about him in a way that he couldn't, from my own perspective, and keep up my typing skills.

I never went to college. I did graduate from high school, and I did write for the school paper and for the yearbook. Some people thought I was a pretty good writer, but I haven't tried in a few years, so please be patient with me while I get used to it again. Trying to tell his story feels a little awkward, but I'm not sleepy; I even feel happy here in the quiet, with the smell of spring wafting in the window, since the wind has swung east toward the river. Don't know how it warmed up so quickly after that rain.

Willie's father left me a long time ago. He wasn't a bad man, but he was like a lot of men, restless, and I must admit he was a little cold-hearted. Things are tough in the mines, especially when you thought you were going to be somebody: serving in the Navy, starting college. Then a wife and a baby come along. He never could handle responsibility: too heavy to carry. When the going gets tough, the tough get going, my father-in-law always used to say. Well, when the going got tough, my husband got going, and he never came back.

He did, once, beat his son. I don't think Willie even remembers it. He was teaching Willie how to box—I didn't approve of that to begin with—and I think he got carried away. I know he wanted his son to fit his definition of a tough guy: the one who cuts up the other guy in a bar fight. I married the man because he was handsome and looked more than a little like James Dean. We were both young.

Well, Willie was just a little boy, too little to box, and I think he wasn't living up to his father's expectations, so my husband started to slap him around a little bit to make him mad, and when Willie did get mad, he started to hit him harder. When Willie cried out, that was all

I could take, so I went after my husband and tried to pull him away. He knocked me down, but then I screamed at him, and he came to his senses and quit. Thinking about it now, I don't even know if he realized what he was doing. He just stood there and looked at Willie, didn't even look at me. Then he turned and walked away without a word to either of us. I was shook up and I could tell Willie felt ashamed, as though he hadn't done what his father wanted.

About a week after that, the two of them were in the back yard. Willie had been playing with a whiffle ball and bat. Willie had been trying to toss up the ball and hit it, and his father went out to help him. As I told you, he really isn't a bad man. Well, Willie always liked to learn how to do things by himself, but he seemed happy enough when his father started to pitch to him. But his father threw the ball much too hard for Willie to hit it, and I could see him getting frustrated. Then his father started to tease him, and Willie just tried harder and harder, but he couldn't do it, till finally he struck his bat against the ground in anger. Then his father went for him, grabbed him hard by the arm, and was just about to hit him again, and I yelled out with all my might.

His father looked up at me, and his own look of pleased rage turned to one more of perplexity. He just dropped Willie's arm and walked out the back gate. Willie looked after him practically in tears, not knowing whether to be mad at his father or himself or me.

After that, my husband's drinking got worse, and he left us a few weeks later.

But I was going to tell you about Willie. He loved baseball from the time he was about five. Before that he never seemed to do much of anything, and I don't know what he was thinking about. He'd just sit in a chair and rock, or walk or play by the edge of the woods, but he seldom spoke full sentences, and he'd seldom play with other kids. It was like the world changed when his uncle gave him a baseball glove and a ball one day, even though his hand wasn't nearly big enough to fit the glove.

I thought then he was silly to do that, but I don't think a day has gone by since that Willie hasn't picked up his baseball gear, if only to practice throwing a ball against the garage wall. For the first month after he got his glove he slept with it by his pillow, and he would sit for hours and turn the ball over and over in his hand and just stare at it, as though it were a diamond or a Leonardo or some marvelous invention that could save the world. My friend Thelma from work told me all boys are like that.

He would breathe in the musty smell of the leather glove and sit in a meditative bliss, still as a statue. I think at the center of his little soul there sat some kind of cosmic baseball waiting to be taken out and thrown. Don't know who'd be there to catch it.

From that time on he could never get enough baseball. I went with all the other parents to little league games, but the games didn't satisfy Willie. He would come home and try to find kids to play some more. No one could tire him out. He would want to play until long after dark, long after the other kids would get bored and one-by-one wander off home. Finally he'd be out in the field or in the back alley tossing the ball up himself, hitting it, and chasing it as it flew.

The only times he'd ever worry me came when he got older, when he'd started to walk for hours in the woods above the hill or along the river bank. We live in a pretty safe town, as towns go, but Willie would go walking day or night, and he liked the nighttime, and he'd stay out walking till long after the moon blanketed the river in silver, when you can hear the lonely sound of coal barges feeling their way down south. From where we live, down at the base of the hill, you have to climb up some streets, more in the summer when the trees are in full leaf, to see boats on the river. Years ago steam ships used to come this far, but now hardly anyone but a few barge pilots and some hometown fisherman hooking catfish spend much time on this old river anymore. Most of the boys fished when I was a girl. Now boys with the bamboo poles are far fewer than they once were.

It's like that late-night talk show host—what's his name? Mutch Humbugh, that's it—says: we've lost so much of what used to make America special. The friendliness, the easier pace, the belief that you really could trust not only your neighbor, but nearly anyone you might run into: we used to believe that everyone was basically good. (I guess that's not what he says, but what I hoped he'd say. Mutch is pretty nasty these days.) Now I don't know. I have friends in the city who tell me they don't even know their next-door neighbors. They're either afraid or unwilling or just too lazy to go over themselves, and no one has ever stopped by to welcome them. And not that our town, Harmon Falls, is much better anymore. Why, people will even snub me on the streets, people I've known for years, though thank God that doesn't happen too often. People here may be a bit backward, but as a rule they won't do any harm and may even occasionally do some good.

Please don't get me wrong. I'm no big fan of Mutch Humbugh. I never listened to him when he was on the radio. He seems to me more than a little proud of himself. But when people you went to high school with won't even greet you on the street, something must be wrong with our society. I think he's right about that. What I wonder, though, is why we need him to tell us about it. Can't we see for ourselves? My friend Josie says the problem is that no one will take responsibility for anything anymore. That hits close to home. Everyone blames everyone else and looks for an easy way to make money rather than working and caring and saying, "Here's what I'll do to make things better for everybody." When I said that to May Spender, she just said, "Well who are you to make things better for anybody else? You've got all you can handle just taking care of yourself and that son of yours." But I said, "May, who do I have to be? Shouldn't we all work for each other's benefit instead of thinking only of ourselves? Isn't that what Christianity is all about?" And she starts back, "Well just who are you to be telling me about Christianity?" And then I started to get a little angry, and I said…. Well, you don't want to hear this. Suffice it to say that I wasn't going to convince May of anything. Josie understands better, but even she believes in looking out for herself first, after her kids, maybe. Anyone who's ever been a mother knows what it's like to put the children first and try to get them to go to church on Sundays.

And we certainly don't need Mutch Humbugh to tell us how to think and whom to vote for.

But you wanted to hear about baseball, so I'll tell you a story that will give you all I know about baseball and a little of what I know about Willie, too, and one that I'm sure he wouldn't tell you.

When Willie played little league baseball, all the parents would go to the games and cheer. Those games were whole-town events, even though the kids were small, and people would yell and blow horns and stand and applaud for good plays. Willie played shortstop in those days, and he was very good at it. But after little league, he played on a team where the coach's son wanted to play shortstop, so they moved Willie to the outfield and sometimes to catcher. I never liked when he'd play catcher, because he'd come home with his face so dirty you'd think he'd been digging in the mines with his fingers and wiping them on his cheeks, and he'd always brood over every little play for hours afterward, so he'd forget to wash and his face would break out.

Outfield was better for him. The other kids tell me he stands out there and sings. I've never heard him do that, but a couple of times I would have sworn I could see his lips moving out there. I suppose he could just be chewing gum—thank God it's not tobacco. Yes, some of the boys do that already.

When Willie was just a baby, I used to hold him in my lap and sing to him: lullabies, folk songs, children's songs, you know, like "Kukaberra" and "Wee Willie Winkie," songs that all mothers sing to their children. He'd never listen much to me, though, but then I'd put on a record, Frank Sinatra or Lena Horne or Tony Bennett or Nat King Cole, maybe, and all of a sudden he'd get attentive. He'd start to bounce and wave his arms, or just sit wide-eyed and quiet for the slow ones. He must have listened to those records a thousand times, and I could always use them to calm him down, something else indispensable to mothers.

He'll never sing in front of me, though. Sometimes I'll hear him singing in the shower. He'll really turn up the water, and he thinks no one can hear him. Usually the same old songs, Tony Bennett, that sort, sometimes something new off the radio. I never hear him play the stuff the other kids play, though, heavy metal, acid rock, that sort of thing, though I like the Beatles and Earth, Wind & Fire myself. I don't know whether he really doesn't like what the other kids like, or he just likes to be different. I do know that from the time he was small he never liked loud or harsh noises, only smooth, melodic ones, except maybe for the sound of the trains at night, which would without fail lull him to sleep. But then that has a kind of melody of its own, too, something old and constant and down-homey.

Willie always liked green grass and the sun and blue skies, even rain and snow, actually. He loves to be outside, anything natural, and once he goes out it's hard to get him to come back inside, even for dinner. I think he's just out walking and sometimes running to stay in training; I don't think he's chasing girls yet. When he was small even he used to watch them real close, almost stare, then blush if he knew I'd noticed. He's very shy about that sort of thing. If I'm lucky, he won't start chasing for another three or four years, till he's away from home, and I won't have to watch him turn into his father.

That's not fair: Willie isn't his father, and I don't assume he'll be like him. There's something different about Willie, something solemn, gentler, something lighter, but stronger. His attention span, when he's doing something he likes, is astonishing, and when he's out on the baseball field, he has all the gall and confidence of Sinatra in front of a New York audience.

I did it again, didn't I? Back to baseball. In the summer league before he started high school, Willie played for a coach who thought he would make a good pitcher. Now Willie can really throw the ball, all the way from centerfield to home plate on the fly, but he never had any desire to pitch. He told me once it was beneath his dignity. I think he was just kidding about that, because he has to face the pitchers and hit them, but it throws him into the part of the game where his body hasn't caught up to his talents yet. He can run and hit and throw, and he does everything in big, fast, fancy, graceful movements, like a dancer almost (don't tell him I said that), but when he tries to do something like pitch, he doesn't have the control yet, the fine tuning of muscles to discipline the flight of the ball. Well this coach nagged at him and teased him all summer so that I almost told him to quit rather than put up with it, though I know that would have been a waste of breath. The coach kept saying, "Come on, you're scared of it. You could do it. The team needs you. Don't you care about the team? Only babies and prima donnas don't care about their team." I could have hit him myself. And finally he talked Willie into it in the last game of the summer on a hot August Saturday afternoon. It was actually the last time I got to see a whole game, because of work.

Now that Willie's in high school, they play before I get off work, and sometimes they play as far as fifty miles away. Oh well, maybe I'll get to see him on TV someday.

So I got to the game a couple of minutes early and sat next to Linda, Lenny and Lana's mother. She always went to the games even though Lenny didn't play much. She always said she wanted to be there for the time he did get in, since she'd been there for all the times he hadn't. She had the fear that the one day she didn't make it, Lenny'd play and hit that home run she said he's been talking about since he was eight years old and starting farm league.

I don't know if she gets to the games much anymore, either.

So when I got there, I saw the coach and Willie arguing off to the side of the field. The coach was squinting and getting red-faced, and Willie was standing determinedly with his hands on his hips. Finally, Willie hung his head and shook it "o.k.," and when the players took the field a minute later, there was my only son going to the pitcher's mound.

If you think it's hard pitching, try being a mother watching your only son pitching.

So Willie took his warm-ups. He threw the ball really hard, much harder than most of the other kids, but you could tell right away that he had a tough time getting it over the plate. And the other team, of course, noticed and they started taunting Willie right away. He acted like he didn't notice, but I could tell it hurt him. Whether he wins or loses, there's always one thing with which you can credit Willie: good sportsmanship. I don't know where he learned it, unless his upbringing had something to do with it, because these kids so seldom have it these days. They harass other players, they fight with their coaches, they make fun of the other team—they don't even shake hands after games anymore. Didn't they used to do that? Well, I don't know whether the problem comes from the coaches or the parents, or maybe television, or maybe the kids just have things too easy these days, but good manners have passed the way of spats and the waltz. So Willie just went about his business and tried his best to pitch.

He walked the first batter on four pitches. Frankly, his pitching made me nervous, whether he was or not, and I think he was. I'm much happier when he's playing centerfield, singing away out in the grass, than when he's the center of attention on every pitch. I don't really like it too much when he's batting either. When he strikes out, he'll brood for days. Thank God he doesn't strike out often.

The second batter went to a 3-2 count, and then Willie struck him out. The batter and their coach chewed out the umpire good, saying the pitch was a ball, but you know how baseball is: once it's called, it's fact, whatever may have happened. The next batter, same thing: three and two, then he struck out looking. Boy, could you hear the screaming then. Fourth batter: three and two, and Willie threw a pitch in the dirt. Are you starting to get the idea here?

Well, he walked the next batter on four pitches—upset by the bad ball, I'm sure—to load the bases. The funny thing was that not one of their players had swung at a pitch yet. I don't know how the coaches expect the kids to learn if they won't let them swing. But I suppose learning isn't the purpose of sports anymore, or even having fun; coaches and kids alike have accepted, what is it that football coach said: "Winning isn't everything; it's the only thing."

Well I never bought that, because winning can mean different things to different people, and you can't win every time and every day. As Willie says, "Win six out of ten, you win the pennant; hit three times out of ten, you're in the Hall of Fame." And as Willie's mother says, "Go play and have fun. You'll have to do real work soon enough."

So there is my only son on the mound, bases loaded, two out, and his mother sitting in the hot August sun trying not to pass out from baseball, the heat, and the worry. Next batter: ball one; ball two; strike one—we cheer for our team. Then on the next pitch their batter swings, the first swing yet, and hits one foul past third base. You should have seen their coach glare at that poor boy. Certainly I didn't want to see him get a hit off Willie, but I had to feel sorry for him. There he is, trying to play the game the right way, and all their coach wants to do is make a fool out of my son.

So their coach called the boy over, whispered something in his ear, and hit him hard on the rear end. That's something I've never understood about baseball: why do they do that, hit each other on the rear end? Coaches do it to the boys, the boys do it to each other, sometimes playfully, sometimes hard, like they want it to hurt. Is it a punishment? Are they making up for getting spanked? Is it that stuff they call "male bonding"? Personally, I don't like it; it looks like abuse to me, and I think discipline's the parent's job.

So their boy went back to bat, and everyone was cheering, shouting out directions on both sides, "Fastball," "Curveball," "Swing," "Wait for a good one." Everyone is always full of advice. But I have to say I was proud when Willie threw one right down the middle and their boy swung and missed. Then I hoped that Willie wouldn't have to go back out to pitch the second inning.

But he did. In fact, he pitched the whole game, and every inning went just like that, except in the second inning he hit one of their batters. And in the fourth, and twice in the sixth. I got mad at him at the time, thinking he was getting even for their taunting him, which was cruel, if you ask me, but he told me later that he was trying his best to get the ball over the plate, and hitting them hurt him as badly as it hurt them. I don't know about the hurting part, but I do know Willie, and he was telling me the truth. I've also heard him say he loves it when the opposing pitcher hits him, because that's an easy way to get on base, but I prefer when that doesn't happen. Why get hurt and lose a chance at a scholarship? That's the very reason I made Willie promise he wouldn't go out for football. He didn't, but then I don't think he likes football that much anyway.

They did get one hit off him, an infield single. I counted two infield errors and ten walks, four ground outs, one pop out, and sixteen strikeouts, not to mention the four beanballs. Their team scored two runs, and ours got one. I think the thing that bothered Willie the most was that he didn't get a hit. He grounded out once, hit a nice long fly to left that they caught, because the outfielders play him almost all the way out to the coal piles beyond the outfield, and stuck out once. He hates it when that happens.

They never made him pitch again, but I have to say the game was exciting. I bit my nails and yelled like everyone else all the way through. Not at the other kids, though: only to Willie to do his best. I am glad he doesn't pitch anymore. I mentioned it to him on the way home, asked if they would make him pitch again, and he said, not if he could help it. I said that would be fine by me.

I'm sorry I said that, since actually it doesn't matter if I get nervous. The important thing is that Willie plays and has a good time, and that he and the other boys grow up right. That's what I should have said: pitch if you want, but preferably when I'm not there. Though now, as I look back and ahead, I'd be happy to watch him pitch or do anything, just so I could see him playing the game he loves.

Oh, if you're curious: I think he took about a week to get over that strikeout, though he tells me that he can remember every time at bat he ever had since he first played little league, even farm team. Imagine living with all that in your head. And Willie says that baseball is fun. At least I get dinner right about eight times out of ten. Does that mean I'm ready for the Hall of Fame? And I did get a raise on my job last month, though there's not much future for me in it. I wish I could start again and go to college myself, but as the boys like to say, "Not in this lifetime." Life may be simple but it isn't always easy growing up in a mill or mining town.

I'd like to tell you a little more about myself, get acquainted, but that's not what I'm here for. I suppose you'll learn more about me by learning about Willie, and if you like these stories maybe I'll have a chance to speak for myself sometime.

The moon has risen in the sky, and it's past one o'clock—and I do have to get up in the morning. The air is still, but cool, and the sky is shimmering with stars. Looks like tomorrow will be a baseball day. I'll just check the door, leave the window open a crack, and turn off the light.

("I found this story when I got up in the morning. I get the feeling that my story isn't just my story anymore. Ma's a good egg, but she doesn't understand baseball that much. The beanball is part of the game, everybody knows that, and I don't mind when they hit me. The guys only called me "The Bean Machine" for about a month after that. Or didn't she tell you that part?

She was right about one thing, though: I'd rather get stung by a hive-full of bees than strike out. Oh, and I do remember every at-bat since little league. Doesn't everybody?

And her handwriting is amazing, like something an artist would do, so too bad she typed her story. Good thing you don't have to read my handwriting, or you wouldn't think I was smart enough to be writing this. But then again, maybe you don't think I'm so smart anyway. Well, whether I'm smart or not, you just find yourself on third base someday and me playing centerfield, and a fly ball hit to me, and you go ahead and tag up and head for home, and we'll just see who gets to home plate first, you or the ball. But don't expect to see me ever again on the pitcher's mound. I swear."—Willie)

5 The Homer That Was Only a Double

I hear ya been talkin to That Damn Willie. Now I jus wanted to tell ya what it's like to coach a buncha these kids, so ya don' jus see his side a things.

Ya gotta scuse me, but when ya been round baseball long as I have, ya get ta talkin this way, y'unnerstan what I mean? Ya forgit about things like verbs and apoxtraphees, as yuns'll fine out when yuns get older. I'm Coach, case you didn't figger it out.

So we's playin at Wormwood, see, that's this little town across the river where there's a steel mill my daddy used ta work at for a while, years ago, back when people used ta work hard an you'd see barges on the river any time a day or night, an you could smell the mills workin three shifts, any time ya woke up. I worked there a bit, too. So like I say we's at Wormwood for a game, an they ain't none too good an we ain't none too bad, but that don't garn-tee we's goin to win, baseball bein' baseball, an when ya got kids like That Damn Willie on yer team, they're likely ta find a way ta lose if they can.

Coupla years back I kin remember we lost 6-1 when our kid pitched a no-hitter, this kid called Scuz, that's what the kids called im, but 'is name was Blanik or somethin Polish like that, not that I mind, the Polacks being as good as anybody else, workin in the mill and makin money so their kids can play baseball an all. That was even back before we had That Damn Willie, who dammit is only a freshman, which means I got ta put up with im four years, though I must admit 'ee ain't that bad a player, though 'ee does stupid things like sing in the outfield even though 'ee don't know I know. An I got this black stain on the seat of my pants now an I know 'ee had something ta do with it, prob'ly pine tar or lampblack he put on the bench when fer a minute I wasn't lookin. You always gotta look. Remember that. But as long as mostly we win I'll play 'im, cause 'ee can run an throw, an fore long 'ee'll learn ta hit pretty good, too, though some days I hope we'd lose so I can just put 'im on the damn bench an be done with it.

So we're playin in this little town called Wormwood an takin b.p. before the game an Coach Luke is talkin ta That Damn Willie who's takin b.p. with is hat on backwarts damn im an says to im how about that short rightfield fence, you like ta hit ta rightfield, an That Damn Willie stops fer a minute ta look an I say don' even think about it or ya won't hit nothing, just hit like you hit an maybe ya won' strike out an maybe even you'll git a hit if yer lucky today, an he jus kinda looks at me wide-eyed an then tries even harder ta hit one over the rightfield fence.

Ya don't wanna give 'em big heads, ya know, these kids. They got it so easy today, anything they want. We had ta work hard. I carried water at the railroad yard when I was fourteen, an milked cows when I was younger. Times was tough, so ya couldn' even drink any a the milk.

Sometimes That Damn Willie ain't such a bad kid. Like 'ee runs up the hill ever day before practice when the other kids ride up in cars. He could be a pro someday if 'ee growed a little an got better an didn't smoke cigarettes like so many kids is doin today, though I don' think 'ee does, 'ee's not that kind a kid. Damn things burn up yer lungs. I seen what they did ta my father along with workin in the steel mill, galvanized an bucket line, forty years. The way these pros play today it takes three hours for a game an they make so damn much money they don't care bout nothing.

They don't love ta play the way we did when we were kids.

Today with the kids ya gotta kick their butts or they all start ta strut real cocky like they was major leaguers, an smokin cause they don' know what the steel mill does ta ya.

So we're takin b.p. and Luke puts one on the outside corner an That Damn Willie pops one out ta the base a the fence in right, which means he'll probably strike out three times today tryin ta do it again so I better bat him eighth. Pecks, our shortstop, takes the next one, a hot one, off the chest. Now there's my kinda ballplayer, like we was in the old days. Charges every ball like is life depended on it, an in a way, it does. Ya always got ta hustle. Ya always got ta care, or ya might as well just dry up an blow away cause ya might as well be dogshit.

We finish batting an I fill out the lineup card. Bud, this big, tall, strapping kid warms up Lowry, our lanky left-hander, but Samula puts on the gear ta catch fer the game. I thought that damn Samula was a good kid, but 'ee damn near choked hisself last game when 'ee took a chaw from one a the other kids. I don't say much cause I like a chaw now an then maself, but I shoulda suspended im a game. But with Bud havin one a them band-aid things on 'is finger an tendin ta faint at the sight of is own blood, I gotta give Samula the go. He does catch good, an 'ee knows how ta git on base. He could teach That Damn Willie a thing er two. You tell im I told ya so, y'unnerstan what I mean?

So we got about the same lineup as usual, which ya already know, but then we bat first since we're visitors, so I pat Lowry on the back an says go get, 'em, kid, then tell Samula ta take a few pitches an tell all of 'em especially That Damn Willie ta make im pitch, Wormwood's pitcher, that is, so what does Samula do but swing at the first pitch, a ball outside. Whataya sposed ta do with these knuckleheads? I swear.

So I notice That Damn Willie is starin at me kinda tri-umphant like, like to say, see, I tol ya, ya shoulda batted me first, an I wanna throw something at im from the third base coaching box, but Samula walks on five pitches an I feel better, if y'unnerstan what I mean.

So Slick's up next an he's a smart player if you can believe that, even if 'ee ain't the best we got, an 'ee takes two an two, then I give Samula the run sign an 'ee does an Slick takes outside an Samula runs hard like real hard but 'ee ain't none too fast an damn 'ee actually gets thrown out at second.

An whattya think but That Damn Willie is starin at me agin an I'm gettin madder and madder when Slick chips a single inta right so's I'm feelin better agin. Maybe I should retire an buy me a little boat out on the lake an jus spend all day fishin, y'unnerstan, a little perch, a little bass, maybe now an then go trout fishin up north.

Then Pudge takes one an two, an Slick steals second though I don' remember givin im the singnal, but Pudge pops out ta short center an we got two down. Burger is up next an ya never seen a slower guy in your life, slower'n dogshit, an 'ee takes two, fouls one off, then grounds out ta short, an we git nothin outta a walk an a hit.

I go inta the dugout an our kids go on the field an That Damn Willie kinda glares at me as he goes by an I come that close to tellin im jus ta stay on the bench an sit this one out, but instead I think maybe I'll find a way ta git even.

Lefty Lowry heads for the mound an I tell im ta throw strikes, he got a team behind im, an that ain't far from right cause these kids play pretty good defense for a buncha knuckleheads.

Lowry looks smooth today but 'ee throws too many curveballs. I tell im not ta do that, save is arm, he may need it when 'ee grows up, but who can tell a kid anything, y'unnerstan what I mean? I swear.

("By the way—Lowry's name is Clem, and we call him Clem, and he ain't got no nickname, cause with a name like Clem, who needs a nickname?"—Willie)

So Lowry ain't got much speed but is ball moves, an all these Wormwood kids can't wait to get at im, which is good cause they git overanxious an swings at bad balls, an they do get an infield hit, but that's all, an their cleanup guy bloops one inta left-center That Damn Willie catches backhand on the run just off is shoetops fer the last out. An all the guys cheer but I jus head for the third base coaching box an don't say nothin' even though 'ee stares at me. He's one a those kids hits better when ee's mad, an ya know ya don' wan' em ta git a big head.

Since these is jus kids an I don' want ta bore yuns, I'll quit the play-by-play an jus give ya the highlights, like they do on TV, but these Wormwood guys ain't that good an we start ta hit em. Stud gits a double down the line an Pecks moves im ta third with a single. Pecks steals second, Mange grounds out an the run scores, Pecks moving to third.

Who's up now but That Damn Willie, an I wanna kick his butt, but I jus tell im "Make im pitch." So what does 'ee go an do but swing at the first pitch, high an outside so he has ta stretch ta git it, an he pops it inta center, but deeper'n I thought at first, takes the guy almost back ta the fence, then back ta the fence, then up agin the fence—then 'ee starts running in an catches the ball an wings it home, but Peck scores easy an we're up two-one. Ya gotta love this game.

That Damn Willie looks at me again like, look, I got a sacrifice fly, but I think, if you hadda ounce a brains you'd a waited a pitch or two an got a hit, an then I think: shithead. But Lowry grounds out an the inning's over an I go back ta my spot on the bench an say good job, men, an sit down in my spot an this puff a white smoke rises aroun me like a cloud, sticks in my nose like the dusty smell in yer basement in August, an I know somebody put a pile a rosin on my spot an I cough an cuss an I hear snickerin' as they go out an I jus know it had to be That damn Willie.

Doke an Smoke is sittin in the corner a the dugout actin like they didn't see nothin, but I know it couldn't a been them. They's both pitchers, an pitchers wouldn't do that ta somebody, only hitters. I used ta be a pitcher in my time, not bad if I do say so maself, but my arm gave out from too many curveballs too young, y'unnerstan what I mean.

Well ta be short about it we git another run in the fourth, an woulda had another but That Damn Willie strikes out. Not only that, but 'ee fouls off about ten balls first, usin' up just about every one we got, an we got to pay for those damn things. An then 'ee fans on one in the dirt.

Knuckleheads, I swear.

Wormwood too gets a run in the fourth an it's a long inning, Lowry walking two an in the hole on ahmost every batter. Jus throw strikes, I says, but 'ee don' listen. I could swear I hear That Damn Willie singin in the outfield, an I wanna yank him so bad I could piss, but he runs down a flyball at the fence ta end the innin, so I let it go. These is after all jus kids.

I wish they had a sense, y'unnerstan what I mean, a' the history of baseball, how ever time they go out there they play right longside Ruth, Gehrig, Dimaggio, Mays, Clemente, Aaron, Ryan, all them guys, dead or alive. Maybe then they'd take it serious. Maybe not.

Then we git the bases loaded in the fifth an two out. Yoo guessed it: That Damn Willie again. He's hopping around the batter's box like a jackrabbit in heat, but 'ee akchaly maneeges ta take a coupla pitches, then fouls off some an runs the count ta three an two, an I yell down don' be anxious, let im come ta yoo, then 'ee swings at one damn near over is head but gets just a piece, an then I don' know why gits a fastball down the middle an drives it ta left, deep, deep, an the leftfielder snags it on the run. Hellava catch, I swear, an in another park it coulda been a homer.

That Damn Willie rounds second and comes toward me with this look on is face like to blame me, like I caught the damn ball. I swear.

Well in the sixth our Lowry falls apart. He pitches a good five, but 'ee isn't strong enough for six, so 'ee walks one an I call Smoke to warm up, an Lowry gets one out an then gives up a hit, an I go slow out ta the mound an when the ump starts ta squawk I call in Smoke, who gets one out, then gives up a hit ta right ta tie the score.

Throw strikes, I says, but nothin too good. An their leftfielder lines a single ta center, an the runner rounds third an heads fer home, an That Damn Willie picks it up on the hop an shoots one fer the plate, an Samula takes the throw on the fly an blocks the plate, an that runner ain't goin nowhere but back ta the dugout disappointed. That Samula is really a ballplayer.

An the kids come in an I say, o.k., o.k., good job, we're due for a run, an That Damn Willie stares at me again so's I'd like ta bust im, but 'ee is justa kid, so what can ya expect?

So we got ourselves a tie ballgame inta the seventh, an with two runners on—I know ya can't hardly believe this—who's ondeck but That Damn Willie. I call Bud an say git ready ta hit if we need ya, an That Damn Willie looks at me like if I pinch hit fer im 'ee'd have two strokes an die on the spot, so I figger maybe I better not. He runs up ta the plate an digs in an takes a pitch, a strike, an I begin ta think that maybe it's a good idea ta scare 'em as well as git 'em mad.

An then 'ee looks at me like, see, Coach, I took a strike, ya idiot, an I turn aroun ta call Bud, but I'm too late cause the ball's comin in, an it's outside, but That Damn Willie swings an the ball flies high out ta right an keeps flyin an flyin an the rightfielder jus watches it fly an he's all for-loren like it was a duck 'ee missed with is shotgun an the ball keeps flyin an flyin over the fence an over the trees an inta the park yonder.

An I think homer an then I think, no, double, groun' rule double, cause a the short fence, an kick myself I can't help but feel bad for That Damn Willie, cause 'ee really peppered it.

He rouns second at a run, then the ump stops im an sens im back. I spect im ta let out a whoop an holler, but 'ee doesn't—jus looks at me fer a secon, hangs is head, an trots back to the base. He doesn' say a word. I didn' think 'ee had that much class.

I wanna argue with the ump, but what can ya say? Thems the groun rules.

Well we git two that inning, so we'z up 5-3 an gotta hold 'em for three outs only.

So I sen Smoke in ta pitch the seventh. For you who don' know, we only play seven in high school ball. I bet That Damn Willie din' tell ya that an left ya confused.

An I go back ta my coat pocket ta git a chaw, an grab a hanful outta my Red Man, an stuff it my jaw, an whattya think I git but a cheekfool a' wood shavins an moss. So's I spit it out an cuss an you know as well as I do who did it. Smoke is out on the moun, an Doke like a good pitcher has called Bud ta warm im up case we need an out at the end a the inning. Who else could it a been but That Damn Willie, who's out in centerfield warmin up an lookin as innocent as some damn puppy who jus crapped in yer garden. I swear.

So they git one run with two out an a guy on secon an I'm jus about ta call Doke ta go in for the las out but I can't fin' im an I wonder where 'ee went when Wormwood's guy gets a single inta cenner an my heart starts ta wobble a bit.

An That Damn Willie comes runnin in again an scoops it up an fires it in an Samula gets it right exactly on the plate on one hop jus the way it's sposed ta be an is waitin there long enough he coulda had a samwich an a cup a coffee fer the guy ta come in who slides an is tagged out an we win an I ahmos have forgot about the wood shavins in my Red Man chaw, y'unnerstan what I mean?

It's good ta win, even with a buncha knuckleheads like this one. An baseball is always good, whether ya win or lose, though don' tell nobody I tol ya so, as long as ya care an play like it means somethin to ya, cause if ya play ya ain't in the mines an ya ain' at war, yer playin, an yer workin hard ta play better, which is zactly what life should be like, gettin better an not hurtin nobody an havin a good time. An there ain' no better time than a good day at the ol ballyard.

So they's all congratulatin That Damn Willie fer throwin two guys out at the plate in one game an I don' say nuffink, but I pat 'em all on the back an say good game, cause they all played good and we're a team, an That Damn Willie looks at me like 'ee's goin to say, see, on one hop, jus like it was supposed ta be, but 'ee jus kinda lets outta sigh an says, Coach, I thought I had a homer, it was over the fence, it shoulda been a homer.

An I say, the world's made a shoulda beens an has-beens, but ya got a double an we won the game, an there's another game tomarra, an homers anough ahead. Though, of course, an I don' say this part, ya never really know for sure, so ya gotta injoy every double an single jus like they was homers, y'unnerstan what I mean? An then I spit on is white shoe, curse about my tabacca, an I walk away.

An that's about it, an we won, an that's all I got ta say, othern don' believe everthing That Damn Willie tells ya. We try ta turn them kids inta men, but it's a waste a time.

Though he ain't all that bad. So that's the end a the story, and good-bye.

* * *

"You gotta 'scuse Coach: had to have his say. I think maybe he graduated from high school. He don't write too good, but you got the idea, that we won, an ol' Fast Willie White Shoes didn't have too bad a game for himself, though I will always remember that double as the homer it should've been.

Whatever the world says is real, you gotta remember yourself what you *know* is real, or at least what you think you know is real, cause that's the important thing, what happens right inside your own head, yours and mine both. That's finally all you know for sure.

Though I hope you don't listen to Coach too seriously, cause I didn't put the rosin mound on his spot, and I didn't put the wood shavings in his Red Man. It was Doke who did it, and you can believe it, though I don't say I wouldn't do such a thing. Doke and Smoke were laughing about it after the game, and Doke said it was funnier 'n horseshit. Now I don't know what's especially funny about horseshit, but sometimes guys just say that sort of thing.

And I hope I ain't got no more new nicknames, cause I got more than enough already.

The wind is up and shoots over the field like a fastball, and I'm hungrier than a junkyard dog on Monday morning. So for now, be seein' ya. Matter of fact, why'n't you just drop by the park for our next game. We could use some fans. Me and Sinatra will be waiting for ya, singing in the outfield.

But whatever, I'll know till I die and after that I hit one whamalang homer today, even though it was only a double. And now you know it too, and that makes me feel better."

—Willie

Yeah, Coach does sound like that.

—Stud

6 Facing Up

Things have got out of control around here, with everybody wanting to jump in and say somethin': but I'm back now. This is my story, right, so I should get to tell it?

I suppose you're wondering why I didn't mention what Ma wrote about my father. I always had this image, ya know, kinda in the back of my mind, but I never knew where it came from. Now I know why Ma always insisted I stay outta fights: she didn't want me to turn out like him or worse. But then nobody ever told me that he got in lots of fights. He probably just wanted me to be tough, because he knew I'd need it.

Don't worry: I'm not looking for trouble. 'Sides, who wants to break a hand on somebody's face so you can't swing a baseball bat with a broken hand, anyway?

Sometimes I do wonder where he really is now, the old man. Probably dead on the floor of some bar after taking the butt-end of a bottle upside his skull. Or maybe in jail after using that bottle on somebody else. Or maybe off with some other woman making more baseball players. I just hope they're not pitchers.

Or maybe he's just a ghost.

Maybe I do watch too much TV But I like old movies late at night, when Ma will let me watch them, especially the old black-and-whites with detectives and fog and rivers and stuff.

And there have been times when I could have used some more of those boxing lessons. We don't exactly have gangs in Harmon Falls like they have in the The City, but we got our share of guys looking for trouble. Some of them are football types or ex-football types who never could do anything else, and some of them are dope-heads or metal-heads, but most of those guys are cool and don't really want trouble. Mostly it's guys who grew up tough (probably getting beat by their fathers to start with, or maybe with no fathers to begin with) and never wanted to be bothered with sports or anything else. They just get their kicks outta kicking the shit outta people or scaring people into believing they will.

What a world, huh? I swear.

You probably don't believe me when I tell you that baseball is a civilizing influence. Yeah, there's that Civics class again. You think of beanballs and base-brawls, spit-streams and cheek-chaws and ball-scratching and managers who can string together a line of cuss-words longer than a midnight freight train. But that ain't what I'm talking about. That's just the toughness thing, guys showing other guys they won't be intimidated into backing their butts out on a curveball or dodging a hot liner. What I mean is going to the park day after day to live the game, to play by its rules, to wear the uniform of your own town like you're proud of it, to bunt or hit the ball to the right side to move the runner along, to tell the other guy "good play" when he makes a good play, to shake hands when you win and shake hands when you lose. Every game is a car waiting to be bought, a girl waiting to be kissed.

Now I know you got a tear in your eye, so I'll quit, but you know what I mean: if you're out on the diamond playing ball, you ain't out stealing somebody's hubcaps or worse. And if you get the meaning of the game, you won't ever do that or worse.

But unfortunately the games do end and we have to go back to school, and that's where the trouble starts, for the most part: guys who don't have any reason to be there (they don't play baseball, that is, which as everyone knows is the only reason for going to school, except maybe for looking at girls) and don't want to be there and ain't gonna be there long. But they do hang around long enough to try to make some other guys feel small.

Like one morning me and Lenny were walking into the school building around eight, and there's this bunch of guys in their beat-up leather jackets hanging around by the door. You know the type. There's Norm Jackson, their leader, who lives down by the river, and Steve Presnick, who used to play football but gave it up for drinking and head-bashing, and Billy Hines, a tall, thin guy who always wears sun-glasses, and Jimmy Darrell, a guard on the basketball team—I never figured out why he hangs with these guys, since you can look into his eyes and actually see somebody behind them.

Well, as usual, Lenny was talking away, this time about his latest musical favorites, Led Zeppelin and Def Lepard. Now don't ask me when Lenny got into heavy metal, but he'd been walking around for a while doing the air guitar thing, and he was really going at it on this particular morning, and good old Stevie Presnick wasn't about to let us by without saying something. He walked right up in Lenny's face, with his big empty eyes wide and staring, his hands on his hips, and he says to Lenny, like, "Well now, here's a real head-banger, what say we butt heads right here, big man."

Now Lenny is just a little guy, and I ain't none too big yet myself, and we are definitely in the wrong place at the wrong time. Now Steve Presnick has a forehead as wide as a snow shovel, and not much brains behind it to be protected, and head-butting ain't the safest thing to do even if you got a padded helmet on, so I'm trying to think fast how to get outta there with Lenny's head still stuck on his shoulders and my brains still intact.

As if things aren't bad enough, Norm starts up, too: "Little guitar man, why don't you play some for us. Maybe some Jimmy—you know some Hendrix?" Then he laughs, and they all laugh with him, except Jim Darrell, who is looking at me out of the corner of his eye.

Now Jim hangs out with the toughguys, but he ain't like them. We used to play baseball and basketball together when we were kids, though he was older and better than me, and we'd work each other out, and we have a mutual respect that you get when you realize that you're both athletes and you both want to win, but you know the other guy is good, too. Jimmy's good at basketball, and I'm not, and now I'm good at baseball, and Jimmy's not. But just then the look in Jimmy's eye said, so why did you have to come along right now? And worse yet, Lenny and me are just out of freshman year and bound to get hazed anyway, but today looks like something worse.

So Lenny says, "Whattya want with me, Steve? Go bang your brick head on somebody else." Lenny musta heard somewhere that if you stand up to bullies, they'll back down, that all they want to do is make you afraid, and if they can't, they leave you alone. Now let me tell you something: it ain't so. Whoever said that didn't have to face real bullies. You can get away with leading with the jaw when you're eight years old and nobody can hit hard enough to break it, but when you get these older street-tough types, you could break a bat over their heads and they'd hardly notice.

So now Steve is advancing on Lenny. "Tough little boy, huh? Why don't you show me how tough? Why don't you just punch me? I know you want to. Come on, little boy. Come on." You've probably heard the whole bit. I think they have to rehearse it to get into the idiots' club. Then Steve pushes Lenny hard in the chest and almost knocks him over.

Well I'm moving now to try to get in between them, and before I realize it I'm saying, "Steve, just leave Lenny alone, and he won't bother you," but he just shoves me away with one big paw and says, "You're for later, baseball boy," and keeps after Lenny, and Lenny says, "Get outta my face, Stevie," and Steve moves in toe to toe and says, "Whattya you gonna do about it, punk," and Norm is just watching all this and smiling, and Lenny is saying something else and a small crowd is beginning to gather and things aren't looking too good for the home team and before I realize what has happened Steve has smacked little Lenny right in the face with that snow-shovel forehead of his and Lenny goes down like Skylab falling and there's blood squirting and now I'm really mad and I'm about to go for Steve and from behind somebody tackles me and is lying on top of me and it's Jimmy Darrell, who whispers in my ear, "Just sit tight. You can't stop Steve now. You'll only make it worse or get yourself killed." And now everybody is getting in to it and bodies are beginning to fly every which way and teachers are running out the door waving their arms and Jim helps me up and pulls me aside and about three guys are holding Steve till he breaks away from them and runs straight out the front door and somebody is standing over Lenny, who is trying to sit up, with a bloody handkerchief in his hand.

And you think it's great to be a kid.

I expect Lenny to be having a fit, but he isn't. He's just sitting there calmly, looking at the blood. And who should be standing above him but Mr. Sanders, the school principal, who has something called a master's degree. I don't know what it is or why it helps, but he has one.

Jim lets me go now, so I go to help Lenny, but Sanders just looks at me and says, "Haven't you done enough already?"

Now what did I do? I was trying to help, and Norm and Steve are already probably going to kill me, and now the principal's after me, too. But I try anyway to help him help Lenny up, but Lenny gets halfway up and nearly faints away. A large, blue bruise is appearing in the middle of his forehead.

"Let him down, just let him lie down," Mr. Sanders says. "The nurse will be here in a minute. Now who did this? Was that Steve Presnick?"

The guy blew it. He should know we can't tell.

"Who else," I say, not realizing I'm saying it out loud, wondering if someone should get a priest to say last rites or something like that over

Lenny. Then Lenny looks like he's coming to, so he probably won't die, and I realize what I've done: the worst thing possible: I told.

I look up, and nobody's looking at Lenny, or Norm, or Mr. Sanders, or for Steve Presnick. They're looking at me.

We may have had a fight, and someone may have been hurt, but I did something far worse: I told who did it. I blew it.

The first law of the schoolyard: never tell.

Die first, but never tell.

Even Jim Darrell turns his back on me. "Ain't nothin' I can do for you now," he says, and strolls away. And I know the horror of my sin.

The nurse comes to get Lenny, but she just leaves him lying there, too, since someone has called a doctor. Mr. Sanders shoos us all off to class, since the bell is now ringing in the background. I go up to Lenny, tell him not to worry, and I'll see him later.

"That's o.k., Willie. I'll be all right."

Mr. Sanders just glares at me, so I go.

I know that it is likely I will live till the end of the school day. Once school is done, I'm not so sure. By third period the word is around that Steve Presnick is after me. I don't know how anyone could know that, because Steve took off at a jackrabbit run when Mr. Sanders showed up at the scene of the crime, and I doubt they'll find him for days. Maybe it's something you just know, or maybe there's some kind of underground where guys like Norm hide guys like Steve, where they bring them food and water until things blow over, and they take messages to guys like me who are going to get it when they come out of hiding. Maybe it's dark there, and they all smoke cigarettes and scrunch their eyes up like Humphrey Bogart in old movies. And they come back, with hats pulled low over their eyes, ready for vengeance.

I go home from school watching behind me, listening, checking every tree. I have a feeling he's out there somewhere. You can never tell where.

As I get near home, I can see, casually, a foot sticking out from behind our maple tree.

It must be Steve.

What am I going to do? No good to run. I could outrun him easy, but what's the point? If he's that set on getting me, he'll get me, so I'd rather it'd be here where I might be able to get medical help or at least where I've got the home-field advantage. So I stop to think. In my gym bag I've got a big, thick biology book, a real heavy *somebitch*. So

I drop my satchel and grip the book tight, ready to whop him upside the head, and I approach real quiet. The foot isn't moving. That's just a little too cool for Steve. Maybe he's so sure he can whip me that he doesn't even give it two thoughts. Well, I'll show him. Maybe he'll kill me, but he'll remember who hit him and planted the word *Biology* in large, unfriendly letters across the side of his face. So I work up slow, quiet, almost to the tree, smooth as a lion, and I wind up and I start to swing and I turn the corner and there he is but it isn't Steve and the book is swinging and his eyes are big and he lets out a yell and I let go of the book and it goes flying past him and he ducks and I try so hard to hold up that I slip in the grass and fall on my butt and here I am looking stupid again and there's Stud looking down at me.

"Sorry, I thought you were Steve Presnick."

"Thanks for the compliment. The day I look like Steve Presnick is the day I shoot myself. Get up. You look like a fool."

"What were you doing behind the tree, Stud?"

"Waiting for you."

"Why?" A chill went up my spine as the thought crossed my mind that Stud was here to do Stevie's work for him. No, not against a fellow baseball player, and not Stud.

"Don't insult me, little brother. I'm on your side. Outfielders gotta stick together. Just wanted to warn you to stay away from any place where you might run into Presnick or one of his friends, at least till things cool down. Steve got suspended from school and the police have picked him up, so you're safe for now. But stay low for a while and don't expect much help for a while, because nobody wants to get on the wrong side of Norm Jackson's gang. Hear what I'm tellin' you?"

"Thanks."

That evening my mother gets a phone call. I worry when she gets a phone call but doesn't say much, and this one is especially quiet.

Then she pokes her head in my door: "I need to talk to you, young man."

When she says "Willie," I know I'm o.k.; when she says "young man," I'm in trouble; "Joseph" is worse yet, because if she remembers my name, she must really be mad. "Joseph Everett" is just about as bad as it gets; but "Joseph Everett Smith" comes only with severe yelling, tears, and some serious attempt at punishment.

So now I'm bad off, but not too bad.

And I can't believe I told you my middle name.

I can't help it. I didn't name myself that. Just don't go tellin' anyone else.

So I go out and sit down at the kitchen table with Ma. She doesn't waste any time.

"Willie, sometimes you drive me crazy. What happened at school today?"

"Who was that on the phone?"

"The police. But you talk first; I asked you a question. And tell me the truth."

So I tell her what Steve Presnick did to Lenny, and how I was an innocent bystander, and how I tried heroically to help my friend, but couldn't, and got blamed by the principal anyway.

"Nobody's blaming you," she said, "except maybe Steve Presnick, because he needs someone to blame besides himself. But, Willie, you know how I feel about fighting."

"But Ma, I wasn't fighting...." She waved me off before I could say any more.

"The police called to tell me that they have Steve in custody, and they tried to scare him good, but they're going to release him."

Panic.

"But they also told him not to come within a hundred yards of you or Lenny, or they'll arrest him again and try him as an adult for assault."

Hope.

"They said he seemed to feel bad for what he did. He may look a little weird, but they think he's a pretty good boy, really."

Pretty good actor, maybe. They must be nuts.

"So don't go looking for trouble, and maybe this business will blow over."

Now what motherly sayings have we left out, here? How about, "Someday you'll grow up to be a doctor, and everything will be fine"?

"You're the only son I have..." I'd forgot that one, "...and I'm counting on your growing up to be a lawyer so I can retire and take things easy for a while."

Sorry, lawyer, not doctor.

So stay out of trouble and don't always be trying to fight other people's battles for them."

Have you heard this list before? And isn't that what lawyers do?

"All right?"

"But I didn't even..."

The wave again.

"No more. Go finish your homework. And if it's not too late, maybe you should call and check on Lenny."

All I'd have to do now is say "Yes, Ma," and give her a kiss on the cheek, and they could turn this into an episode of *Leave It to Beaver*. But no matter how hard she tries, she's not going to get more than a nod on this one. It might take all the brains Stevie has in his head to do it, but he'll remember what happened and find a way to get even. Maybe I should start going to Bruce Lee movies and taking notes before it's too late. Hoooaaaah...

7 Partytime

Small, old mill towns like Harmon Falls don't have much in the way of excitement. In the summer, when you're not playing baseball, one night a week they have a moonlight swim at the pool, where you can go to swim or just go to look at girls. In spring there's the Riverfest, but that's just mostly greasy food and beer, so not many kids go there, and when they do they're with their parents, and it only lasts two days anyway. Around midsummer there's a Strawberry Festival that lasts for about two hours. They have a parade, and people eat strawberries, strawberry pies, and strawberry cakes, and they drink strawberry milkshakes. In early October there's the Pumpkin Festival. They have a parade, and people eat pumpkin pies and pumpkin cakes and drink pumpkin milkshakes. In the winter people complain about the weather.

Otherwise, in the summer you can walk in the park if you don't mind staying away from motorcycle gangs, but that only takes about three minutes, unless you stop for an extra minute to look at the goldfish in the fountain beneath the World War I memorial. You can hang around the donut shop, or get pizza if you have money, or cruise if you have a car, or go to the movies if you have money and want to walk four miles to the bigger town across the bridge. Or you can spend the evening throwing baseballs against your garage, which I try not to do so much anymore since it just beats up the balls, and last year I knocked a block out of the wall last year that left a hole I had to try to mix and Ma finally ended up hiring a neighbor to do it. Major league fastball, I'm tellin' you.

If you don't like any of that, there ain't much to do. Old people grow flowers or vegetable gardens when they're off work, or they bowl or drink and play softball or listen to radio or watch TV

Sometimes I walk to the top of the hill to the cemetery. I know that sounds morbid, but wait till I tell you about it. The dirt road winds up the hill like a string on a top, past layers of gravestones that get newer as you climb. The place is filled with old willows and uneven stone walls that climb the hill like a drunk with a fresh bottle: stumbling and slow, but tight to the road. The trees bend and sway with the road and make the place seem more alive than it is.

If you go just before sunset you can watch the sky redden over the hills to the west and see the silver light of the rising moon skim off the river like tinsel on a Christmas tree. From the very top of the hill, where there are few gravestones yet and few trees to block the view, you can see the river wind for miles, till it cuts and disappears into the hills south gentle as a bad curveball. The birds will chirp loud as a storm till the light dies, and the red from the sky and the green of the grass and the blue of the spruces and the gold of the moon fold one by one into the black of the river till they all close tight as sleep. And layer by layer the houses stack up along the sides of the hills, fade first into the mist from the river, then into the rising night, till you can see only a few that emerge out of the light of street lamps limp as smoke. Then you have to wait for the nighttime coal barges that shoot their lights off the hills as they float south or the one riverboat that still gets this far on its run. Then the blinking lights and the jazz music and the sound of the paddle wheel filter up the hill till they're light as wind chimes on a bare summer breeze.

The top of the hill is cooler than the valley, and when the wind is right, you don't get the smoke from the mill, and you can actually fill your lungs with the real air and think about what it feels like to breathe.

A dark path cuts off the back of the cemetery over through some trees to the baseball field, and if you're really brave, you can walk past there over the jagged stones to the rock quarry, which glows deep blue under the steadily rising moon. Lance told me there are copperheads around the woods and the quarry, so I don't go there often—only when town is so quiet that I feel like I'm dead already and I don't care if I meet one or not.

Most nights lots of people go to the center of town, off the park, to the little league baseball field. By dark most of the little league games are done, and men come in for slow-pitch softball games. They have leagues for old men and young men, one now for women, too, but mostly for ex-high school athletes and miners and steel workers and guys who spend their nights drinking at bars, and some pot-bellied lo-cal businessmen who think they can make more money by mixing with the working crowd, and guys you've never seen before and you wonder where they come from to a little town like this just to play softball. There's talk about somebody starting a girls' softball league, too, and I hope they do, but they haven't done it yet.

Almost everybody comes out then: wives, kids, bikers, bums, third-shift workers on their way to punch the clock, but mostly ex-ballplayers with bad legs and beer on their breath and young guys like me who don't know what else to do and figure that one day we will be here, too, fatter and slower, and everyone in town will finally come to see us play.

This is where the real party is: beneath the lights and the lazy drifting softballs that float up into the night and hang there like stars. People bring beer, even though it's against the law in the park, but the policemen, being polite, don't notice, even though they sometimes stroll by to watch for a few home runs, too. A lot of guys just go for that, the beer, because they know that somebody will have an extra one from a six-pack, or some kid will have snuck a few from home or will have got some old drunk to buy him some at the store in exchange for sharing a few. And people drink and joke with the players and boo the umpire and ooh and ahh all the home runs that fly gracefully and easily out of a little league park often till as late as midnight—that's what they come for, the home runs. Everyone has a good time but the pitchers and the umpires, which sounds just a little bit like heaven to me.

So tonight I get to the park and it seems half the town is there. It's a hot night, and moths circle endlessly under the lights. I see Pecks, but he doesn't talk to me; he's our shortstop, so he thinks he's too good to be seen talking to a freshman outfielder, even though pretty soon I'll be a sophomore outfielder. Burger is there with his girlfriend, and Stud with his, but they leave soon. They show up, let everybody know that things are cool, and then go somewhere and do something that fresh-man outfielders don't know anything about. Probably someone with a car drives them to the movies.

Lowry is there. He'll be a good pitcher—that's right, you heard me say it—someday if he grows enough to get some steam on his fastball he will be a good pitcher. Lance is there, but he lags back in the dark, drinking beer with his buddies. I run into Samula, and we go back behind the backstop to watch balls and strikes, to see how the umpire will call pitches.

Slow-pitch softball is not like baseball. No fastballs, curveballs, bunting, stealing, and the bases are only sixty-five feet apart. No bean-balls, few strikeouts: the ball's easy to hit, though I must admit, it's harder than you'd think to hit it well. I once saw this old guy, must be thirty-five or so, Fred Wilson, hit five home runs in a game. Imagine that, five homers, each one high and long as a rainbow, disappearing into the night so you couldn't even see where they landed, somewhere out in the park. Course, the fence is only 200 feet down the line to left, a little farther in center and the power alleys. Still, he hit five straight balls right on the button, I mean cleaned their clock: boom, boom, boom, boom, boom, rising like a rocket and falling into nothing. I bet you he could never hit a curveball, but that's slow-pitch for you. He made the front page of the sports section of the next day's paper. Not his picture, mind you, just his name, but to me five homers was worth a picture, if for no other reason than because he went home with that pitcher's respect, with everyone's who saw the game, and with his own.

This game is between Drift Inn and Beans Foundry. If you'd never in your life seen a game before and you seen this one, you'd think softball was closer to Custer's Last Stand than any sport you can imagine. I mean, this is a bunch of young beer hounds, the Drift Inn team, guys who've played a lot of ball, against foundry workers, guys who look older than Father Time. The Drift Inn guys have beer bellies the size of kegs, but they also have arms the size of basketballs, and they haven't lost all their speed or much of their hair yet. They have one good player that people around here remember from his high school days, George Jakovich, and a bunch of tall guys named Emil who look like their chins were carved out of the sides of mountains. The Beans boys look like souls that even hell forgot: skinny, whiskery, whiskey-eyed Elmers who've played softball since before their opponents were born. The Beans pitcher is so old he can't even put much arc on the ball—he just can't throw it that high. The slow-pitch is supposed to drop from about twelve feet up straight down on the batter—that's what makes it hard to hit. With this guy, it barely gets above the top of the batter's cap. But he's maybe the only guy they got who can throw it that far. If you think this is going to be one of those stories where the underdog comes back against a huge enemy to win an impossible victory, sorry to disappoint you. When the first Emil walks up to the plate for Drift Inn and sees a pitch coming in letter-high from a codger older than his grandfather, his eyes pop big as gum-bubbles, and he's so surprised that he only knocks it off the fence for a double instead of burying it in the fountain in the park out beyond the left-field fence. Now the others from Drift Inn don't hoot and holler like high school players would, but don't go thinking they're gentlemen and will take it easy on the old coots. Each one walks up with a big, silent grin on his face and a big bottle-bat in his hands and a pretty good idea that tomorrow's box score will show some pretty big numbers next to his name.

The second batter, a lefty, looks really disappointed when he only lines one off the right-center field fence instead of hitting it onto the roof of the bowling alley across the street. Beans' centerfielder looks like he could have run once upon a time, but by the time he gets to it, he's too tired to throw it, so he pitches it underhand to the rightfielder. The better part of the rightfielder's arm hangs below the elbow rather than poking up above, so he's not good for much, and the batter shows probably more embarrassment at himself than pity for him by stopping at third with a stand-up triple.

Samula and I look at each other and realize we're not going to see much in the way of balls and strikes, so we head for the street beyond the outfield. We're not bodacious enough to brave the park and Grim Reapers, the local version of Hell's Angels, but maybe we'll catch a few homers that soar over the right field screen.

By the time we get there, Drift Inn already has a 6-0 lead and it's still in the first inning. We find Lance and Ricky Anders out there just as Ricky snags the fourth homer of the inning. Catching the ball knocks a little beer from the can he's holding, so he curses up a storm, and wipes his hands on his shirt.

Now, frankly, even though Lance is a ballplayer and all, I don't much like to hang around these guys. Ricky has more than a mean streak, and they've always either got or are talking about getting beer. Now I'm no goody, but I don't like to mess with that stuff. I've got a baseball career to think about, and if I got arrested it would just kill Ma.

Plus, you gotta admit, the stuff just smells bad.

Not long, though, before they offer beer to me and Samula. Samula takes one. He's a good guy, but he likes to be one of the crowd, not stand out too much, and since everybody else has one, he takes one.

That is, everybody else but me.

Pretty soon, Ricky comes and puts his arm around my shoulder. "Come on, Willie, don't be a wuss. Have a beer, man, and you'll feel better."

"I feel fine already."

"Come on, mama's boy, just try it. I'll bet you've never tried beer before." His breath smells like sweat from the beer, and he's not too steady on his feet. His eyes have receded deep in his head, so far that I almost want to reach into his eyeball with my hand to see if I can pull the pupil back out.

"Come on, man," Lance says. "Be a man."

I have tried it, beer, when I was a little kid, at my uncle's house, not knowing what I was tasting. Yuck.

Now, before long they're all after me to try one, and pretty soon they're giving Samula a hard time, too, because I won't drink. Ricky threatens to beat up both of us, which of course he couldn't do, since he's nearly drunk, and you can't really fight someone who's drunk, anyway.

Eventually Samula's after me, too. "It's hot," he says, sweat dripping from his forehead, "and you don't have money to buy anything to drink. Just have a beer. Maybe you'll like it. It's really pretty good when you get used to it, and one won't hurt you."

A softball fires down and bounces among us, another Drift Inn homer, knocking Ricky's can from his hand. He curses again, loud and long.

"Beer doesn't seem to have done those guys any harm," Lance says, pointing to the Inn players, and everybody laughs and gulps. He must not have seen their bellies.

"Just give him a break, Lance," Samula says almost in a whisper. "He'll take some when he's ready."

"All right, it's not me pushing him anyway. It's Ricky. Let him just take care of his damn self."

Another kid has just shown up with a fresh six-pack and starts to pass them around. Nobody says a word to me this time. We all turn to watch as another homer soars way over the centerfield fence, hitting the door of the bowling alley on one bounce.

I glance over at the beer, which is actually starting to look pretty good to me. Samula's right, I'm thinking: it has got hot.

"Last chance," says Samula to me, about to pop open the icy, dripping can.

"All right, let me have one."

"What?" from everybody.

"I'm thirsty. Let me have one, please."

"All right!"

"Good job, Willie."

"We'll make a man outta him yet."

With a sheepish smile, Samula hands me a can of beer.

Now I want you to know: I gave in to thirst, not to these guys and their pushing.

The can feels cold. Words and pictures proclaim the virtues of the regal brew within. The top opens with a crack like the sound from a distance of a bat hitting a fastball. I bend over the can, and then some of the fizz gets in my nose and almost makes me sneeze. Frankly, the stuff doesn't smell good. I notice the others tilting their heads back. "Chug ya'," says Ricky to Lance, and they both turn bottoms up at once, so I do too.

The liquid tingles, almost burns at first, like soda pop, but the cold feels so good in my throat that I keep swallowing and swallowing. The can is empty before I expect it to be or want it to be. Upon reflection, I find the taste not as bad as I had remembered and much better than the smell.

I look up, and everyone is looking at me.

"Man. He chugged it, the whole thing."

"On his first try."

"The boy," says Lance, "was born to drink beer."

"Sorry, Willie, that's all we've got," says the kid who brought the last six-pack.

I start to say "that's o.k.," but all that comes out is a loud burp. It snuck up on me like a back-door slider. Everybody laughs, except for Ricky, who is howling with glee.

The funny thing is, only a few seconds later, everything starts to blur. I haven't moved. In fact, I don't feel like moving for some time, but nonetheless everybody looks smaller, and the lights look a little dimmer. A softball whops against the fence just in front of us. The aged right fielder, whose beard seems to have grown longer over the past two innings, picks it up and loops the ball back toward second.

So now I've had my first real beer.

"You o.k.?" says Samula. "You look a little funny."

"A little funny yourself," says I.

I don't feel like a man. My body feels smaller and loopier. Someone is playing music.

Pretty soon we're all arm in arm, even Ricky, singing Beatles' songs, and I'm wondering if any of these guys knows Sinatra or Tony Bennett. The scoreboard has Drift Inn up about 35-0 after three innings, and they're batting again.

One by one, they step up to the plate, and "pop," the ball arcs high into the night and over the fence. Then another, "pop," and another, "pop." "Pop," "pop," "pop," they sound like champaign corks popping and fly like Fourth of July rockets. "Pop," "pop," then one makes a sound more like a whip cracking and zips high down the left field line. "Crack," it hits a bulb on the left field line light pole, and the bulb shatters in a thousand pieces, sending sparks that spray round and bright as the best fireworks and fall to the ground in a fiery flower.

"Ooh," the crowd says together. "Aah."

I notice that the fence is starting to imprint my face with a series of squares, and I'm starting to taste metal. I didn't realize I was leaning against it.

"Pop."

"Ooh."

Singing: "All the lonely people, where do they all come from?"

I wonder how I came to be leaning face first against the fence. I try to collect myself, and I figure if I run a few laps around the park, maybe my head will clear. Drift Inn in up 52-0 now, and the crowd is starting to thin, so maybe I won't run into anyone. Once around the field, and I look again at the scoreboard: 59-0. Three times around: 65-0. Five times around: 71-0. "Pop."

About now, the cheers have died down considerably, and I have a terrible need to relieve myself. So I finish my next lap and head for behind the concession stand. As I'm about to turn the corner: "Hey, Baseball." There's Norm Jackson, sunglasses and all though it's pitch black out, and on one side of him Undo Purdy, a defensive tackle on the football team, and on the other side Steve Presnick.

I ain't lyin' when I tell you I almost peed right there.

I start to move back nice and slow. Norm says, "What's your hurry, Baseball? The game's over anyway. Stick around and maybe Steve will teach you a little boxing lesson." Steve's already got his fists clenched and his mouth foaming, but he's either too mad, too drunk, or too stupid to say anything. I keep backing up.

Then I feel something behind me. I damn near leap away like a frog, but I'm doing my best to keep my composure, and my legs feel like limp noodles. I turn around and look, and there's Billy Hines and Jim Darrell behind me. I also notice that more people are leaving the park. I thought the game had two innings to go, then I remember the ten run rule: if one team is up by ten or more after five innings the game's over. I look at the scoreboard and read 72-0 just as the lights in the whole park go out.

I turn: Steve Presnick's coming at me. I turn again. In the moonlight I can see Jim Darrell's eyes flipping back to his right, toward the crowd. Is he leaving an opening for me? I turn again just in time to see Steve lunging for me like a fullback about to run over a rookie defensive back.

I step to the side and think about letting go with the nastiest haymaker I can muster. But all I do is duck and swerve aside. Steve trips over my foot and falls flush on his face.

Yep: drunk as well as mad. He lies there for just a second, gets up, and puts his hand to his face. Then the hand drops, and his eyes are wide and round, and even in the dark I can see blood dripping from his hand and his nose, and he lets out scream like a fire alarm and yells, "I'm gonna kill you, Smith!" and he's on me like a bear on a fish and he grabs me in a headlock and he's starting to punch at my face but all he's hitting so far is my hands and the top of my head and the sweat from running has made me slick and slimy and I slip out of his grip like soap outta your hand in the shower and fast as I can I run where Jim pointed with his eyes and I'm not surrounded and now I'm in and out of the last of the fans and Steve Presnick is nearly at my heals and I'm cutting and dodging and he's after me and I come to the bleachers and cut fast to the left and I hear him crack his shin on the concrete and he lets out a yell and he's after me again and cursing like a demon but I've got a lead now and I dodge between some people and head for the backstop where a path cuts between the field and the hill behind it and the path leads back to the park and if I can make it to the park I'll have a lot of directions to choose and a chance to kick in the burners and disappear before I'm dead or the Grim Reapers get me, which would be much the same thing.

As I turn round the fence maybe I've lost him and I glance back and he sees me again and I can hear him yell again, "I'm gonna kill you, Smith," and he's on my trail and I don't have long so I sprint down the path and as I pass the backstop there's a slight turn to the left and the moon shines full on the path ahead of me with the fence on my right and a steep hill on the left, almost too steep to climb, and I see two things. At the end of path ahead of me is a group of bikers, the motorcycle kind, in black leather jackets, chains, and sunglasses. Directly before me on the path is a stone about the size of a baseball.

Now whether or not these bikers are friends of Steve's, chances are they wouldn't mind watching a kid get beat up, so they just might not let me through. So it looks like I got one chance: Steve can't see me where I'm standing, so I could pick up that rock and wait, and as he turns the corner I could plug him clean in the face with it.

No time to think. I bend over, pick it up, and poise to throw.

But I can't do it.

I don't know if I'm chicken or what, but I can't do it. Not square in the face.

Up to now I haven't really hurt anybody, whether I broke the Law of the Schoolyard or not, but throwing that stone means taking the chance of killing somebody, even if it's only Steve Presnick.

But I don't want to leave the stone for him either, so with no time to think, I take the only other option: stone in hand, straight up the hill.

Now let me tell you that hill is steep. I've never seen anyone run up it before. I've seen guys try to climb it on all fours and once or twice make it, mostly not. They fall back and hurt themselves.

I have no choice if I don't make it all the way up, because in three seconds Steve will be at the bottom waiting for me to fall... and my feet are spinning and the dirt's slipping beneath me and my hands are clawing above and I'm reaching and straining and one last push and I'm up and up and over the top.

I look down and see Steve charging past me down the path like a freight train, straight toward the bikers, screaming like a steam whistle as he goes.

I don't even pause for breath. I'm on my feet, across the railroad tracks, and sprinting for home with all the energy I've got. I run maybe half a mile before I remember that I have to piss, but I'm too close to town now to find some trees or a place to hide, so now I gotta run the rest of the way home gripping the water in and stumbling and running stiff-legged and feeling the sweat pour down my groin and feeling like the pee is gonna burst out my belly button at any minute.

It might have been easier just to go ahead and get beat up.

Maybe not.

But finally there's my street, and there's my yard, and I jump the fence and I'm in the back yard behind a tree and my fly is stuck oh god I got this far and my fly is stuck and I yank and yank and I've finally got it and just in time aah.

I take a few deep breaths and compose myself, check for cuts or bruises that might get Ma alarmed, and head for the porch. The moon is round as a turnip and bright as the lights that flash when you get punched in the eye. But I made it home alive. But somewhere under that same moon Steve Presnick is still looking for me.

Ma is lying on the couch in the living room watching TV "Wille, you're late. You had me worried."

Yeah. Me too—I think it but don't say it.

"You shouldn't be out so late by yourself. You could get into trouble. You could... ooh! You smell of sweat. Have you been out running in those clothes? What am I going to do with this boy? Go get a bath right away and put those nasty clothes in the wash. Hurry up now. I'll pour a cold drink for you for when you're done."

Of course, I do just as my mother says.

"What are you watching on TV?" I ask.

"Mutch Humbugh."

"Why are you watching that idiot?"

"It's nice to know somebody's dumber than I am."

"You're not so dumb."

"Thanks a lot for the compliment. Go get your bath."

"What's Mutch raggin' about tonight?"

"Oh, how the streets aren't safe because of all the young hoodlums and the ACLU and women who work and how we waste too much money on educating hoodlums who don't care and on welfare mothers and programs for the disabled. I better not get started if I want to sleep tonight."

"Right, sorry."

She shook her head, changed the channel and put on an old movie instead.

As I run water I notice my heart has finally slowed down and I wonder if I'm one of those young hoodlums Mutch likes to complain about and blame the Democrats for. Tonight, I suppose I was, but then I didn't kill Steve Presnick, even though he would have killed me if he'd caught up with me.

My heart's starting to beat fast again.

I brush my teeth, then merge into the water and try to think of something to calm me down so I can sleep. I drank beer tonight. I don't think I'll do that again soon. Better stay on my toes with my life on the line. For some reason Lana comes to mind. Gotta get her out of my head; Lenny would never forgive me if he thought I was gonna hit on his sister. What made me think of that anyway? I've never thought about hitting on Lana. Not exactly, anyway. Better not think of it exactly or inexactly or any way at all. But Lana's hard not to like.

Through the window blinds I can see the moon again. I watch a cloud mosey toward it and try to engulf it, but the moon shines right through it, like a lightbulb through newspaper.

P.S.: That happened in the summer after my freshman year, so it's a little out of order. Ma helped me with the first few pages of this chapter, but not with the rest: would you show that to your mother?

8 Stud's Tale

Hey, man. My name is Stud. Least, that's what the dudes call me. Willie told you 'bout me. I just wanted to set the record straight on a coupla points, cause Willie ain't gonna tell you everything, and Coach ain't gonna tell you nothing, and anybody else is only gonna tell you my part of the truth.

Now, me, I'm only gonna tell you part of the truth, too, but you can believe that whatever I do tell you is pure truth and nothing but, cause I'm not here to tell you 'bout me. I'm here to tell you 'bout Willie, so I got nothing to lose. Now we understand each other.

To begin with, Coach is a bit of an idiot, but he does one thing right: he puts the best players on the field and lets us play. And if we win, we win, and if we don't, we don't, and it's our fault, because we have to hit and catch and throw for ourselves, and that's as it should be.

And another thing: it's true almost nobody comes to the games, except my girlfriend and a coupla the moms and dads and granddads, but that ain't entirely their fault, either. My dad would come, but he works three to eleven, in the coal mines, that is, *always* three to eleven, and it don't take much brains to see that our games will always come between three and eleven, except a few weekend games, and he comes to those. He's tried to get day-shift, even though it pays less, so he could come to games, but they won't give it to him. They just tell him to be glad he's got a job.

He is, and he works hard, and he's here with me in spirit, and that counts. But one thing you got to understand, things are still tough for black people, even in a little place like Harmon Falls where there ain't as much prejudice as some places. Work is hard to find, and they assume you don't want to go to college unless it's for sports, and they don't like it much if you got a white girlfriend, which I don't, in case you're wondering, and as if it mattered. So you got to be glad you got a job, and you got to work hard, and you got to miss games, and you got to let your kids know you believe in them, which my dad does.

And you got to stay tight with the right brothers: Burger, Split, and dudes like Jim Darrell on the basketball team. Good dudes, every one of 'em. Not everybody can be a Dr. King or a Malcolm or Sidney

Poitier, or a Shirley Chisholm or Barbara Jordan, for that matter. But we can be good people, and we are.

But one thing I got to say, cause I know it ain't true everywhere: there's no prejudice between the baselines, whatever there may be in the stands. It's not like the old days with the Negro Leagues and Jackie Robinson, God bless the great man's soul. Once you get on the field, people are people, and we all play together.

It ain't much, but it's a start.

And the guys you play with, and the guys you play against, you're all brothers really, whether you know it or not, and the people who watch are your brothers and sisters, and there are no colors and three are no creeds, except for baseball. And that's also the way it should be everywhere, always. Though you and I know it ain't, always.

And it's the same when the women play softball, except that *really* nobody goes to their games. I would, but my girlfriend plays volleyball, not softball, and yes, I go to her games when we're not playing baseball.

And one more thing, in case you haven't got it yet: Willie's a better ballplayer than he lets on. He don't hit a lot of home runs, but if he grows, he may get to The Bigs, God willing. I mean that.

And here I am sounding like Reverend Ogletree. Well, you know what I mean. You're probably saying, C'mon, get to the game, man, so all right, I will.

So I'm a senior, and I'm sitting in the corner of the dugout rubbing up a bat handle and saying my *Om*, and listening with a corner of my mind to the shit people are talking on the bench.

"So, Lenny, you gettin' any good stuff?" says Lance, who is always picking on both Lenny and Willie because he's an upperclassman and he thinks he's better than the freshmen and sophomores are. "Whatta you mean?" says Lenny, looking perplexed. That's a nice word, ain't it, *perplexed*? He thinks Lance means drugs, and Lenny ain't that type. Fact is most of us on this team ain't that type.

"You know what I mean," says Lance, and moves his hips like he's, you know, doing the deed. Lance ain't got no conscience and he ain't got no taste, though he does have his share of girlfriends, sad to say.

"You asshole," says Lenny, trying to sound tough, but he's no match for Lance when it comes to insults.

"Oh, you like assholes," says Lance. I thought you might be that type."

"I ain't your type, and you ain't mine," Lenny says, "so just leave me alone."

"Lenny don't even know what his peter's for," says Lance to Pudge. "Neither does Willie. He thinks it's for pissing on his shoes." Lance is a shithead, but he don't miss much.

Then Lance grabs Burger by the arm. "Burger, look at Lenny's face. He don't even shave yet."

"I been shavin' since I was nine," Lenny says, falling into it.

"Who ya been shavin'?" Burger says.

"Dad must own a barbershop," adds Pudge.

"Make sure ya shave the right end, Lenny," says Lance.

"Ain't no right end in baseball, so just stick to playing shortstop where you belong and shut up," says Bud to Lance. Bud is big, he don't like this kind of jawing, and he will stick up for the young guys, so when he talks, guys listen, though he faints away every time he sees his own blood. I guess no one's willing to take a chance on drawing it first. It's a strange world, and that's also the truth.

So we're playing Hollywood tonight, and don't get on me for the name. I didn't make it up. Strange thing is it's just this little podunk town south along the river with a stamping plant and a meat-packing business, not much else. I hate to play there because their fans ride you from the beginning of the game—yes, their fans, parents mostly, actually come to the games, usually dozens of them, and they don't just cheer for their own. They also jeer and hoot and cuss at and threaten the visiting players like they was hardly people at all. That kind of shit makes you really want to beat their team, which we usually do, since most of their players are more show than go and more shit than hit, fortunately.

Strange thing, I played on an all-star team with some of their guys once, and all of a sudden their parents treated me sweet as strawberry pie, like we was blood friends forever. Until Harmon Falls played them again.

I think that's what Reverend Ogletree calls hypocrisy, but you may argue if you like.

So before we play today's game, we have to finish a game that we started two weeks ago at our field but that was called because of darkness. We were tied in the bottom of the last inning, which means, fortunately, that we get to bat first, and all we need is one run and the first game's over and they lose their confidence for the second game ahead. Don't let anyone kid you: confidence is ninety percent, and, as Yogi Berra says, talent is the other half. Right.

Well, Willie's leading off for us, then Slick and me, and we're about to start, so Willie is in the on-deck circle loosening up and saying his *Om* like I taught him, and I stroll up and put my arm around his shoulder, and I say, Look, why don't you just get a single, Slick will move you along, I'll knock you in, and we can mark up a "W" and start game two?

Willie says, "How 'bout if I get a double, Slick singles me to third, you hit a homer and we all score."

For Willie, nothing in baseball is ever quite enough, and that's both good and bad: he's never happy because he always wants to do better, so he always tries to do better, but—he's never quite *happy*. You've got to know the meaning of *enough*. And if you have to try too hard, just keep it to yourself, because most people will think that you think they're no good, that *they* don't try hard enough, which is not what you think at all. What do you think?

So whattya think happens? Willie gets a walk, which as we know don't happen much, because he loves to hit so much that he won't take pitches unless he knows that taking pitches *specifically* will help us win, which we're about to do. Then Slick takes a pitch and Willie is off for second quick as a ball off a bat, and he slides head first four feet easy ahead of the throw. Now Slick knows how to play ball, and he grounds a ball between first and second that nearly slips through, but their second baseman knocks it down, and you know Willie rounds third hard and looks like he wants to score and Coach nearly has to chain him to third to keep him from getting thrown out at home like a fool and spoiling my chance for a game-winning rbi—which of course I get on the second pitch when their lefty puts one on the inside half of the plate, and I line it into left center for all the hit we need, and, as they say, this one's over.

So everyone congratulates me and Willie and Slick, every one of our guys does, cause the Hollywood fans ain't none too happy with two minutes of game and already a big one in the loss column. But they'll get used to it, cause they're about to get number two for the day and no mistake. As I said, a big part of anything is confidence. So we do not go hopping around like a bunch of ten-year-olds. We check our gear and get back to rubbing up bat handles, since as visitors we will lead off game two in about five minutes.

The smell of pine tar rises in my nose, and my muscles feel loose and strong, and I know that this, baseball, is what God made us for, among other things, of course, if you know what I mean—no, I don't mean what you were just thinkin'.

I know Willie has told you that I have girlfriends, but what do you expect? It's no big deal, so don't think it's worse than it is. I am no ladykiller. Right now I have one girlfriend, Melita, and she is just what I have been looking for. We treat each other right and we get along great. She is a lady, and I treat her like a lady, and that too is as it should be. Someday Willy will have a girlfriend, too. Now he's too young, and he knows it. 'Nuff said.

So Willie leads off the second game, he's batting first now, and we knock helmets, and he steps up to the plate. Hollywood is pitching a lefty, and Willie doesn't especially like lefties, mostly because in high school we don't see too many of them. They don't specially bother me, but then I have a different philosophy of hitting than most people. I figure it doesn't matter what he throws and how he throws it and how hard he throws it. If he wants to get me out, he has to throw it across the plate. So I pick out a particular zone over the plate that I like, and I wait for the ball to hit that zone. When it enters the zone, I just think of it as though the ball was sitting on a tee waiting for me to hit it, and I swing as if the ball was suspended in the air right where I was expecting it. Now and then I don't get what I want, and on rare occasions I strike out, but more often than not when I don't get what I want, the pitch is a ball, and I walk, cause in high school, the pitchers' control ain't that good anyway. I don't know if it would work in the Big Leagues, but it works now, and that's good enough for me, now. I'll worry about the Bigs when I get to the Bigs, and if I don't, I'll go to college like my father wants me to, or I'll work in the mines like he does and play ball in the miners' league, or I'll join the Army. Yeah, the mines have their own teams here. It doesn't matter. It's all a state of mind, and Melita will love me either way, though I think she got this idea that she's gonna have a fur coat and a Corvette someday, and that I'm gonna buy them for her, though I could be wrong, though I kinda hope not.

Sorry, I was telling you about the game. Willie is a more experienced player now, though he's still too eager, and he's calmed down a lot since last year since I taught him to say *Om*, but he doesn't entirely relax in the box yet. Even though he's a lead-off hitter, he doesn't like to take pitches like he's supposed to, but he's found a way to get around that: whenever a ball comes inside, he just turns his shoulder and lets it hit him so he gets first base. Then he falls on the ground like he's kinda stunned, then he gets up, dusts himself off, and hobbles kinda unsteady down to first. I taught him that part. At first he used to just stand there and let it hit him like he was some brave dude facing a firing squad, but the umps caught on quick and started not giving him first base, since the rule says the batter gotta at least make an effort to get outta the way. But that rule's like most rules in life: you gotta know how and when to break it. Notice I said most rules. Some you don't break. Others, stupid ones, you got to know *how* to break. Got it?

Funny I should mention it, because Willie takes two balls and a strike that barely nips the outside corner, when the next one comes inside and drills him right on the tricep, and down he goes. We run over to him and glare at the pitcher, who looks like he's actually feeling kinda bad, cause he really didn't mean to do it. Then he turns away cause he doesn't want to let us know we have the edge, but it's too late, we know, and Willie gets up looking a little woozy, which is ridiculous, cause the ball didn't get near his head, but it is effective, and the ump gives him first base. Of course he's fine, which everyone else finds out when he steals second before the first pitch. That's right, before. The pitcher tries to pick him off and fakes him out and Willie is already on his way to second and they should by rights have him, but the first baseman takes a second to realize that Willie left and starts to sweep the tag and then notices that Willie is gone and starts to make the throw and stops himself because it's already too late: Willie's sliding into second with a stolen base when he should be hustling back to the dugout with his head down and his tail between his legs for making a bonehead play. Two things you have to say about that young man: he's hell on the bases because he can fly, and he manages to squeeze out of sticky situations smelling like anything but shit.

Well, before you know it, Slick's singled in Willie and I've doubled in Slick and stole third and Burger has brought me in with a sacrifice fly, and we're up three-zip, simple as that. Ain't baseball wonderful? And Hollywood is looking like it's slipping into the earthquake-fault, and no movie-style happy ending for them today.

We add a run in the third, and not much else happens into the fourth, when dark clouds begin to creep in over the hill. Hollywood is nestled right on the side of a steep hill, as are most towns around here, and their baseball field sits right at its ankle, high enough so you can almost see the river from here. That can be pretty nice to look at, but it can also bring rain in a hurry, which is all right if it's past the fifth inning and you're ahead, but pretty bad if you're like Willie and you'd prefer to play extra innings every game just so you might get to bat again. Well, in the fourth the rain begins to leak from the clouds, not a problem yet, just enough to settle the dust, but not boding well for an inning or two ahead.

Things begin to get a little more complicated when Flap, our pitcher, starts to unravel with one out in this one and another inning to go. He walks one, then Pudge boots one at third, then one of their big guys, Malabraga or some Italian name like that, rips a double to right. Another walk, sac fly to center, single to left, and it's 4-3, and we're not out of the inning yet.

Then this little right-handed batter pops one back of second base that looks like trouble. Mange darts back, eye on the ball, and Willie and Slick sprint in, eyes on the ball—in fact everybody's eyes are on the ball, which creates the problem, because nobody knows where anybody else is, and Slick pulls up, but Willie and Mange don't, and nobody calls, and the ball falls, and you can hear an Oof! as Willie running full speed leaps into the air and his glove envelopes the ball, and he and Mange collide and they both go down, and Mange is looking painfully at Willie and Willie looks like he's outcold except his glove hand is sticking up in the air with the white of the ball showing at the very top.

We help Willie up, and you can tell his ribs are hurting. Mange looks o.k., and we're out of the inning, and one centerfielder ain't much to lose for the sake of ending a dangerous rally when the game's at stake. Willie'd tell you the same thing.

The darkness is thickening now, and the rain is clouding into a fog that nearly steals the fences from sight.

So back in the dugout everybody's either saying "good play" or yelling at Willie for not calling for the ball, and Willie says, "How could I call when I didn't know if I could get to it?" and Coach is mad, but that, my Friends, is the state of the world, since you should know by now that you can't please everybody, and in fact you're lucky if you ever please anybody.

And the most unhappy of all, you know, are the Hollywood fans, who of course moan and cry because their rally got snarfed like Sunday dinner. And they get even by booing Willie. That's the kind of people these Hollywood folk are: he gives up his body and makes a great play that any decent fans would cheer whether it was their hometeam player or not, but they boo like he just beaned their star freshman for the third time. People like that don't deserve baseball, because they don't know its beauty when they see it, how it all comes together from a quiet breeze over the grass into a moment of dangerous, frenzied dance, back into quiet again, just like their very own lives.

Well, as you expected, the rain continues to fall, a little harder and a little harder, and we take the score to 5-3, then they take it to 5-4, and the field is getting muddy and a little dangerous, but the ump isn't about to call the game, because we're ahead, and he doesn't want to have to deal with a bunch of irate Hollywood folks after a loss.

So we take the field in the sixth, and Flap gives up another walk and Hollywood gets a couple of line drives, one by that Malabraga guy, that skid on the wet grass, and before we can get them out, we're down 6-5, and the thing I hate most about it is listening to those Hollywood jeers. I want to get a bat in my hand, and I want to hit one all the way to Atlanta, which if you ain't realized is a long, long way from here.

So we're still playin', and Samula leads off for us in the seventh, and we gotta get a run. I don't know that I could deal with losing to these people. Samula gets a pitch to hit, and he nails it, but too high, a long drive to left that falls about ten feet short and gets caught just shy of the fence, their outfielder nearly disappearing in the fog. *Close* don't amount to much in baseball. I don't know that we'll get a better chance, cause the field is getting muddy, and now that Hollywood's ahead, the fans are screaming for the ump to stop the game. He wants to, but he'd rather let us make three outs first so he can be sure we won't complain. The umps around here aren't much good, and if enough managers complain, they can lose their jobs. What a world, huh?

But then the ump's job gets harder, cause Lance and Mange both sneak singles into wet the outfield grass, and things are getting interesting again. The ump keeps looking up at the sky, then at the Hollywood coach, and then our coach, and then he shrugs, like he wants to say, what can I do but call it? The Hollywood fans would love it, cause they don't care how they win, as long as they win. They have no honor.

And in a sense the ump is right, because the batter's box is getting muckier and muckier, and the outfield grass slipperier and slipperier, and the sky darker and darker. Maybe if we can get one run to tie we can finish the game on another day and all go home to supper. But I would love to beat this team twice and send them home hoarse and wet and 0-2.

Then Flap gets up and tries to move the runners along, but he hits it in the air to the second baseman, not deep enough to move the runners, so it's two on and one out and Willie steps up, Hollywood's fans yelling, "Call the game, Ump; call the game!"

Now the ump knows that Willie can play, so he is just about to raise his hand to call it when Coach dashes out of the dugout as fast as he can. *Dashes* is an exaggeration. Waddles would be more like it. Coach can't go very fast, but when he gets riled up, he tries, and he looks so damn sincere that you can't help but think he's going faster than he really does. It's a kinda optical allusion, I suppose.

So Coach talks to the ump for just a minute, whispers in his ear would be more accurate, then the ump kinda plays with the dirt with his foot, his head down, then he shakes his head just a little, and Coach, hands stuffed into his back pockets, starts back toward third. The ump calls, "Batter up," Willie looks at Coach then at me, then he shrugs and heads for the batter's box. I call over to Coach and ask what's up, and he says to me, just hit, kid, which is kinda stupid, since I'm not even on-deck yet, but you can never figure exactly what Coach is thinking, if anything.

Don't ask me what he said to the ump, cause I can only guess. He may have said, if you call this game now, I'll kick your butt, which was certainly an empty threat, though Coach can make that kind of thing sound, like I said, sincere, or he might have said, only a shithead (Coach likes that word, *shithead*—I could live without it) would call the game now, cause it'll look to hell like you stopped it right as we was rallyin' (that's kinda how Coach talks, though I can't get it exactly on paper), or he mighta said, I know about you and the mailman's wife, or he mighta said, look, Warren, how's the fishing at Big Bear Lake, as I was thinkin' about goin' down there this weekend?

Whatever he said, it worked, so Willie steps up to bat.

Now Willie can make any game exciting. He's just that kind of player. He can make some wild Flying Wallenda catch to save a game or he can boot a simple play to blow a big lead, but more often than not, he'll come through in the clutch, and that to me is what makes a real player. With the game on the lane, there's no one I'd rather see at the plate than Fast Willie White Shoes, except for me: I like to hit just as much as Willie does.

So Willie takes a pitch low in the dirt for ball one. The ball gets muddy, but we're long past having any fresh balls to put into play, so the muddy one, brown and slick, goes right back to the pitcher, making him more dangerous than he ought to be, both because of what a slick ball might do and because the air is getting darker and darker to see through. The pitcher glares in at Willie and smiles, and the next pitch knocks Willie on his butt. It doesn't hit him, but it does get away from the catcher far enough that Mange can move to second, though not far enough for Lance to score, since the footing around the plate is treacherous. I almost hope Willie will bunt and let Hollywood's infield scramble for the ball. But he doesn't: on the next pitch, which is high and inside, Willie swings from the heels, trying to hit the ball to China to make up for getting the brushback. Of course he misses it, and he gets up with a muddy butt, but he growls at the pitcher like some professional wrestler, trying to let the guy know he wasn't intimidated, which, I can tell you, he wasn't. He would have let the ball hit him, like he did before, but he wants to hit this guy. He wants to win standing on his feet rather than sitting on his butt, and you can't blame him for that, however you like smart baseball and bravery and all that shit.

We all yell at Willie to wait for a good pitch, but it's no use: when Willie wants to hit, Willie's going to hit, or at least swing. The guy just loves to hit. What can you say? You got to appreciate him, even if you don't think he always plays smart.

So the next pitch comes low over the outside corner, and Willie fouls it into the Woods along the edge of the hill. Count even at 2-2, he gets tough, chokes up an inch or two on the bat, and moves a little closer to the plate. The next pitch comes in high, and he manages to choke himself into not swinging, though for Willie that may be the hardest thing in life to do, or not to do. Coach is standing in the third-base coaching box with his head in his hands.

I yell to Slick, who's on-deck, to call Willie for me. Willie steps out of the box and looks over at me. I mouth "Om" at him, and he looks at me for a second, heaves a sigh, shrugs, and steps back in for the 3-2 pitch. I can see his lips move, as if he's saying *Om*.

The ball comes in high and tight, definitely ball four, close enough that Willie has to dive out of the way again, but as he's going backing off, his feet slip out from under him, and he begins to fall backward. Then it all looks like slow motion: his eyes are glued to the incoming pitch, and he manages to swing the bat even though his feet are off the ground, and he makes solid contact even though he got no leverage, and no matter what the physics teacher may say, the ball sails over the shortstop's head, and the infielders run out, and the outfielders run in, and Willie is flat on his back in the batter's box watching, and we're all yelling, get up and run! and the ball falls, and two players dive, and Willie is motating for first, and Lance is waiting to score, and the ball falls into a puddle with a thhhht! and the ball skids, and their center-fielder picks it up and throws it to first, but Willie beats it, the run scores, and Mange moves to third. And whoever said that baseball ain't dramatic and exciting, even high school baseball on a cold, rainy spring night in small-town U.S.A.?

As I told you, Willie is the kind of guy who will get you home to dinner. But so am I.

The rest, of course, is silence (I've read more than you think I have), or almost that, as Slick gets a walk to load 'em, and I get a single to center to score two. The rain eases up a bit, but it's nearly pitch dark as we take the field for their half of the seventh. The ump wouldn't call the game now even if Gabriel blew his trumpet. To keep it short, they do get one run, but me and Willie both run down shots that they hit out into the gloom, and the final batter pops to Burger at first, and it's over. The Hollywood fans pick up their chairs and head for their cars, and neither their fans nor players stop to tell us "good game."

So we stop to tell ourselves. You always got to be sure to do that and never to take one inning of baseball for granted. Every inning is immortal, and every win lives in your memory, in baseball more than in any other sport. Just ask anybody who plays or has played. My dad remembers games from twenty-five years ago, and I remember every inning from every game of my life, clear back to little league. A little part of the diamond always stays with you, and you leave a little of yourself there, and other people remember you, if nothing else as an excuse for their own losses. And we return tomorrow and every tomorrow to this sacred place where we are all live forever, as immortal as Clemente, or Mays, or Bach, or Ellington, or Shakespeare.

I catch up to Willie on the way into the dugout. Big shot, Willie White Shoes, I say, and, Bigger shot yourself, Stud, says Willie to me. And life is good for this moment, and someday me, and Willie, and even Hollywood will all pass into the gray dusk, immortal.

Don't ask me how this story got to you. That's more than I know.

9 The Fifty Excuses for Missing a Fly Ball

I'm back. Willie, that is.

Now I'm going to tell you something really important, something not about me. You can use if you're a baseball player, and if you're not, think for yourself! and adapt it to your own needs.

Don't say I never gave you anything.

Not that I ever need them myself, of course, but just about everyone can use one of the Fifty Reasons I Dropped the Fly Ball at one time or another. Here they are, in order of frequency of use:

1. The sun was in my eyes.
2. A bug flew in my eye.
3. There's a hole in my glove.
4. I stepped in a hole.
5. My spikes got caught on something.
6. My foot slipped.
7. The ball was wet.
8. Man, he hit that ball hard!
9. I lost it in a cloud.
10. I sneezed. ("Coughed" is o.k., but never "choked.")
11. I was concentrating on my hitting.
12. My girlfriend dumped me.
13. You shoulda seen the spin on that ball!
14. The ball's got a corked center. It felt funny.
15. I couldn't see: the fans all have white shirts. (Only useful if you have fans.)
16. I think there are alligators (snakes, bears) out there.
17. A girl got caught in my eye. (This one doesn't work. Trust me, but I heard someone try it.)
18. My dog died.
19. My grandmother died. (Not an honorable one, and not useful more than twice.)
20. I was getting a message from God.
21. My glove fell off.
22. My shoe was untied.

23. I have a headache from the sun.

24. I have a headache from the rain.

25. Just then I farted.

26. I farted and something came out.

27. Just then the rightfielder (or leftfielder) farted.

28. I had to piss so bad I could have died.

29. My feet were stuck in the mud (sand, water—be creative).

30. I was thinking about my homework. (Available only during the school year.)

31. The batter is my cousin, and he was in a slump.(Sometimes works with teammates, but never with coaches.)

32. I swallowed my chaw.

33. I swallowed a bug. A big one. With a stinger.

34. I realized at that moment what life is all about. But now I forgot.

35. Coach, I just got the joke you told us.

36. I got lampblack in my eye.

37. I forgot to use lampblack under my eyes.

38. I was abducted by aliens. Well, they put me back.

39. That wasn't me. That was the rightfielder (or leftfielder—this one is difficult to pull off, but plausible).

40. I just remembered that I forgot to go to church last week.

41. My pants were falling down.

42. I forgot to wear my cup. (This one can sometimes confuse them because it works for catchers and infielders.)

43. I had to chase it so far I ran out of steam. (Makes a close friend of the pitcher.)

44. A raindrop landed in my eye.

45. My glasses fogged up. (Only some guys can use this one, obviously.)

46. I couldn't judge the ball because I couldn't hear the crack of the bat because the fans were cheering too loud (not very artful, and only for use, for us, at away games).

47. My socks fell down—we need new uniforms!

48. I didn't want the rightfielder (leftfielder) to feel bad because of the one he missed, since we're going to win anyway.

49. My dog chewed on that part of my glove.

50. I was tired from spending last night with the rightfielder's (leftfielder's) girlfriend. (I never heard anyone try this one, but it just

might create a diversion.)

As I told you, you can adapt them to your needs. Many of these same excuses, *reasons*, if you prefer, will also work as explanations for Why You Didn't Get Your Homework Paper in on Time, which if you're a baseball player may be important if you don't get drafted out of high school and want to go to college. I'll give you a few more specifically for that purpose at no extra charge to you:

1. The dog ate it (the old classic).
2. The cat peed on it (also classic, but less familiar).
3. My mother accidentally threw it away.
4. My father intentionally threw it away. (This one can really get them, if you have a father.)
5. My grandmother visited, and I lost it in the confusion.
6. My typewriter broke.
7. They ran out of pens at the store.
8. I got blood all over it when I used it to wipe my face after a gang of kids beat me up.
9. I had it five minutes ago, but someone stole it. Check the other papers for my writing.
10. I already gave that to you. You didn't lose it, did you?
11. It's on your desk under Miss Simpson's stockings. (This one can really throw a scare into a male teacher.)
12. I have it all in my head if you'll just give me till tomorrow to write it. (It worked for Mozart, they say.)
13. It was so good, my brother took it for *his* class! (Obvious limitations.)
14. It flew out the bus window on my way to school, and the driver wouldn't stop.
15. The bus driver ran over it and got roadkill on it.
16. I got the flu and puked on it, but you can have it anyway.
17. My (blank) died. (The oldest one in the book. No self-respecting student would use it anymore, but I list it for the sake of completeness.)
18. I couldn't finish because I was on my deathbed. (My personal favorite, from Lenny.)
19. I had a near-death experience, and God told me He was sure you'd give me an extension.

20. My aunt is a history teacher, and she told me it needed more work.

21. My aunt is a history teacher, and she thought the paper was so good that she took it to show *her* class.

22. I accidentally dropped it in the Care package we sent to starving children in Central America.

23. I used it to stop the bleeding of a kid who got hit by a car on the way to school.

24. We ran out of toilet paper at home, so we had to use everything twice. Here's a note from my mother. (This one's better than it looks at first glance.)

25. I dropped it in the garbage disposal. (Only if you really have one.)

26. It accidentally got shredded. Here are the pieces.

27. Some seniors stopped me on my way to class. They hadn't done their homework. I bought my life with that paper. (Powerful with sympathetic teachers.)

28. I sent it to the *New York Times*. They told me it will appear in the Sunday edition.

29. I was abducted by aliens. They took my paper, too, to learn more about us.

30. I thought you had enough grading to do already. Would you like an apple?

If you're smarter than a baseball player, or even smarter than a baseball, that should be plenty for you. The main thing is, don't panic. Like, don't walk in to see your English teacher and say, "I lost it in the sun!" Remember to use the right list. And never give more than one excuse at once: "My dog ate it, but my mother would have lost it anyway!" If you try too hard, they tend not to trust you. Deliver the reason naturally and calmly, and you'll have your best chance for success. And remember that people have been doing it for generations, so you can, too! Maybe you'll even be one of those special people who add one to the all-time list. I wish you good luck.

Now, to tell you the whole truth, the list, as good as it is, will not always help you. It doesn't cover every possible instance. Your best bet is to study the list, have something ready, but then go with your instincts when the time comes. As for each excuse: as they say in the math textbooks, the proof is left to the student.

Like one time late in my freshmen year, when Spit was pitching the best game of his life.

He has a one-hit shutout going into the last inning, and we're up two-zip. He gives up a walk on a bad call, then, angry and all, moves the runner to second with a wild pitch. Coach goes out to calm him down, which he does, and then the next batter on 0-2 hits a looping liner to leftcenter. I'm charging, but the ball is dropping fast at a funny angle, ahead of me and just to my right, so I'm trying to decide whether to take the ball forehand or backhand.

Everybody knows that on a play like this, you don't have time to decide anything.

So I dive for the ball.

My hand goes almost forehand, and the ball hits off the tip of my glove and falls in. The run scores. Spit loses his shutout.

On the next play, Stud makes a great catch down the left field line to save the game, so we still win. Stud is a helluva player, let me tell you.

As I come in, I can tell that Spit is hopping mad. He really wanted that shutout, and he's probably blaming me more than the umpire, because it's easier to get even with me than with the umpire.

"Stud, why don't you play center field, too, so flyballs will get caught instead of dropped out there," Spit spits.

"Be cool, man. Willie almost made a great play. That was a tough ball," Stud answers.

"You woulda had it."

Stud looks at him, then at me. His look says, yes, I would have had it. "Well, we won," Stud says, and that's enough. You'll pitch your shutout next time."

"Shit," says Spit. Baseball players make the most sense when they say the least.

"Now, you goof-offs pack the gear so we can go home," says Coach Luke. "We won the ballgame. It's a team game, not about who did what."

Spit disappears around the corner of the dugout so Coach Luke won't hear his stream of cuss words. Coach Luke thinks about winning, not statistics, and he doesn't like guys cussing their own team, especially when we win.

But I know Spit is partly right. I look up from the ground, and everybody is looking at me, including Stud and Coach Luke.

Now is the time when I need the excuse.

I quickly scan the list in my mind. Nothing quite works.

"Sorry," I say. "I wanted it so bad for Spit. Guess I tried too hard and just muffed it. My fault all the way." Everybody knows that even if I miss, I always give it my best.

"I know it's your fault, boy" Spit says from behind the dugout. "That don't help."

"That's o.k., center," says Stud. "You always hustle. No harm done."

My reason works, sort of. You can add that one to the list: sometimes, just tell the truth.

"Spit'll throw his shutout next time out, right Spit?" adds Burger, but Spit has already gone off to sulk.

The guys pat me on the back and make me feel a little better, but not much. That's the bad thing about baseball: everybody knows when you make a mistake, and sometimes there is no excuse: you've just muffed it, and your error has cost the game or somebody's stats, or sometimes the catch is just too hard to make. Funny, though, how Spit doesn't remember that I led off the third with a single, stole second and third, and scored the first run of our two-run inning that got him his win.

One mistake can take you from first to worst. But there's always another game. Unless you die before you get to play it.

I don't know what happens after that.

Just so you know: Spit got his shutout. In our last game of the year against Central Catholic, really a better team than we were, he beat them 7-0. Burger and Pudge hit homers. I did not.

But I also didn't make any errors.

I did snag a sinking liner in leftcenter field, and I threw out two guys, one at home and one at third. I'm glad I did, because I was out of excuses. I had used up the very best one on my first try, so there was nothing worthwhile left.

Funny how those things work out.

But I also went 0-4 and dropped my batting average about twenty points. I had a fly to the base of the fence in right, flew out deep to left, bunted a little too hard and got thrown out by half a step at first, and lined to shortstop for our final out of the season and the last of my freshman year. After the game everyone congratulated Spit, including me. He didn't say anything back to me then, and he hasn't since.

People say baseball is a funny game. But people are funnier yet. The funniest game in town.

By the way: I'll be back for three more years of baseball. After that, who knows?

And you're welcome for the lists.

10 What to Do When You Don't Understand

You noticed I'm telling you this like I know what I'm doing. Well, I don't, not about life, anyway. Not that I'm dumber than most guys. I guess I'm about as smart as most baseball players. Maybe that ain't saying much.

But then you never know what's going to happen to you till it happens. Like I read this story in an old book where a guy went on vacation. While he was gone, some other guy went up to his house and acted like it was his. He told a policeman he'd locked himself out, called up a locksmith, got himself in the front door and moved right in. In a couple of days, he sold all the guy's stuff, sold the *house*, then took the money and left, never to be heard of again. Then the guy who owned the place, who all this time had been having a good time on the beach, comes back home only to find somebody he's never seen before living in his house, and all his stuff gone. Imagine that! Worse yet, I heard of a guy that *really* happened to, and you know what? It was his own son who did it! Guess that's what they mean by an inside job.

Here's where I heard it: Lenny told me that happened to his cousin. The guy was gone on a business trip, and when he got home, there was a "sold" sign on his lawn and his house was empty. So he called his son, who was away at college, and said, "What happened to the house?" And his son said, "I sold it! Made a nice profit on it, too." Lenny said his cousin was so happy that his son had done something, since the guy was practically flunking out of college, that he let him keep the money to quit college and start his own business. I swear.

I suppose that's the kinda stuff you find when you read old books, and then you find out that life is like that, too. You never know what you're gonna learn next. And sometimes it's worse than just finding that your house got sold when you were gone. Sometimes it's things you just can't understand. Then you have to figure out what to do next. Or you just feel like Stud said, *perplexed.*

That's where I am now. I guess you could say this is where things get confusing, or maybe you'll just say that things are always confusing: that's the way things work. When I was a kid, a little kid, I always thought the world was simple: you eat, you sleep, you play ball. Everything else you did was so you could eat, sleep, and play ball without anybody bothering you. Now I don't know anymore. So here it is, this story, and you can decide for yourself.

Well, it's the end of my sophomore year, and this year's team is the best I've ever played on. I'm leading off and hitting about .350, which ain't great, but ain't bad for my second year. We've got five guys hitting well over three hundred, and six of us have made the league all-star team—that is, if you include me as an alternate. All the guys say I should have made the team straight out, but this year Coach picked the all-stars, and naturally he left me off. Next year I'll hit .400 and anybody will have to pick me or not pick me, and anyone who leaves me off will get arrested for robbery.

But for now we're winning, eighteen and five: like, that's amazing for baseball, and it looks like we're dead set to win the league, sweep the playoffs, and head for Districts. And this is the team that could win it. Our infield defense is only fair, and our pitching ain't none too deep, but we hit and we run and we know how to win, and, most important, we believe we can win, no, we know it, every day we take the field.

So we've just won number eighteen at home on a warm, misty evening toward the end of May, more than this school has ever won before. Spit, our ace, tossed three innings to stay tuned-up, then Pudge came in from third base to throw two innings and gave up only one run, and Flap came off the bench to finish the last two and get the save. Yours truly scored two runs—the fans went wild—and Mange got three hits, which ain't that easy to do in a seven-inning game when you bat eighth. We make a little noise, but for the most part we're cool, professional, you know. Mange, of course, says nothing. Everybody congratulates Pudge on the win and Flap on the save. Everybody's cool except Flap. He's acting all crazy, jumping up and down, swatting everybody on the butt. He comes over and starts to squeeze my shoulders and pick me up, so I just kinda shake him off and try to keep my distance, so he starts following Pudge around like a puppy.

Not too many guys can put up with Flap. He's just too weird. Lenny won't go near him. Burger and I will talk to him, but not for longer than we have to, not only for the jumpiness, but because he's been the only thing to upset our dugout rhythm and make us think about anything but winning. Not that he's that bad a player: he'll throw a couple of solid innings and get his bat on the ball when he has to. But there's something about him that makes him uncomfortable to be around, like something is always bothering him, hiding in the back of his mind but looking around the corner at you, almost as though he doesn't even know it's there.

When we got back to school, he was even worse. He kept going up to everybody and putting his arm around our shoulders, which can be bad enough anyplace, but will really make you self-conscious in the shower. He kept yelling, "Yeah, we showed those wussies, we wupped those faggots, yeah," till finally even Burger told him to keep it down. Now usually Burger is the last guy to get riled up and the first guy to join in after-the-game cheers, so something really has to be bothering him before he'll tell anyone to knock it off.

But we won, and I can go home and forget Flap, almost, and think about hits and runs and how I'm gonna hit one outta the park in our next game on Friday.

Not likely.

In the evening I'm out running, up the hill, down to the river, through the back streets, as the mist is starting to rise, and I spot Stud, who's back visiting from college. If we still had him, we'd never lose.

"What's happenin, Stud."

"Man, did you hear about Mange's dad?"

"No."

"Aw, man, bad accident in the mill. I heard he was dead."

"Dead?"

"Yeah, and another guy hurt bad, I don't know who. They was down on the floor when a cable came loose on a crane. Dropped a couple ton a steel on them. They didn't even see it coming.

"I can't believe it."

"I know. Me neither. But that ain't all of it."

I felt my stomach turning. "What else?"

"Flap's dad was driving the crane."

"No."

"No shit. They said it wasn't his fault, though: old loose cable, just one of those things."

So I hurry back home, and Ma doesn't even say "Don't slam the door" cause she's just heard about it: one of the other mothers called. Mange's father died, and another guy got his leg totally smashed, probably crippled. They didn't say anything about Flap's dad.

Ma says, "Tomorrow I'll call Mange's mother to see if there's anything I can do for her. Tonight no one could do anything."

"You don't even know Mange's mother. In fact, I don't know if anybody knows Mange's mother. I didn't even know he had a father."

"Somebody must know her. And everybody has a father."

"What about me?"

"Go get a bath and eat your dinner."

The next day was Saturday. The sun rose early, round and yellow as daffodils. We were supposed to have a game, but it was canceled because of Mange's father. I went up to the field anyway, ran up before breakfast to keep my legs strong. When I got to the top and crossed to the field, Mange was there, standing by second base.

I took a couple of laps around the field, trying to figure out what to say. Mange looked around at me once, but just stood there still as an empty base. Finally I went up to him.

"How you doin'?"

He looked once at my chin, but didn't say anything. I realized that his eyes were about level with my chin. Was I growing?

"I heard about your dad. Really sorry."

I waited for a long time and was turning to go when he spoke.

"He was a shit anyway."

I couldn't believe he said that. I thought you weren't supposed to speak ill of the dead, and all that stuff, and it was his *father*. I don't think I'd say that about my father right after he died even if he was a shit.

But then, what if he was? Should you still be sorry? What do you say to somebody when his shitty father dies? What about your own? My father was probably shitty, too, but I didn't want him to die. But then Mange hadn't said he had wanted his father to die, only that, while he was living, he was shitty. Is it disrespectful to say what's true, if you don't say it in front of your family or to a roomful of people, but to somebody out on a baseball field when nobody else is around? Shouldn't there be some place where you can say what's true without anybody getting juiced?

"Well, I'm sorry anyway," I said. It was stupid, but it was all I could think of. I started to go, and Mange spoke again. That, in itself, Mange speaking twice in one day, may never happen again.

"There's gonna be more yet. You know about Flap?"

I went back. "What about Flap?"

"You don't know?" he said.

"What?"

He just made this kind of coughing noise and half laughed.

"What about Flap? You mean Flap's father."

"He looked at my chin again, then turned away. No matter how many times I asked him what he meant, he wouldn't say anything else. He wouldn't even look at me again. So now I've got this mystery on my mind and no idea what it means. I took two more laps around the field wondering what to do, then just headed down the hill for home.

The sun skipped bright off the spring leaves, and a breeze blew out toward left, not seeming to care if anybody had died. It would have been a perfect day for baseball, if.

But on Tuesday we did play again, our last game of the season before tournament. Nobody was talking to Mange, just patting him on the shoulder or the butt. And nobody was talking to Flap, either. But it wasn't because of his dad and the broken crane, though I didn't know that at the time.

We began the game with a moment of silence for Mange's father. Coach requested it. That almost made me believe that Coach is a human being. Almost. At least somebody had the decency to do it, instead of canceling the game.

When things go bad, you still need baseball, to get your mind on something else.

Well, we got down early 3-1 to Beaumont, that's a town south along the river, but we tied them in the sixth. Yours truly had an rbi double and a hit-by-pitch and scored two runs. But they got this football player who plays left field and bats fourth for them, and he can, man, hit moon shots, balls that disappear into the sky, so we're careful and walk him, and lefty Lowry manages to keep us tied into the last inning.

We load the bases with two out against their lefty, and who does Coach send up to pinch-hit for Clem Lowry but Flap himself.

No one can believe it, least of all, me. Cancel what I said about Coach being a human being. Not only was Flap being weirder than ever, but everybody knew he didn't hit lefties very well.

But he did go up, looking like he really wanted to hit, really determined, but pale as a new baseball right out of the box.

Flap took their pitcher to two-and-two, then fouled off a couple, took a third ball in the dirt, and bounced one to second for the third out. End of possible rally. Nobody said a word.

Well, Coach brought in Treetops, a freshman but a decent pitcher, if such exist, to try to get Beaumont out so we could hit again, but as I've said, you just can't trust pitchers. Tree is always a gamer, but he didn't have much experience yet in tough situations, so he loads the bases with one out and Mr. Leftfielder-linebacker coming up to bat.

You can't walk him, cause we lose, and you can't give him anything to hit, cause we lose.

Treetops took him to 2-1, then fed him a kneehigh fastball on the outside corner, which the guy sent missiling to left.

Of course, Davey's playing in close so he can make a play at the plate on a short fly ball.

But the guy hits a long fly ball instead.

Davey just stands there. He knows the game is over.

Me? I'm sprinting full-out for that ball cause maybe I'll catch it and the ground is uneven but I'm holding on and the ball is falling and Davey doesn't even turn his back and I'm stretching to make the catch and maybe the guy tagging at third will trip or have a heart attack and I'll catch and throw and he'll be out the plate and we'll have another chance and I'll get to bat again cause I was on deck and maybe I'll hit a homer and we'll win and some girl will come out of the stands and kiss me and say "good play" and TV crews will want interviews but why would that happen cause we're not playing at home more likely some yokel will pull out a shotgun and drill me for stealing the game from his team and I'll die and I wonder if any of the girls from town will put flowers on my grave maybe Lana and the ball is falling fast and I'm diving but I'm nowhere near it and falls cleanly and bounces to the fence and I roll over and the run is scoring and there's nothing I can do and Davey looks depressed but not stupid but I look really STUPID diving for a ball that lands twenty feet away but that's just me I can never give up oh well.

We lost.

I can never get used to those words, even though in baseball you're doing pretty well if you win three outta every five.

But there's something ominous when you lose the last game of the season before tournament.

By the way, Mange went two for three with two runs scored. Who'd believe that, after what he went through?

Two days later I got to class in the morning and Samula turned around and says to me, "Man, did you hear what happened now?" And I said, What? And he said, "I can't believe it," and he told me.

I can't believe it, either. I didn't even know those things really happened. I thought they were just some joke that people used to make fun of somebody. But it wasn't a joke. As if things hadn't been bad enough. Man, the world is a screwed-up place.

Flap shot himself.

Dead.

Seems he snuck his father's pistol and hid in their garage, and sometime in the middle of the night, he pointed it toward his head and pulled the trigger.

I asked Samula why. He just turned red and turned around wouldn't say another word. For the whole class I couldn't think of anything else, even after Miss Ripley threatened me twice with death by geometry problems. After class Samula hustled out before I could talk to him.

I searched the halls until I found Davey on his way to class. "Davey, did you hear what happened?"

"Yeah, I heard. Idiot."

"Just because of a little ground-out? It doesn't make any difference. We're gonna win the tournament anyway. Everyone knows we're the best team in the league this year. One loss is no big deal. Or was it because of what happened with his dad?"

"Aw, man, it wasn't the game or that. Don't you know?"

I thought for a minute. "Not Mange's father? Everybody knows that wasn't Flap's dad's fault. He even went to the funeral."

"Ain't nobody ever told you about stuff? It had nothing to do with baseball or with Mange's father. It had to do with Flap. He should have learned to live with it. We ain't living in the damn Dark Ages. And he shoulda been more careful or changed himself or stopped himself or something." Davey wouldn't say anything else. He slipped into class before the bell, leaving me alone in the hall, late.

By then the whole school was buzzing about it. There was a policeman in with the principal, and teachers whispered together in the hallways, but no announcement came over the PA.

All day everybody whispered, but nobody would talk out loud. How could they expect us to understand?

I mean, Flap was no great friend, but he had been a guy like the rest of us, and a baseball player, and now he was dead.

At the end of the day I chased down Pudge before he could catch the bus home. Pudge was a senior and a smart guy, so I figured he would tell me what happened.

He laughed at me.

"Look, Willie, I gotta get the bus. Ask your Mom or somebody. I'm not gonna explain it to you."

On the way home, Lenny wouldn't say a word. He just blushed and kept walking. Imagine a baseball player blushing.

One of our teammates puts a bullet through his own head, and nobody will tell me why.

Practice was canceled, but I went to the field anyway. Whatever else I didn't know, one thing I could count on: finding Mange out by second base. I walked right up to him.

"Why did Flap shoot himself? Did his father beat him or something? Was he into drugs? Why?"

First, Mange wouldn't say anything. Then he looked over my left ear. "You stupid, or what?"

"Look, no one else will tell me. Just tell me."

"You sure you're old enough to know?"

"Just tell me."

"All right. Flap was a fag."

What?

"You know." And then he let out a string of words that even I wouldn't write down. I never heard Mange say so many words at once, and not one of them printable, even for a guy who has written down *shithead*.

"That's why he shot himself?"

"Some people caught him with some other kid, a guy, down under the bleachers at the football stadium. Man, they were really goin' at it. Everybody in the whole school knows about it but you. The people who caught them told everybody. They said Flap would get sent to jail, cause it's illegal."

By that time my head was spinning and I had to think. I didn't want to think.

Sometimes you just have to think, and other times you need not to think.

That evening I put on my shorts and went out to run. I ran and ran, musta been a couple of hours. I couldn't get myself to stop. And I couldn't stop thinking about Flap, and as hard as I tried I couldn't understand.

Why does life make such confusing stuff?

When the darkness was thick as flannel uniforms and the streetlights burning so bright that Zane Street looked like a night game, I saw Stud, back from College, walking home from his girlfriend's house.

I stopped him. "Stud," I said, "I just don't understand, about Flap."

Stud sighed, looked at me like I was some stupid little kid, which in some ways, I guess, was right. "Look, Willie, some people are just like that, you know? The world isn't always perfect and easy. But I don't know why the idiot shot himself. More people are like that than you'd think. Who knows why? Maybe he should have just accepted it, and we would have accepted him."

"But wouldn't everyone in town know about it? Mange said they might send him to jail or something."

"I doubt it. They'd have to send a lot of people to jail, even in this little town, people you might never suspect. It's not as if he raped somebody. Then I could understand his shooting himself. But once he got caught, I guess, maybe he thought he wouldn't have had much chance living around here anymore."

Stud went home, and I kept on running, running until I was too tired to think, damn near too tired to move. Then I stumbled home, took a bath, and went to bed. I didn't tell Ma what I'd heard. Maybe she knew already. Ma had a way of not talking about things that were too hard to talk about. Can't say I blame her. Some things are just too hard to tell your kids, I guess.

The next morning in school the principal made an announcement on the PA, that Flap was dead, and when and where the funeral would be. "Our grief goes out to the family," was about all he said. I guess he didn't need to say more—what would be the use? I guess he could have said "Pray for him" or something like that, but maybe even that would have been too much.

Then school went on like normal.

Two days later we took out 18-6 record to Marshall for the first game of the tournament. We were seeded first. We lost 4-1. I went 0-2, got beaned twice, stole two bases, didn't score. Davey and Slick and Mange got our only three hits. Slick made a great catch in right field, and I made one in center. Marshall played lots better. That fast, our season was over.

I guess I felt worst for Slick and Burger and Pudge, the seniors, who played their last game, losing in the first round when we had been talking about making it to state and putting our little town on the map. I really thought we had the team to do it. Sometimes even that isn't enough.

Nobody said much after the game. Nobody talked much on the way home on the bus, just the usual jokes and comments about people on the streets: some guy's fast car, how beautiful somebody's girlfriend was, the major league standings, somebody's date that night. Somebody asked Pudge what college he was going to. Somebody was surprised that Stud had gone to college and thought he'd quit to go into the Air Force after all, which he had told us he might do. Slick wanted to go to school for psychology and Burger was just going to try to get a job at the mill and take classes at the Branch campus because he wanted to stay close to his girlfriend. Other guys were looking for summer jobs or wishing school would end so we could start up summer baseball leagues. Nobody said much to Mange, and nobody mentioned Flap.

When the bus got back, we showered and went home. As we left, Slick and Burger wished me a good season of summer baseball. The rest filtered home. I wanted to say something to the guys who had played their last game, but what do you say? We had promise, and we blew it. No, not even that: we didn't really blow it. We didn't play that bad, make errors, strike out with the bases loaded. We played a game, did our best, lost to a better team, and it was over. Maybe that was what I couldn't get off my mind, that word: *over.* Yogi Berra said, "It ain't over till it's over." Well, Yog, it was over. The season for me, high school for the seniors, life for Mange's dad and for Flap, and what about Flap's poor dad, too? What would he do after all that?

And here's where I'm supposed to be a man, to say something important, like I sort of said I would before, about what to do when you don't know what to do. And you know what? I don't know what to say any more than I know what to do.

On the way home I stole a flower out of Mrs. Scarfo's garden and left it on the kitchen table for Ma. I took a bat and two beat-up old dead baseballs from my room and walked down to the river. When I got to the bank, I took the bat and one ball, wound up, and hit the ball just as far as I could out into the water. "That's for Mange's father," I yelled.

The ball splashed and disappeared.

Then I picked up the other ball, and hit it even farther. "That's for Flap," I yelled again.

Somebody had to do something. He was a baseball player, just a guy. We should all know that.

The river bubbled on, as it always does, not taking the slightest notice that I could see. I turned for home, listening. I stopped: no sounds but the river and a car passing in the distance.

I had a hard time thinking of stories to tell for a long time. I just couldn't write anything down, couldn't understand and couldn't forget. And to this day I still don't fully understand why all those things happened as they did. That's life in Harmon Falls, or maybe anywhere.

11 Homecoming

You may notice that I'm not telling you everything. Sometimes months go by, and I don't tell you anything at all about them, and sometimes I tell you a lot about a couple of hours.

Fact is, sometimes there's not much to tell, even for someone like me, who lives a life of constant excitement and adventure. Right. Especially the months without baseball are slow, maybe even pointless. But sometimes even in the offseason things happen that are worth telling or even thinking about.

If you're only interested in the baseball part, you can skip this chapter. But you might want to read it anyway. But WARNING: the Surgeon General has determined that this chapter may be hazardous to your health. It's not a pretty story, but I'll tell you anyway. Hell, some of the others haven't been pretty, either, but you made it through those, or you wouldn't still be here. And it's better to know that sometimes death doesn't go away, even after roadkills and Mange's father and Flap.

It was in the fall of my junior year, around a couple weeks before Homecoming in football season. Now, as you know, I don't much care about football, but at Homecoming, a good time can be had by all, even me, because everybody's excited and all the girls are fired up and lookin' for somebody to go to the Homecoming Dance with them. And word was out that Angelina Zamboni had her eye on me, and if I was interested, I might get a date with her, and if that doesn't sound interesting to you, then you ain't seen Angelina Zamboni.

Now I know her brothers ain't much: decent guys, but kind of big and slow, destined to drive a truck or run a pizza shop even with rich parents, which ain't bad if you ask me. But Angelina is something different entirely. As Lenny once put it, she's everything a boy could want from A to Z. Lenny's no great connoisseur of women, and maybe you think I'm not either, but he happens to be right this time. Angelina could make you melt on January ice.

She is the kind of girl who can make your pants too tight just by your looking at her. Not even looking; her smell, her presence around a corner is enough. All you have to do is know she's somewhere near. And sometimes you know without knowing—know what I mean?

But not too many guys get too near. For a while she dated Harry Kuschner, who plays a mean trumpet, and for the last year she'd been with Pervis Easly, who plays in a local rock band. She likes the musical but tough types, and Harry and Pervis are both athletes, too. But about the only music I can do is Sinatra or Tony B., and maybe some Nat King Cole and a little James Taylor, which doesn't go too far with girls these days, so maybe about now you're as confused as I am.

Why would anyone *tell* me Angelina is interested in me?

Got to be a joke.

And Harry and Pervis have the only bands in town that can play their way out of a paper bag. So she can't find another musical type unless she goes to The City.

Now, why, you ask, would Angelina *be* interested in me, when she can have her pick of the local rock stars?

Answer: damned if I know, and damned if I care. If it turns out she is, I'm not asking questions.

At the end of last baseball season, she and some of her friends actually came to one of our games, probably to make Pervis jealous, because nobody comes to our games just for fun. I made one diving catch, one of my best ever, mostly out of instinct, but I couldn't hit for shit, mostly because every time I came up to bat, I couldn't think about anything but Angelina Zamboni out there watching me, and I wanted to do something spectacular like I've never wanted anything ever before. So maybe I had some impressive swings and hit some huge pop-ups that went nowhere.

Well, nothing more came of it then, but by a couple of weeks before Homecoming this year we, that is Angelina and I, were doing some weird kind of dance in the halls at school: you know, she circles me, I circle her, by chance we almost run into each other then we blush and spin and hurry the other way.

Finally we're about a week away. Pervis, nearly ready to graduate, is chasing older girls now, they say. Angelina wants to make sure she's gonna get asked by somebody, so I'd better make my move or forever hold my peace.

One morning I run into Alberta Donally, one of Angelina's buddies, by my locker. So what's she doing there, huh? She says, kinda coy, "So, baseball man, you goin' to the Homecoming Dance?"

"Not yet, I'm not. But you know that already."

"So what's wrong? Don't you wanna go?"

"Yeah, I'd like to go. You askin'?"

"Sorry, boy, I got a date. But I know someone who might not mind goin' with you."

"Who might that be?"

"You know that already yourself. But you better hurry, cause she's not gonna wait much longer, and A. Z. can go with anyone she wants. Then don't say I never warned ya."

Then Alberta Donley flounced off down the hall, her hair bouncing and her butt wiggling.

I had to walk to class with my books hanging directly in front of me, partly because of Alberta's wiggle, but mostly at the thought of the real possibility of a date with Angelina Zamboni.

Now here's the thing: I told you I know a little about girls, but not much. Here's my experience: getting turned down for the Freshman Dance three times. One girl said "Ick," one girl said "Yuck," and the third one said, "Go away, baseball geek." So you can guess my confidence was running high.

I suppose you know what I thought about all through class. It wasn't algebra, that's for sure, more like solid and circular geometry, and lots of other good things of Angelina Zamboni's. By the time class was over and I had to get up and leave, I was damn near ready to faint. I was stumbling down the hall feeling kinda like you do when you're getting the flu, not quite thinking of where I was going, then all of a sudden I notice that the hall has cleared out except for one person standing at a locker, replacing some books.

Angelina Zamboni.

She turns her head and looks at me, her dark hair flops to one side, and then she turns her head back toward her locker, her face pink as a rose and a little smile crossing her lips.

I wonder, can I get by without saying anything? Maybe if I just hang my head low enough the floor will absorb me and I'll disappear, and Angelina will think, huh, I guess that wasn't him after all. Then I'll call her. Or send her a letter. Or move to Tahiti and open a hot dog stand and never show my face here again.

But that would be rude. I go by, smooth as I can manage, and by the time I'm almost past her, I gotta say something, so I search for something dashing and devastatingly charming.

"Hi, Angelina." I don't even turn my head.

Very quietly: "Hi, Willie."

Now I turn my head, and I get one long look at Angelina Zamboni, from head to toe, facing me, her brown eyes flashing.

This may be my last chance, and I may not even get it if I faint first. Think of something cool, something suave, but think of something. Keep your composure. Come on, boy, it's the World Series, last of the ninth with two outs, and you're behind. Your behind is on the line. Just don't think of Angelina's behind, cause then you will faint.

"Would you wanna think about going to the Homecoming Dance with me?" I blurted it out. I think that's what I said. I'm not sure. Pretty awful, no?

"All right, I'll go with you."

She turns to close her locker, tosses me a quick smile, flips her hair dark as a wave at midnight. The bell rings for class, she disappears into the nearest classroom, the door closes behind her, and the hall is silent, except for the ringing in my ears and my heart thumping like a stereo with the base cranked all the way up. I am once again late for English class. How do I always manage to do that? And what new insult will Mrs. Brickhouse have for me today as I sneak in after the bell?

More important, what do I do now that I actually have a date with Angelina Zamboni? I don't think I've said two dozen words to her in my life, and a dozen of them were just a minute ago and I'm not even quite sure what they were.

I always thought getting the date was the hard part. Once you have it, what do you do next? I don't know when to pick her up, or where, or how. My God, I don't even have a car. Don't you have to have a car? What do you wear to a Homecoming? Do you have to dance? What do you do if you don't know how to dance? What do you do if you get a huge zit the day before the dance? What do I do if she ends up Homecoming Queen? Do I get to kiss her? When? How much does the dance cost? Where do we go after for dinner? Where am I going to get money, anyway?

And you thought you had problems.

Well, maybe you do, and maybe I don't. I *do* get to take Angelina Zamboni to the Homecoming Dance. Oh, no: what will her brothers say? Suggestion to readers: always date an only child, or at least one without enormous older brothers.

Come to think of it, why does she want to go with me, anyway? If I were a girl, would I want to go with me? No way to answer that. Maybe she thinks I'm good looking. No accounting for taste. Really, what does it matter why she wants to go? She's going, and I'm going to enjoy it, if for no other reason than I can spend the evening staring at Angelina, and I can bet she will look her best for Homecoming. You should be so lucky.

Word gets around quickly. When school's done, Lenny comes up to me with this huge smile on his face and swats me on the back. "You dog, you dog of a dog. Angelina Zamboni! How'd you do it?"

"Natural talent."

"Yeah, for being a dog. You are the world's luckiest dog. Man, I'd give up cars, baseball, and *Playboy* magazine for a date with Angelina Zamboni. And pizza. And my dog. And my whole family."

That struck something strange deep in me. At the time I couldn't quite tell what. But I felt a little bit awful.

"What do you say, Willie? I'll trade you the whole thing, car, mom, sister, food, great literature, dog, and I'll throw in my autographed Billy Williams baseball in exchange for your date with Angelina."

Something in that list, I'm not sure what, made me hesitate for just an instant.

"Sorry, she's not mine to trade. I just have a date with her, anyway; I didn't win her in a poker game."

"You dog. You dog of a dog."

"Where did you get *Playboy* magazines, anyway?"

"I traded Dirk Jenson some car parts for them." Dirk and Lenny had become fast friends since Lenny got interested in cars.

I almost said, let's get you a date and we can double. But something stopped me, something I'm not proud of. Would Angelina want to be on a double date with Lenny and a girl who would go out with Lenny?

I like Lenny, Lenny is my friend, but Lenny is not the kind of friend who would impress a girl, especially one with a lot of class, like Angelina Zamboni.

"So, Len, you goin' to the dance?" I didn't say it intending to be offensive. Just, hopeful, to make myself feel better. But I could tell it made him feel bad.

"Naw, I'll just stay home and work on my car."

Lenny had just got hold of a '67 Chevy, a real junker, but he had been fixing and painting bit by bit, part by part, until it was starting to look not so bad. The thought passed into my head that I might ask him to borrow his Chevy, if it would run, to take Angelina to the dance; at least it's cool, better than Ma's old Ford. But the thought sunk right out again loaded me down with a chain of guilt.

"I don't really want to go anyway," Lenny said. "I don't know how to dance, and there's nobody I want to take." He looked at me with a little bit of envy, but hidden behind years of our friendship.

"Come on, Len, let's go throw a little baseball to work off the excitement," I suggested.

"I think I'll just get my homework done so I can work on the car tonight. Thanks anyway." I wondered if he might not just offer me his car himself, but he didn't. Better not to think of that.

"Well, let's get on home then, cause I'll need to go for a run. Man, I feel like someone just injected me full of steroids or jet fuel and I'm gonna shoot off like a rocket if I don't get ridda some of this energy." We jogged home, and I had a hard time not leaving him behind, I was so full of anticipation.

That night I ran like I was on fire, and partly I was.

Homecoming came around quickly. I checked with everyone I could think of to see how you do a Homecoming dance, asked as casually as I could so's I wouldn't look like a complete geek. I ordered a corsage of big mums and made a dinner reservation at La Traviata, the only place worth going to around here, and Italian at that, which I thought would go over well with the Zambonis. I did a couple painting jobs on a Saturday and rented a tux jacket, tie, and shiny black shoes, and when Ma was out I pressed my best pair of jeans to wear with them—you can't change your style entirely, or, even if you look good, you'll feel stupid.

I cut the last grass of the season and picked up a couple more jobs cleaning out some people's garages to earn enough money for tickets, dinner, and a new white shirt. I got my hands almost clean in time for the dance. The only problem left was a car.

Ma was so excited when I told her I was going to the dance that she offered me her car right away. I didn't know how to tell her that I couldn't take out Angelina Zamboni in that beat-up old Ford. I think Ma almost shed a tear at the idea of my first big date—you know, her son growing up, her getting old, all that stuff. I hardly saw Lenny all week long. One day he asked me to ask Angelina's friend Wendy Chance to go to the dance with him, but I tried to explain that it was hard enough for me to ask for myself, let alone for him. Then he said I should use my influence with Angelina, but I said, what influence?

Well, he said, you are going to the dance with her. Then I realized that I hadn't talked with her since that day in the hall and it was Tuesday before the dance and I wondered if I really was going with her after all. Wednesday morning she came up to me before school and said hi and I should talk to her Friday about plans. The whole thing could have been a little warmer, if you ask me. Almost sounded like a funeral.

But all this stuff was new to me. For all I knew, that's how dates always go.

Wednesday night I took Ma 's car over to Dirk Jensen, Lenny's friend, to see what he could do to take care of the engine knock and spruce up the old beast. That boy really knew his cars, but even he couldn't turn chicken shit into a chick magnet.

"Give it up, Smith. Rent a limo or something, cause you wouldn't want to be seen in this old pile a' shit. Can't you borrow one from somebody?"

"Not unless you got something you could lend me cheap."

"I ain't havin' nothin' to do with that damn dance or that damn school, and nothin' a' mine is gonna show up at that shithole."

It was common knowledge that Dirk's girlfriend, Gloria Hankins, had dumped him a couple weeks before. Now Gloria ain't much, unless you especially like someone who could use an extra front tooth or two and who looks like she hasn't slept in about two weeks, but Dirk and Gloria had gone together since junior high, and word was out that they did the deed, you know, regularly. They say you can get mighty quarrelsome when you're used to getting it and then all of a sudden you don't anymore. What would I know?

Frankly, Dirk didn't look any too good either, with grease all over him, a cigarette hanging from his lip, and a nasty bruise around his left eye, so I left quick as I could, thinking it hadn't been very smart of me to go to see him of all people. Things were looking bad for ol' Willie in Mudville.

By the time Friday of Homecoming week rolled around everyone was too excited to think of anything except football, the dance, or parties, so school was a total washout, which, frankly, it is about all the time anyway. As for me, I still didn't have a car, and I was beginning to get worried: I don't mind hitting in the clutch, but the coach has to put me in the game before I can do it. And I hadn't seen Angelina all day long to set up things for Saturday.

Friday night I walked to the football game, stewing and praying. I got there as the band was coming in, and I began to search the stands for someone I knew. I saw some of the baseball team here and there and waved. I spotted Lana, Lenny's sister, sitting with Harry Kuschner, of all people. I wondered what that meant. Lenny was not to be found—at home, working on his car, getting more and more silent by the day. Then I saw Angelina, sitting with her friends, Alberta and Wendy and Jenny Gathers and some members of Pervis Easley's band, not far from Lana and Harry. They were clapping with the band and cheering with the cheerleaders and looked to be having a good old time. I pushed my way through the crowd, snuck up next to Angelina, and sat down.

"Hi."

She was singing the school fight-song with the others. She didn't stop singing, but flashed me a nervous smile. When the song was done and everyone had clapped and cheered, she turned to me and said, sweet as can be, "How are you?"

"Fine. How are you?"

"Great. It's gonna be a great game. I know we'll win." I knew that, too. Everyone knew that. We had about an average to decent football team that year, but the school always tries to schedule the Homecoming game against a school they know we can slaughter so everybody feels great and nostalgic and proud to be a Harmon Falls Lion for at least one day.

Did I ever tell you we're the Lions? Big woop, huh?

So I sit with Angelina for a while, and damned if I can think of anything to say, and she doesn't say much to me, either, but chatters on and on with her girlfriends and occasionally flashes me a smile, which, you're thinking, ought to be enough to keep me happy, and it nearly is.

Nearly.

But I still have to figure out what to tell her about tomorrow and Ma's car and a thousand other things I can barely remember. I'm just about to spill my guts or get up and leave, I just make the slightest move in my hips, and Angelina turns to me and says, "Don't worry about tomorrow. Everything's taken care of. We're going with Alberta and Brian and Jenny and Phil in Phil's new Camaro that his dad bought him. After the dance we'll drive up to The City and eat at La Boheme, it's like the greatest place there is. Brian's parents made a reservation for us in their penthouse dining suite, and it'll all be great. Just come by at six-thirty to pick me up. See you then." This time I get a big smile, and she touches my wrist, and my head is spinning again, and the tone of her voice says, you are excused now, loyal subject; I'll ring if I want anything further. So I mutter o.k., bye-bye, try to smile, and disappear into the crowd.

Boy, does it ever sound stupid when a guy says "bye-bye." And I didn't know much about Brian and Phil: they come from the up-the-hill fancy-houses-with-swimming-pool, tennis-playing vacationing-at-the-beach crowd, and neither had ever bothered to speak to me, but I guess we'll get real chummy tomorrow, I thought. And I guess "pick me up" means show up at my front door, but don't bring that awful car and you'll spare us all some embarrassment.

I'm tingling all over with something, but I don't know what.

By halftime our team is up 14-0 and not looking back, so I head for home. I run up the hill, past Lenny's, where the garage light is on late, down past the river, up into our tiny downtown where the time and temperature blink all night long all year long for no one to see, and I get home just as the crowds are celebrating their way back from the football game. The band will march all through town playing the fight-song and cheering, and sleepy people will cheer back, half-dressed, from their porches or yards as the band goes by. I jump into the back yard over the fence and do some incline push-ups on the porch steps. I lie in the cool grass for sit-ups, but the grass feels too cold and damp, so I just lean back on the steps and look at the stars. Did you ever wonder how someone figured out that this or that group of stars looks like a horse, a hunter, or some ancient queen? And why did we still believe them?

Later, on the kitchen table there's a note waiting for me: "Dominic from the flower shop delivered these mums for your date. They're really sweet. Have a good time. Mom."

In the morning I get up early, no small feat for me on Saturday, take a workout and a bath, and proceed to spend my day worrying. What do I know about dances? What do I know about girls? What do I know about anything but baseball? Ma has left me some lunch and gone out, so I'm eating and trying not to toss my cookies when who should knock at the back door but Lenny.

"How ya' doin', Willie?"

"Fine, ol' buddy. Come on in and have a sandwich."

"No, thanks, I don't want any."

"Too bad. I'm just gonna throw them up anyway."

"What's wrong with 'em?"

"Nothing."

"Oh, big Casanova, huh, chickening out on his date tonight, tossing his cookies?"

"Damn near. I think I'm in over my head."

"So learn how to swim. What's this?"

"Corsage for my date tonight."

"Big mums for her big mams."

"Cut it out, man. Try not to be disgusting."

"There's nothing disgusting about her. Boy, I'd like to take her flowers and..."

"Len."

"Oh, all right. You're no fun anymore."

"I just hope Angelina doesn't say that."

"Oh, it'll be great, man. Just think of it: you and Angelina Zamboni. Just think of it like throwing a baseball, and remember, don't squeeze too tight. And no matter how good she looks in her dress, just think of how good she'd look out of it. Too bad we couldn't have double dated."

"Yeah, that would have been great."

"Well, I just came to bring you this. It's my good luck charm, and you can keep it till tomorrow and bring it back and report to me on how you did, if you're home by then."

He reaches into his coat pocket and pulls out his autographed baseball. There's the script in black ink: "Billy Williams."

"You'd trust me with this?"

"Only for a day. And I want a full report. Everything."

"Everything a gentleman can tell."

"You dog. You Casanova of a dog."

Lenny left, and I concentrated on trying to keep my lunch down and watching a dance show on the TV, trying to pick up some moves.

About one, Ma pulled in, but not in her own car. She got out of Uncle Fred's Pontiac Le Mans with a big smile on her face.

"What have you got Uncle Fred's car for, Ma?"

"For you," she said. "To take Angelina to the dance."

Once again, I nearly fainted. I'm not that weak, really, that I'm near fainting all the time. Remember, this is the guy who runs into fences and up vertical hills. But all this dating stuff was nearly too much for me. After a moment of nearly jumping outta my shoes, I wondered how I was going to tell Ma that it wouldn't matter what I was driving, because we were going in Phil Johnson's Camaro. Answer: don't tell her.

"Thanks, Ma. This is great. Better than I could have ever expected."

"Don't thank me. Thank your Uncle Fred. Call him now, if you want to."

Of course I had to, which meant I also had to put up with Uncle Fred's out-of-date advice, although Uncle Fred had a reputation for being a lady's man in his day. I listened just in case. Trust me, nothing worth reporting. I picked up another dance show on TV about three, tried to keep Ma out of the living room so I could practice. Now and then she'd poke her head around the door and laugh and laugh.

By five the nerves were settling in. When I appeared dressed at five-thirty, Ma had a fit at my clothes. Yelling: No jeans! That's not how to tie a tie! What color are those socks! Where's your comb? Were you raised in a barn?

Now how am I supposed to answer that last one?

So I just tried to do everything Ma told me and not throw up. Had to wear the jeans, though: they were the only pants I had that looked pressed. Ma had got me a nice tux jacket from a garage sale, so you'd hardly notice the jeans anyway—saved some money not renting.

So I'm back trying to find another dance show on TV, and a car pulls up in front of the house.

Not just a car: a Lincoln Continental. Now I'm watching this guy sling himself around the front of the car and come up to our porch. He calls my name.

The man's broad, hairy chest is hanging out of his shirt, which is unbuttoned about three buttons down with the shirt collar turned over the collar of his jacket. He's wearing a thick gold chain around his neck, his hair is neatly combed back, silvery black, and his deep voice booms like a foghorn. He looks around the corner of the house as though in anticipation of my flight, then comes up the porch steps. He looks like the kind of guy who would spend all evening slapping you on the back, forcing Chianti down your throat, and figuring out how much concrete it would take to cover your feet entirely so you'd sink in the river never to be heard from again.

The guy calls my name again. Then, "Get your ass out here, kid: time to go to the dance."

I have no idea what to say or do, so I get my ass out there.

"I left Angelina's corsage in my car."

"What's that in your hand?"

"Oh. Sorry. Guess I'm a little nervous."

"Nervous? Nervous about what? It's just a little date, kid, no more. Mums, huh? Nice. Don' worry: I'm just here to see you get there safe."

"Yes, sir."

"Well, Mrs. Zamboni will have something to say about those mums. You got a car, huh? Just follow me, then, and park right behind my car at the house. *Capisce?*"

Everything went fast and blurry after that. I don't remember driving there. I'd hardly driven at all before, just enough to pass my test about a month before. But I remember sitting in Uncle Fred's Le Mans, parked behind that Lincoln, outside the Zambonis' house.

Then the Godfather slings himself around the front of my car and opens my door for me.

"Come on, kid. Don't be so nervous. Come on in and have a drink. You look like you need it. Soft drink, that is, though you won't be driving. You'll have a good time. You play baseball, right?"

So he hauls me up to the front door of this big old fancy house, the door swings open magically, and there's Mrs. Zamboni looking like an older and slightly heavier version of her famous daughter.

The Zambonis are one of the classiest families in town. They made money years ago running a concrete business, then went into general construction, then they built a bunch of pizza places. Pretty great stuff, *capisce?*

So you about get the picture. Frankly, I swear I can't remember much of the rest. The house was big as a rock quarry and as bright as summer, or maybe I just think it was because people like Angelina should live in places like that. Angelina's mother, she must have looked exactly like Angelina once, tried to be nice, but she looked at me like I was a day-old hamburger when she had ordered Filet Mignon. Angelina's brothers were there, big and intimidating, but they didn't say much, just shook hands and looked at me suspiciously, told me how much their sister meant to them. The mother pulled me discreetly into the kitchen, saying "What nice mums, but let's try these roses, since they'll go so well with black. That's it, elegant. I'll just get rid of those for you," and she whisked my mums into oblivion.

After what seemed like time enough for me to have become Italian by osmosis, Angelina came slipping queenly down the central staircase.

You ain't never seen anything like her, or if you have, I congratulate you. I could have spent forever just watching her come down that staircase: poised, smiling, feline, her midnight-dark hair shining and brushed back thick and rich, her soft, black dress low-cut in front but not too low, just enough to set off the simple gold pendant on black cloth around her throat, her skin olive-pink and smooth, her eyes black and round as night. To tell you the truth, wimp or not, I must have fainted twice, on my feet, before she got to me. Big smile: "Hi!" Soft, simple but moving. She touched my wrist. "What lovely roses! Did you bring them for me?"

The roses that Mrs. Zamboni had forced into my hand. "Well, sort of. Can't think of anyone else they'd look better on."

I meant that as a compliment, but I'm not sure how it sounded. "How sweet," Mrs. Zamboni said without any real emotion. "Here, I'll help you, dear," and whether *dear* meant Angelina or me, she pinned the flowers deftly at Angelina's neckline.

Then the doorbell rang, and the room was filled with happy, jostling people, and in the background could I hear something like "must be the new style, tux jeans" and "wrong side of the tracks" and "nice boy, though, maybe" and insincere welcomes from the rich kids, and then we're out the door and Brian and Phil are talking and Angelina is chattering away with her friends and I'm wondering, for some strange reason, what Lana thought of my going out with Angelina, and what I thought of it myself. Don't get me wrong: Angelina is more beautiful than a new baseball field lined and trimmed and shining in the sunlight, but I felt like a salmon who was working and working and all of a sudden took a good sniff and realized he had come up the wrong stream.

The dance was great. I guess. Angelina sat with her friends. She talked with her friends. She danced with her friends. She danced with Brian and Phil. She danced with Harry Kuschner and Pervis Easly.

Pervis came with a sophomore girl I didn't know. I'm not even sure he knew her, because he spent the whole night staring at Angelina. At least that's one thing we had in common. Worse yet, Harry Kuschner came with Lana Simms—that's Lenny's sister. Lana spent the whole night with her arm in Harry's, sitting almost in his lap while he stared along with Pervis and me and everybody else at Angelina Zamboni. As close as he sat to her, Harry ignored Lana almost completely.

Everybody watched Angelina, danced with Angelina, hugged and kissed Angelina. Everyone but me.

In fact, Pervis had his hands all over her. He pretty much just grabbed her by the buns while they danced locked together close as pine tar on a bat handle. She cried. He cried. They kissed each other on the cheek. They kissed each other on the mouth.

That nearly did it for me. Hotshot or not, Pervis nearly ate a few knuckles for that one.

But you know, what's the use? Win or lose, I'd ruin the dance for Angelina, and I wouldn't feel any better about it, either. And Lana would see me make a fool of myself.

The only thing that made me feel better was that Lana had just as bad a time as I did.

No, that's not true. That didn't make me feel better. It made me feel worse. I wanted to take an ash upside Harry's head, too. I imagined some tall, thick, mustachioed pitcher winding up and chucking Harry's head toward the plate. I imagined my own tremendous swing. Contact: his bean headed for the gap in left-center, bouncing off the wall. I'm rounding for third. The centerfielder wings Harry's head toward the bag. I'm there, sliding. The head arrives, takes a bad hop off the third baseman's shoulder, and bounces over the fence into the stands. I stand up, dust off, and trot for home. Why did he ask Lana, anyway, if he didn't want to go with her? And did she really want to go with him?

"How you doing, JES? Looks like you're having a great time." Lana wakes me from my dream. Sometimes she calls me *JES* for my initials.

"Great, yes, great, that's the word, LAS." I call her LAS for her initials. "I see you're dancing the night away yourself." She squinted at me, but didn't say anything. I wanted to show that at least I was paying some attention to her, even if Harry wasn't, but did a damn poor job of it. I have to admit, Lana looked pretty good in her Homecoming dress: deep green, floor length, simple, to set off her yellow hair. But her eyes, icy blue even in the dim Homecoming light, looked tired and distant, not like normal Lana.

"Poor Willie, come dance," a voice said from behind me. Finally Angelina took pity on me, or maybe she came over because she saw me with Lana. I looked on the floor, and Pervis was having his obligatory dance with his confused but eager sophomore babe. Everyone else was about danced out, except the cheerleaders who had a corner of the hall all to themselves while the football players half watched and half recounted their heroics from the night before.

Why don't they have Homecoming in baseball season? Isn't baseball more like Homecoming than football is, eternal spring, eternal youth, always green and new, the stuff that *homecoming* really means?

I wonder if anyone's ever even thought of that.

So Angelina gives me her hand. It feels warm, smooth, almost small in mine.

If this is the moment I've been waiting for, why don't I feel better about it? I'm dancing with Angelina Zamboni, the prettiest girl in the universe. She looks flushed and tired, dazed, almost drugged, as we bob and weave, swing and sway, step and spin.

I tried desperately not to step on her feet. I think, at least, I didn't embarrass myself dancing.

"Willie, you dance real well." She seemed surprised and matter-of-fact at the same time, just as somebody might say, look at that gorilla: he really does have a short forehead, doesn't he?

We danced one fast and one slow. In addition to the afternoon dance shows, I'd seen some old Fred Astaire movies, but I kept it simple. It didn't mean much. Angelina spent the rest of our dance watching Pervis grope his date. She briefly put her head on my shoulder. I think she may have cried a tear or two. But when she looked up, she smiled, thanked me for the dance, and led me off the floor. She returned to whisper with Alberta and Deb and Jenny, their heads close as bats in a rack.

Homecoming Dance came mercifully to an end. I watched the last dance, Lana draped in Harry Kuschner's arms, Angelina talking with her friends, then rushing for a quick rendezvous, a few whispered words and fervent nods, with Pervis Easly at the door.

Leaving the hall I followed Angelina like the good dog that I am. Lenny knew what he was talking about.

We went to a very late dinner at Luigi's Supper Club across the river—I hope someone canceled my reservation at La Traviata and the one at La Boheme. I spent every last cent of my money to buy Angelina's dinner. You know, she looked genuinely appreciative. When she went to the bathroom, I had to swallow my pride and ask Brian Schwartz to lend me money for the tip. Honestly, he did, and without making me feel stupid at all. In fact, he even said, "You're a patient man, Willie. It can't be easy watching every guy in the world drool over your date. I don't think I could have done it. You're o.k., baseball man. And no matter what anybody else says, I like the jeans and tux look. Man, it's you, no compromise." If nothing else, I came out of this evening with more respect for Brian, which is more than I could say for any of the rest of them. He was infinitely patient with Alberta and answered her every whim, while she spent most of her time danc-ing and chatting with her girlfriends and eating up most of his hefty allowance. I guess we all have our problems.

As for Luigi's: sort of like living in a big-budget movie. Give me a pizza and an old *noir* film and Angelina in a pair of faded jeans and a tight t-shirt lying with me on an old stuffed pillow in front of the TV on a long Friday night with the wind blowing in lilac fragrance from the yard.

On the long drive home the girls sang songs and hugged each other and cried, and Brian and Phil talked about their tennis games and the football team's chances of going 7-3 this year. I hummed to myself all the Sinatra and Nat King Cole songs I could remember and thought how disappointed I was that I wasn't even going to get to kiss Angelina Zamboni good-night.

That could have made up for the whole thing.

Except maybe for seeing Lana there with Harry Kuschner. I'm not sure anything could have made up for that.

Brian took Angelina home first. He paused to be properly im-pressed with my uncle's Le Mans and with the Continental still parked in front of it, then pulled quietly in front of Angelina's house. The porchlight was shining bright. She kissed her girlfriends, cried some more, pecked Brian and Phil on the cheek, and purred out the door. Almost as an afterthought, she looked at me: "Willie, would you walk me to the door?"

I slid out behind her, my stupid heart beginning to beat fast again.

"I had a marvelous time. You're such a dear. Thank you so much," she kittened. I couldn't think of anything to say.

The air was cold, and morning wasn't too far over the hill. Brian's car remained poised out front. So much for privacy.

"I know tonight wasn't always easy for you," she explained. "But I hope you had some fun. Tell me you had some fun. Please."

"Being with you, even for tonight, was all I could have ever asked for." I lied. So shoot me.

"You really are such a sweetheart. Some girl will really appreciate you someday."

Ouch. Eeeee. Oooof. Oooooh. I could feel my skin beginning to crawl off my body and go back to my car without me.

"Well, it's cold, and Mama and Daddy told me not to stay out to late," she said uselessly.

Isn't it funny how whatever happens, we sing the song and dance the dance?

I started to turn for the steps.

"Willie."

I turned back.

"Thank you."

She came close, closed her eyes, and touched her lips gently against my mouth.

The world stopped for just that long.

Before I could recover, she had disappeared through her front door. I have to admit, the girl had a great talent with stairs and doors.

As I came down the walk, Brian honked his horn very quietly, and I saw several hands wave out various windows at me. I waved back, and in a few seconds they were gone down the street.

I eased into the Le Mans, started it up, tiredly and carefullyturned it toward home. I slipped in the back door of the house, took off my shoes, and crept upstairs so as not to wake Ma, as much because I wouldn't have known what to tell her as because she needed her sleep. I don't think I even undressed before I was asleep, though my jacket and tie were hanging over my chair in the morning. From that night I can remember a thousand confusing dreams to go with a thousand vague memories. Did I have a good time? Hell, I don't even know. I kissed Angelina Zamboni, and one thing I'll tell you, that kiss gets even better the more I think about it, and at the time it was pretty darn good, though I wouldn't say I was in love with her then or now. But my dreams were full of all sorts of people saying and doing all sorts of things. Angelina and Pervis; hundreds of people dancing, twisting like drunken tops; Angelina's roses; Lana sitting with her arm wrapped around Harry, an empty look spilling out of her eyes like tears; Angelina kissing me under the bright porchlight. Yours truly caught in the middle of a bunch of girlfriend/boyfriend soap operas.

Funny thing, all this stuff isn't even what I set out to tell you about.

Sunday I didn't make it up for church, and, mercifully, Ma didn't wake me. In the late afternoon I returned my uncle's Le Mans and went from there for a long run, up the hill, out through the country, looking at the turning leaves burning with color, thinking about Angelina's lips and Lana's eyes. I got so lost in my thoughts that I got lost on one of those country roads, too, and I didn't find my way back to the road to town till nearly dark. My feet felt like lumps of lead. Or concrete.

By that time I was tired and walking, and I heard a rumble in the distance behind me that got louder till it pulled up beside me at the edge of the road.

A car window rolled down, and out poked the head of Dirk Jenson, a cigarette hanging from his lips. A strange smell poured from his car.

"Hey, baseball, you look tired. Need a ride?"

I did, but I wasn't sure I should say so. Dirk didn't look so good, and he didn't sound so good, and he didn't smell so good.

"Come on, man, I ain't got all day. Get your ass in."

Reluctantly, I did. Bad idea. But Dirk looked like he needed help, and that overcame my fear of riding with him—as if I could do anything.

When you're in high school, you can't be afraid to ride with somebody you know, anyway; it's against the code, shows fear and lack of respect. Damn the code, anyway., and somebody outta change it.

But I got in, all right, and the strange smell got stronger.

"What you doin' way out here on the edge of town, boy?" Dirk peeled out in a cloud of dust.

Dirk called me *boy* though he wasn't much older than I was. That's just the way people talk here.

"I'm an idiot. I was out for a run and I got lost up over that hill. Now I'm going home."

"What you runnin' from?"

"From? Nothing. Just running, you know, to stay in shape."

"Shape? What good will that do you? You just gonna die someday anyway."

Something about the way he looked made me think it might be sooner than I'd thought.

He lit another cigarette, and in the light of the match, I could see that his face was full of cuts and bruises. Then I realized what the smell was and that the cigarette had a funny shape. Dirk was smoking grass.

He took a puff, then grabbed a bottle next to him and tilted it bottoms up. The bottle read: "Jack Daniels." Where did he get this stuff?

The bottle was empty now, but the smoke filled the car like fog spreading over the river.

That meant that by now the smell was all over me, and the smoke was filling my lungs, too.

Now, no matter what you think of kids today, I've never done that stuff, except for unintentionally, riding that night with Dirk Jenson. I don't like things that mess with your brain, since I got nothing I can afford to lose, which maybe is why I don't go out with girls much, either.

"So what are you up to?" I ask Dirk, tentatively.

"Just drinkin' and drivin', drinkin' and drivin'. And smokin' a little, too." Then he laughed loudly and pushed down harder on the gas pedal.

I am no daredevil, and I could feel the hair on my neck stand up and my stomach sink as Dirk flew around the turns up this side of the pike, past Dead Man's Curve, fortunately going the other way, hugging the hill, puffing and laughing as he saw me grip the seat and the dashboard.

"What's wrong, Baseball, no guts? You think that's fast, you ain't seen nothin' yet." By the time we hit the top of the hill, Dirk wasn't the only thing smoking. I could have sworn I smelled rubber as we burned around those curves. Surprised to feel a seatbelt, I tried to ease it on without Dirk's noticing. He saw me and let out a howl of laughter.

Then we started down the other side of the hill.

The steep way.

Dirk was pounding those curves, screeching through one by one. On my side, I could see the town appear over the ledge at the edge of the road. It was a long way down.

I tried to distract him. "Dirk, what happened to your face?"

"What happened to *your* face, fool?"

"No, I mean those bruises. How did you get them?"

"Go to hell," he said, and screeched around another curve. Then: "Be glad you ain't got no old man at home with a bad temper."

"But your father's a preacher, right?" SCREECH.

"Only on Sundays. The other days he works in the mine, drinks after work, and comes home ready to hit somebody." SCREECH.

"Why would he do that?"

"You need any more proof than this? He does it cause he likes to do it. The whole shitty world likes to do it. Ain't you figured that out yet? Your girl dumps you and your old man uses your head for a punching bag. And everybody else is even worse." SCREECH.

Maybe there *are* worse things than not having a father.

Now we're heading straight for a house that sits right near the road at a sharp curve. Dirk speeds right for it, yelling out the window, "Look out, you bastards!"

When we're almost to their porch, he yanks the wheel back, we skid, miss the stone of the house, and we're back on the road.

This is what I think happened next. I'm not entirely sure. I do remember that fear clawed up my back heavy as some huge animal. I felt like I was getting eaten alive.

When Dirk jerked us back on the road, he pulled too hard and we crossed the centerline. A car, coming up the hill in the other lane, was right on us before he could spot it. Dirk swerved to miss it and ran us right into the guardrail over the cliff. I heard the sharp scream that comes with the tearing of metal, and I remember looking out my window and seeing a shear drop right beneath me over the cliff and onto houses below. When we hit the rail, Dirk must've pulled the wheel with all his strength, and we shot across the road and cracked head-first into concrete wall that lines the road against the side of the hill. Only some fireworks and then darkness after that.

The next thing I remember is the wailing of the car's horn. My head hurts, and I try to move, but that isn't easy, and I don't know exactly where to go, anyway. Then I think about Dirk. I look over, and he is slumped with his belly over the steering wheel. There is a huge crack in the windshield, and the side of his head is smashed in. I hope you never see anything like it. I still dream about it. He must have gone through the windshield, against, the wall, and back, like a line drive off a brick outfield wall. There is blood everywhere. My head feels hot, and I can taste iron on my lips.

Slowly, I got out of the car. I felt like I had stepped onto the high seas and they might roll me off the cliff at any instant. I almost fell. Steam was pouring out of what used to be the car's engine, and something liquid was running thick at my feet. I touched my head to try to steady myself, and my hand was sticky and hot with blood and shreds of skin.

The only thing I could think of was the houses: go to get help. I stumbled to some steps, a walkway through the concrete wall, and tried to climb. Man, that was one of the hardest things I've ever done. I felt like someone had cables on my legs pulling me down, like I should just give in and fall and tumble over the cliff to the valley below.

I fought it off and kept climbing. A funny thought went through my head: I just wanted to see Lana again. Just not right then.

At the top of the steps was a porch. The house loomed above it big as a castle. It seemed to disappear back into the darkness of the hill. The light was on, and people were just coming out, peering to see what had happened. You'd have thought the noise of a car crushing itself flat would have scared them silly.

"It had to be a wreck. What else would sound like that?" a voice said.

"Who is that?" I heard someone say.

"What does he want?"

"Was he in that wreck?"

"My God, that's Willie Smith. He's bleeding. Call an ambulance or something."

"Your dad already did. Come inside."

"No. Don't you understand? That's Willie, I know him. Come help me get him inside."

"You can't bring him in. He looks awful."

"He might die out here. God, get some help."

Now I'm sitting on the edge of a porch. Brian Schwartz is looking down at me, his hand on my shoulder. "I'm o.k., I think."

"You're not o.k. You've got blood pouring out of your head and mouth. Here, use this to stanch the flow. What the hell happened?"

I didn't want to answer. I felt like I had been running for days with no sleep and I needed a rest.

"That's all right, don't answer. Let's get you in a chair here. Is there anyone else in the car?"

"If there was, there isn't now," his father said, coming out.

"I'd better go down," Brian said.

"You'd better stay here. It's dangerous out on that road. You watch that boy, and I'll see if there's anything we can do, though I doubt it. He smells like pot. Damn kids, smoking up and driving. The police will be here in a minute, and they'll want to question him."

I feel like I am fading in and out of time.

"You'll be o.k., Willie, all right?" Brian says. I notice he is wearing a long baseball shirt, which is odd, cause he doesn't play baseball anymore. He is looking at me uncertainly.

It strikes me what Brian's father just said. They may think that I cracked up the car, or that I was smoking up with Dirk. The police may arrest me.

"Look, Brian, I gotta go, call my mother or something. No, better not do that. Look, I didn't do anything. I just hitched a ride with Dirk and he was all crazy. Someone should help Dirk."

"It's all right, o.k., I believe you. Just take it easy, and the ambulance will be here soon."

I was thinking it had been less than a day since I had kissed Angelina Zamboni. What a way to go, huh? One kiss and you're dead. I wondered if I still might die. Or end up in jail.

The police got there a couple of minutes later, then an ambulance. They took a while with Dirk, and a paramedic looked at me. The police took me to the hospital. The officer sniffed when he helped me in the car. "You're gonna live," he said, "but you may end up with all the trouble you asked for."

What am I gonna do?

I called Ma from the hospital. She damn near broke down, even though I insisted I was o.k. When I hung up, the policeman asked me why I would do something like that to my mother. A nurse shooed him away and told him that he didn't know that I'd done anything wrong at all.

"Just sniff his clothes," the policeman said. "What more do you need to know?"

Ma got there. Big scene. Half mad, half relieved. Man, I was tired, felt like I could sleep a thousand years. They kept me in the hospital overnight. Slight concussion, cuts and bruises, loss of blood, not dangerous, worth keeping under observation.

Dirk was dead on impact. They called his parents to identify what was left.

I wondered if I wasn't, in a way, dead, too. What if people believed that I was smoking and drinking with Dirk? Or that I caused the accident. I wondered if in some way I had. Would Dirk have driven that way if I hadn't been along? Would he have gone somewhere else? He's the only dead person I've ever seen, and he damn near took me with him. Where?

My head was hurting, and my left knee and thigh were swollen and throbbing.

"It wasn't your fault, was it?"

The nurse was standing there looking at me.

"I don't think so."

"He was driving, right?"

"Right."

"Were you smoking?"

I looked straight in her eyes. "No. Absolutely no."

"I didn't think so. It's gonna be tough, but you were lucky, yes lucky: you looked death in the face, and you'll live to tell about it. Your friend wasn't so lucky, if he was even your friend. You said you were hitching?"

"Not even hitching, really. I was out for a run. I got tired. Dirk rode by. He offered me a ride, and I couldn't say no. I was in before I knew what he had been doing. Some awful things happened to him."

"Pray he's in a better place now, and pray that people will believe you like I do. Stick to the truth and be brave: that's best. That poor boy. Yes, I know your head hurts, but you'll be all right if you don't let them blame you and, most of all, you don't blame yourself. Hard as it is to understand, sometimes things just happen. Thank God you're alive."

I thought for a minute, and when I looked up, she was gone. That nurse was one nice lady. When she came back later, she didn't have time to talk. I wanted to ask about death and blame and Angelina and Lana and Ma and a bunch of other things, cause I had a feeling she might know, but I never had the chance. I went home in the morning.

Ma was mad for two days, then got over it, mostly. I think she knew I hadn't done anything wrong, except that to her taking a ride from Dirk was wrong. Lenny didn't even call me. I think he thought that I must have had something to do with his friend's death, that Dirk was too good with cars to have killed himself.

That's what I think he did. He killed himself, and I just happened to be there at the time.

Everybody was talking about it at school of Monday. Angelina Zamboni wouldn't get near me. She just looked at me with a kind of horror and walked away with a tear dripping down her cheek. People looked like they thought that if they'd get too close to me, they'd be the next to go. Or maybe they thought I was a druggie and deserved what I got and worse, because Dirk died. I don't know.

After first period I got called to the principal's office. A policeman was waiting for me, and Mr. Sanders was there while I told him again the same story I had told after the accident and at the hospital. He said this wasn't a trial; he just wanted to go over the facts. Mr. Sanders said, just tell the truth. Like I would do anything else.

Then they called in Coach.

I couldn't believe it. Of all people for a character witness.

And do you know what?

Coach said that he knew I would never smoke pot or put someone else in danger. "He's bad sometimes, like most kids, mis-chee-veeus, y'unnerstan what I mean, but he ain't a mean kid who would cause any real trouble. Y'unnerstan what I mean? He's a ballplayer, not a hood."

The old man left me speechless. Then, I thought, here's curtains: they called in Mrs. Brickhouse.

"He's not my most conventional student. He's got an imagination, and he's not afraid to use it. He acts tough, but he does his work and doesn't"—looking at Mr. Sanders—"for the most part, fight with other kids. He actually has some writing talent, and I don't believe he'd lie to you. I think he's an honest boy."

She really did say the writing talent thing. I swear.

When she left, Mr. Sanders said, "Look, officer, he did get into some trouble a couple of years back, but that may not have been entirely his fault. He said he was trying to protect his friend, and he may have been telling the truth. He has a decent record for school work, and no history of drug or substance abuse or even use problems."

I didn't say anything about the beer in the park, though with all this stuff about honesty I almost felt obliged.

"The hospital didn't find any alcohol in his blood, and the boy's mother says she's never seen evidence of use, and the kids I talked to all said he shuns marijuana like poison. I really think what you have here is a case of someone being in the wrong place at the wrong time and making a bad decision."

Who'd have believed it? Mr. Sanders, too. They all bailed me out.

And even the police officer admitted that a couple people who lived along the road where I had been running had seen me. I always wave at people when I see them sitting on their porches. Thank God for that. They had remembered.

I got off school to go to Dirk's funeral. People said I shouldn't go, but I felt like I had to. Closed casket. His parents wouldn't even look at me, let alone talk to me. I think they thought it was my fault, or wanted to.

Ma was back to normal soon, though every now and then she'd look at me like she was mad at me for nearly dying.

Gradually, most of the kids at school forgot about what had happened, though I think some always suspected I was a druggie or in some way tainted with death.

Two weeks after the funeral I was out walking at night. I hadn't been running because my head and my leg still hurt. But I couldn't stay inside out of the air, and the night felt especially close and cool and necessary. No stars shone through the clouds, and the first snowflakes of the year fell tentatively, dying before they hit the ground.

I walked by Lenny's house. Lana was sitting on the front steps.

"Hey, crashman."

Will I ever hear the end of nicknames?

"Cut me some slack, Lana, please."

"Sorry. How you feeling?"

"Great. I'd be out running four-minute miles if it weren't for the snow, so I'm just walking."

"Want some company?"

"Sure."

"Nice lump on your head. Complements your profile. You should keep it."

"Just what I need: an art critic." With Lana you can actually say things like that, and she understands.

We walked for quite a while in silence except for the sounds of our shoes scuffing against the street.

"So, did you have a good time with Harry at the Homecoming Dance?"

That was the wrong thing to say. She didn't say anything for a long time, and neither did I.

Finally she said: "So what's wrong with you and Lenny? You haven't come over in a long time."

"I think he blames me for Dirk, partly."

"It wasn't your fault."

"I know, but I'm glad to hear you say it."

"You should come over some time and talk to him. He's just my stupid brother, but he is your friend."

"O.k. You're right, as always."

More walking. I begin to feel cold, because I came out without a jacket. Lana is wearing a zippered coat and leather gloves.

"I didn't realize it was this cold when I left home. The wind is starting to blow winter in. Early this year." Unconsciously, I shivered.

Lana linked her arm in mine and walked close to me. We went on walking for long time.

I think I've told you enough of this story. It's too long already.

12 Why We Play Baseball

Spring comes early this year in Morgan Falls. We are playing baseball by mid-March, and by the first of April, the breeze carries warmth so the dew on the morning grass leaves only silver tips on the grass. The rains come regularly, but the ground seems eager to dry quickly.

I am glad to be playing baseball.

I am lucky to be alive.

Who would have believed that the hospital nurse and Coach and Mr. Sanders and Mrs. Brickhouse would have rescued me?

I am in my junior year. Lance and Spit and Lowry and Mange are our seniors, so I'm not the team leader yet, officially. But I am the one who can fire us up and make the play to jolt us out of 1-1 ties to win games that would otherwise be losses, and I am the one that other teams' fans hate and boo—yes, they do that at high school games—because they know, too, that I am the one who will beat them.

Not by myself: we have a good team, but not a great one. We will win a lot of games, but not our tournament, the one that determines how far we can go. We don't have that much heart or that much will. But more important for now: this year I will play not only to win, but for pure joy in the game, more than ever.

I have always played, I know now, with unconscious joy. This year it is also conscious joy. I am back from the dead. I am new. I am still alive.

Joy is a funny word to say, but it looks just right on the page, and that is what I feel. Today is the eighth of April, and the major league season is beginning. Because of the school year, we start our season early. We are already 4-3 for the year, and we are going to win today. I know that as I know the feel of grass under my feet, as I know the smell of spring in the air, as I recognize the perfect balance of a bat made for my swing, better than I know that tomorrow will come, better than I know my own name.

I sniff the leather of my glove, and the pine trees around the parking lot, and the exhaust of the bus. I feel each muscle tighten and loosen, tighten and loosen, as I warm up. My white shoes, old friends, conform to my feet, though they're beginning to gray with wear. My right arm and fingers feel strong and certain, as though I could swing a sword in battle or carve the most intricate scrimshaw figures on a tiny piece of ivory, or throw a baseball into a peach basket from three hundred fifty feet. My leg has healed completely. I don't think I have ever felt more real.

We are playing at Barnwell, a small country town north and across the river. People say it got its name from how the town was founded, when the first people settled here, how they all met to build a huge barn, the first thing they did, together, and then dug a well for underground water. And the town has been here ever since.

Lots of fans come to see their games. Beside their field are tennis courts where people play in perfectly white outfits, girls in short dresses even in the cool of spring. The grass is already bright green, and the turf is soft, because we have had rain, but not too much rain.

This game will be a special game for me.

This year, every game is special for me. But two things will happen today: Lenny will play in his first varsity game. And Lana, Lenny's sister, will come to the game. She will come by chance, more with the feeling that by some strange coincidence Lenny will play, not to see me play. She will see both, and I will be happy. I feel happy now whenever I see Lana.

And I will play well and feel like I am playing well. I will have no doubts.

The dry, chalky smell of rosin rises in my nose as I work it into the pungent, tacky pine tar on my bat handle. By the time I finish mixing them, the grip will be so sticky that I almost can't release the bat to put it down. The handle squeaks with tension as I screw my hands tightly to it to lead off the game.

Barnwell has a concession stand, and the buttery smell of popcorn wafts to me as I step up to the umpire's "Play ball!" All the fans clap and cheer their pitcher. They don't boo me here. I don't think they boo anyone. Behind the right field fence a park with great oak trees stretches into the distance. To the west, just beyond hearing distance, lies the river, the same river that lips the banks not half a mile from my house. Left field has no fence at all; it disappears into football bleachers four hundred fifty feet away. I glance back at Lenny. He seems to know it is an unusual day, and he gives me the thumbs up. He has forgiven me for Dirk's death. I glance into the visitors' bleachers and see Lana, quiet, her arms folded across her chest. She is dressed in blue jeans and a black and white striped crew-neck shirt. Her hair is loose around her shoulders.

Today the bat feels perfect in my hands. Coach will not get mad at me, I will not get mad at me, and the field and I will absorb each other like the river and its fish.

I step into the batter's box. The box is smooth, still flat and even, since no one has batted yet, and I cut the first heel marks in it, because the Barnwell people take care of their field. Their uniforms are a modern clean, bright white with green and gold trim. Ours are old-timey gray flannel with blue numbers and red trim. I wear the number ten. Did I tell you that?

At Barnwell they even have a PA to announce the pitchers and batters: "Now batting for Harmon Falls, Will Smith."

"Will?" Hmmm.

There is a song going through the back of my head, but it will not come to the front, and just now I don't want it to. I want to think of nothing but baseball.

I check the fielders' positions. I am still no great homerun hitter, but I have learned to shoot the gaps. No matter: outfielders are playing me deep this year, as though they believed I could hit the ball a hundred miles. I feel like maybe I can. Barnwood's left fielder is almost out of sight.

I am completely relaxed, because I know I will hit the ball every time that I bat today, and I will bat often. The pitcher doesn't even matter. I barely notice him. I see nothing but the ball, hear Stud's *Om*. I take the count to three and two. Without even having to look at him, I know Coach is happy. He always tells me to take pitches, to make the pitcher work. Often I don't—I love to hit and I can't wait and take pitches. Today I wait, because I feel a 3-2 fastball on the way. Our players sit on the bench chattering softly to me, theirs stand in the field, poised, posed, offering the proper swagger, chattering to their pitcher. No one says "He can't hit," or "He can't pitch"; this is not Little League, and something odd about the day wouldn't allow it. Anyone who would say something like that today would immediately be swallowed up by the earth, and everyone else on both teams and among all the fans would think that right and just, and the game would go on as though nothing had happened.

The baseball angel is here today.

I can feel him.

Whoever it is who watches over the events of the world and takes special care to make certain that now and then someone pitches a perfect game or hits a five hundred-foot homer or turns an unassisted triple play, the one whose strength you feel when you hit the ball so squarely that you don't even feel it leave the bat or whose speed you feel when you round second on your way to a stand-up triple, he is here. His laughter is in the breeze blowing toward straight away center field, his fingers brush the grass in waves when a gust kicks up, and he keeps the merest wisp of cloud from the sky, so that when you look up, if you didn't know the difference, you couldn't tell whether you were seeing sky or tropical water. The sky is so blue you can almost look through it and see his face, but he doesn't sit still long enough. He sits in this player's glove to bring in the ball that should go too far, on that player's bat to hurry it to the curveball it should miss, and on that player's knee to brush away the bad hop that might have caused an injury.

He tells me that the fastball is coming, thigh-high, inside corner. Then he laughs and disappears.

The fastball comes, thigh-high, inside corner.

My swing is smooth as the flight of the dragonfly, quick as the dash of the hummingbird. I meet the ball perfectly on the sweet spot of the bat. I hardly feel the contact with the ball, but it leaps from the bat like a bee from a troubled hive, sounding like a zip-gun as it flies. The trajectory is beautiful, like the launch of a mortar you know will not explode, and the echoing sound is like that, too, a deep "whump," not a crack.

The left fielder is running. On another day he may simply have given up and watched the ball fly, because it is going a long way. But as the baseball angel was with me, I know, as I round first sprinting for second, the he is now with the leftfielder, not even thinking of what he just done for me, but doing what he will do for the next player. As I near second I glance out, and the fielder, at a full sprint, catches my rocket like a wide receiver in a football game catching a pass from a quarterback with a Paul Bunyan arm.

He falls. He somersaults. He comes up, more than four hundred feet from home plate in the left field power alley, holding his glove high, the ball just poking out in the top of his glove. He is almost dancing with delight.

I hear the laugh of the baseball angel, so light that if you didn't know what it was, you would mistake it for the wind dipping beneath a bird's wings. He may occasionally play favorites, but not for long.

Barnwell's fans cheer. Even our few clap. They know a great play when they see one.

I round second and return to the dugout. I am not unhappy, tip my cap to the leftfielder. The baseball angel did his part for me: in almost any baseball park in the world, that ball would have been a home run. I have done all I could, and I will bat again today. And I have made Barnwell's leftfielder probably as happy as he has been in his life: he has made as great a catch as you'll ever see. If you don't love baseball, you won't believe that, but I tell you it's true. I would feel the same way if I had made that catch. And someday he will tell his grandchildren about it or maybe write a story about it.

Though I tipped my cap to him, he's too busy to look for me. There are bigger things at stake for him: his own game, his own life, his own self, and his memories, his team, his catch.

In the third inning I come up with Mange on second. I can see the ball so clearly it's as though I were looking it over with a magnifying glass. I swing effortlessly and hit an rbi double off the right-center field fence.

By their half of the third, small clouds are beginning to sneak into the sky. But not to worry: the baseball angel has given me his promise that this game will go the distance.

In the fourth inning, Barnwell's leftfielder hits a two-out double, and their next batter singles to center. I charge, reach down, come up throwing, rear back, let go, and put the ball directly on the plate on the fly. The guy doesn't even bother to slide: Samula is standing with the ball in his hand waiting for him. He does not try to run Samula down. The baseball angel has spoken to him, too, and he knows he is destined to be out at home.

In the fifth inning I line one past the third baseman and down the line, stop reluctantly at second with a double: the baseball angel says don't be greedy. I steal third, and Krick knocks me in with a single.

In the sixth, I hit a drive into center that's so high it nearly disappears. Their centerfielder catches it with his back against the fence.

In their half of the sixth, a runner tries to go from first to third on a one-out single to right center. I snag it, turn, fire on one hop to third, and the third baseman makes the tag: got him. And you knew the even better part? Lenny is playing third. We are ahead, and Coach puts him in for the last two innings. When the ball comes in hard and low, Lenny looks scared. But the hop is true, and he makes the catch plenty early. The runner slides into the tag. Lenny smiles wide as the river at its broadest point and gives me the thumbs up.

In the seventh Lenny bats. He takes the count to 2-2, then bounces the ball past the pitcher. The ball might have got through, but the second baseman makes a good play and throws Lenny out at first.

The baseball angel is always true, but he is not always kind. But I feel good for Lenny. He has waited three years to play. He has made a putout at third base in his first try, and he has put the ball in play with his bat. He looks disappointed, but he didn't strike out. In the bleachers, Lana is cheering encouragement and calling his name.

With one on and two out, they walk me. We don't score again.

In Barnwell's last at bat, their third batter hits one to right center. I can feel the angel with me again. I run, glance at the fence, jump, catch a spike in the chain link, latch on with my right hand, twist, catch the ball as it is just about to drop over the fence, and I drop off the fence onto my feet.

Our guys cheer, their fans clap. This time, even Lana claps.

We win, and life feels right and good, at least to me and for a bit.

"Great catch, Willie!" Lenny leads the cheers as I reach the infield and guys clap me on the back and slap my hand.

"Good game," everybody says, and we shake hands with the Barnwell players.

"You too, my man Lenny."

"Way to play, my man Willie."

"Way to play, my man Lenny." Lana greets Lenny at the fence.

"Oh, Lana, I didn't get to do much. A wimpy groundout."

"But you hit the ball and made a good play at third."

"That's right, Len, you're a gamer."

That seems to make him happy, when I give him a compliment. I realize that I have never given Lenny a compliment about his baseball. I wonder if I have ever complimented him about anything. I wonder if I have ever complimented Lana about anything.

Lenny and I are closer than we have been for a while. "Willie, some day I'm gonna write a book about you," he says.

They walk together toward the parking lot, Lenny toward the bus, Lana toward their mother's car. Lana pats Lenny on the back, and they part. As Lenny turns for the bus, Lana turns just her head and notices

I am following her with my eyes. She gives me the thumbs up sign and, I think, but I'm not sure, a smile, and walks to her car. I just now notice that the sky has clouded over. I feel a drop or two on my face as I look up.

The angel has done his job, and the rain begins to fall. Our custom is that freshman carry the bat bag to and from the bus and the field. I go back to the dugout to load the bats, and even though I'm a junior, I sling them over my shoulder. I feel strong: the muscles in my legs and back feel like they thicken as I sling the bag on my shoulder and hoist it for the bus.

In a few days, a few months, or a few years, no one in Barnwell except that leftfielder will remember that I played here. For him I'll be only the guy that hit the ball that he got with a miracle catch.

I will always remember that I played here.

If I thought about it, I could probably remember every game that I ever played, every at-bat I've ever had, what pitches I missed, which ones I hit, which balls I caught, which runners I threw out, whether or not we won.

Today I went 2-4, threw out two runners, saved a home run ball, and we won. Lenny played, and Lana was there to watch. And I felt the presence of the baseball angel with a certainty I've never had of anything before, and I felt him not just in me, but in everyone else at the park, too. And because, now, I hear the river singing again, singing to me, to all of us, with its own voice.

Suddenly I realize that I did not sing today. For the first game in my life since I began playing centerfield, I didn't sing.

No, that's not right. I didn't sing Sinatra. Something else was going through my head the whole game, and I didn't notice it till now.

I drop the bats in the bus, tell the driver I'll be right back, and since some of the other guys are still collecting their gear and talking with Barnwell players, I run the couple of hundred yards to the river. I need to listen.

My song was taught to me by the baseball angel, and gently, gently, I hear the river singing it now. Why is the river singing that song? I am obligated to listen.

As I close, the song stops, but I know what it is now. I can hear the words clearly in my head:

All you need to do is call,
And I'll get there:

You have a friend.

Why that song? Who is the friend? The baseball angel? The river god? Lenny? Lana? Baseball itself?

"Will."

I hear the word again, clearly, just as I heard it once before, down by the riverside.

"That doesn't answer my question. Who is the friend?"

The rain thickens now, falling quickly in long, fast drops that look like silver string, so I turn and run for the bus.

As I run, the thick raindrops weigh down my uniform, making me feel heavy. I know that we will finish the season with a winning record, but we will lose in the second round of the tournament. I know that I will hit .400 and make the all-star, all-league, and all-valley teams, and I will play summer ball and get better than I have been. I know that I will say something important to Lenny and something to Lana. I know that my confidence is rising, and that it will not always help, but that I would be lost without it.

The wind is beginning to kick up now, too. When I get to the parking lot, the bus is running, the lights are on, and the last of the players are filing in. I climb the steps behind Tiny and find a seat alone. Everyone is cheering and joking, yelling to Coach to stop on the way home for ice cream, which he never does, but which they do to make him mad. He doesn't get mad today, but he won't stop for ice cream either, because he knows he'd have to buy.

"Good game, Willie," several of the guys say. "You played like a pro today. You really had those guys scared."

Scared isn't right. I showed them I could play, and they respected that. But I respected them, too, because we all played with the joy of playing and the will to win, by the rules, trying to do something.

Will.

You got a friend.

Hmmm.

13 Friends

I have this theory about people.

I call it my "shithead theory."

It says that, for the world to work and for people to get along with one another, you don't have to be Albert Schweitzer, and you don't even have to be nice to everybody. All you have to do is *not* be a shithead.

When people really make an effort to hurt each other—or themselves—bad things happen, like when they're thinking about their own selves and figuring, let the other guy take care of himself: I'll just step right over him if I have to. Except for accidents that nobody could do anything about, a simple commitment not to be a shithead, not to grind yellow snow in someone else's face, would keep us all on pretty safe if not chummy terms.

I guess, though, that everybody is a shithead now and then, no matter how hard we try and how well versed we are in the shithead theory. Even me.

That's right. You've been reading: I don't get things right all the time. You thought that just because I'm in a book, I'd know things? Right. I swear.

Well, the summer after my junior year I was playing some of the best baseball of my life. I wasn't hitting many home runs. In fact, I hit only one all summer, even though I had hit three the summer before and two during the school year, my best since little league. But I was hitting the ball hard almost every time up, and there wasn't a ball I let drop in the outfield, and there wasn't a runner who'd try to take an extra base on me, and I hadn't struck out all summer. I was hitting almost .500 playing for two different teams, and our American Legion team looked like we just might be able to go somewhere.

And I was still glad to be alive.

I hadn't heard much from Angelina Zamboni. Through the school year Lana and I would take walks together, sometimes home from school, though by summer we didn't see much of each other, and Lenny and I were friends again, and there was plenty of summer to go and baseball to be played.

As usual, Lenny was at my side, keeping score, but getting into a game here and there, when we had run up a big lead or were too far behind to catch up and not in a league game where losing could make a difference in our standing for post-season play.

Late in July we had a legion game with Northfield, our chief competition for first place in the district. We didn't have to beat them to make the tournament, but if we did, our chances of going in top seed were sealed.

Northfield always plays us tough. They're from one of those old mining towns where people don't do much but work, eat, and play ball: I guess we have a few of those around here. Northfield always has a good team, and they're never out of a game, no matter how far behind they get, because they play till the last out and they play to win. I suppose people from a town like that have learned for generations that to survive you stick to something till it's done.

I led off the game with a walk—not bad for me, since I love to hit too much to take pitches. When I'm hitting plenty and well, I'll get myself to take a few pitches because I know I'll get a chance to hit again. I stole second and third and scored on sacrifice fly by a guy named Radzinski who isn't from Harmon Falls, but plays with our legion team in the summer. Looks a little like Humphrey Bogart with bad knees. Frankly, he walks kinda funny, and he doesn't field all that well, but he's one of those guys who will always get his bat on the ball, so he's good to have in the line-up, and nobody complains about an occasional error, because he does try hard and gets his hits and wants to win.

Northfield tied us up in the second when their big hitter, a tall guy named Haynes, hit a long home run way down the left field line. They say the pro scouts are after this guy, because he's big and can hit the long ones. Let him hit his big homers, I thought, and I'll steal my bases, and we'll see who ends up winning this game.

Well damned if in the fourth inning he didn't go and hit another one just as long as the first, a ball that disappeared into the trees way beyond the left field fence, this time with a guy on, to put us down 3-1.

In the fifth I got a pitch low on the outside corner, the one I have trouble with, on a 3-2 count, so there was nothing I could do but go after it, and I got lucky and made some good contact: it sailed over the first baseman's head and right down the right field line. I got third sliding on a close play, good call by the ump if I do say so. That brought in a run, and Radzinski got a single to center to bring me in again to tie the score.

That's when we got fired up, and the whole offense started to rumble. Two more runs in the fifth, four more in the sixth, and despite Haynes's double off the right field fence in their half of the sixth, we were still up 9-5 going into the last inning.

Since Northfield was home team, they had last at-bat, and no lead seemed big enough to me to be sure we'd win.

Our coach, Bud's father, started to substitute so everyone would get a chance to play. He told Lenny to get ready to go to third, and a couple other guys to play first and right field, and another to catch.

That's when I said something I will always regret.

"Mr. Socco, shouldn't we stick with the starters? We need this game: you know what home field advantage does for you in the tournament."

I didn't think. And Lenny is there with his glove in his hand, ready to go to third, but now with his jaw hanging open, his eyes wide with disbelief.

All I had on my mind was winning this game and not letting their hotshot home run hitter beat us.

Mr. Socco is an old baseball man, played in the Minor Leagues himself, but he usually trusts my advice, cause, believe it or not, I don't give it often. "Maybe you're right," he says. "Can you guys hang in there till Saturday? That's a non-league game and we'll be sure to get everybody in."

A noticeable sigh from some disappointed players—but they understand baseball logic, so they sit down on the bench one more time.

Lenny looks at me, and his eyes say it all: how could you do that to your friend over a baseball game? He shakes his head and looks away. I don't say a word, because I know what he's thinking and I know he's right and I know I couldn't say anything in the world to help now.

Lenny keeps score, but he comes to the park for the same reason I do: because he loves to play baseball. Every day he comes hoping to play, knowing that he probably won't, living for the few innings and occasional at-bats he gets.

I felt ashamed. I still do.

Looking back at it now, I wish I could say another guy said it, but I haven't told you a lie yet. After that, things were never again quite the same between Lenny and me.

Coach Socco went up to each guy and patted him on the back. "We're a team, and a team's job is to win. Right, Len? You play on Saturday, buddy?"

Lenny just nodded, didn't say a thing to him or to me.

"That's the spirit. We'll go in tops in the tournament and win us some ball games. We have the stuff to make it to state."

In their final inning Northfield knocked the spit outta the ball. Our rightfielder, Ropes, playing his first season of legion ball at fourteen, made an outstanding catch on a ball down the line to save a run. With two runners on base, I caught the final out on Haynes's long drive to straightaway center. He musta hit that ball nearly four hundred feet, but center is deep at that park, and I caught it Mays-like over my shoulder. There were no plays at third base, where Lenny would have been.

Northfield scored two runs, but we scraped by, 9-7.

Lenny didn't wait to talk to me. He left for home without saying a word, and he didn't come to Saturday's game.

On my way outta the dugout I noticed a couple of older guys with pads of paper and pens in their hands talking to Haynes. He had to bend his head down to talk to most people—he was that tall. Mr. Socco comes up behind me and puts his hand on my shoulder.

"See those two guys talking to Haynes? They're pro scouts for the Mets—I've seen them before. I hear they'll be drafting him. Surprised they're not talking to you, too. You could make it, you know. You're good enough. They always go for the big kids first, though. The rest of you have to prove yourselves."

He patted me on the shoulder twice and called his younger son, Lon, to help him with the bats.

"Willie, you want to take a bat to practice with?"

"Thanks, already have two of my own at home." One of them was broken and nailed together again so I could still practice with it, but the other was nearly new: Billy Williams model, thirty-five inches, thin handle. I never went in for aluminum bats. They were brand-new then, but they don't sound the same or feel the same. And baseball is a natural game, a game of earth and grass and wood. In the summer I swing the bat at least a thousand times a day, a few hundred with a bat with a lead plug in the barrel, some with standard issue, to get the perfect swing embedded in my brain.

If only my brain were as good as my swing.

The scouts left after they talked to Haynes. I stayed around and watched them leave and almost missed a ride home.

Lenny came back the following week for our last game before the tournament. He batted once. He struck out. We won 4-1. I got two singles, three stolen bases, and scored twice.

After a couple of tune-up games that didn't count, we lost our first tournament game to Wellsville, 10-2, and the summer season was over. I went 0-3 with a hit-by-pitch and a stolen base and my only strikeout of the summer, and Lenny didn't play. I finished one hit under .500 and haven't got near that since. Lenny finished the season with one hit and one error at third and lots of dedicated scorekeeping and a hole in his heart for what his so-called friend did to him.

* * *

Lenny hadn't said a word to me since I embarrassed him. After the Wellsville game, late that night, I walked up to his house. I felt like I had to say: something.

Even if you've faced death, that doesn't mean you'll never say stupid things again. But to hurt a friend is worse than just being stupid. I felt like something too low to get eaten by a worm.

When I got there, the light was on in the garage. Lenny had become a regular grease monkey on all but the coldest winter nights. Usually he was tinkering with his engine or with some borrowed junker, taking it apart meticulously, looking over each piece, putting the whole back together again. On this particular night he was waxing his '67 Chevy and touching up the rough spots by hand with a small paint brush. He had painted a nice thin, red lightning bolt down his driver's-side door.

I stood by the garage door for a long time, but Lenny either didn't notice me or didn't want to. Finally, I spoke.

Still no answer.

"Len, I know you don't want to talk to me. And I deserve that. But I wanted to stop to apologize. You don't have to say anything if you don't want to. But I wanted you to know what I feel."

"Go away, Willie."

"Look, I know I was a jerk. We're ballplayers and we want to play and to win. If you think about it, maybe at least you'll understand why I did a mean thing. It wasn't to hurt you. It was to win. Which, I have just realized, is maybe now and then a stupid reason."

He finally looked at me. "No, Willie." He paused. "We're not ballplayers. You're a ballplayer. I sit the bench. Yes, and keep the score. Now and then the coach lets me in because he feels sorry for me."

I'm about to say "No," but he interrupts my thoughts.

"But one thing I always thought I could count on was a friend, one who'd believe I'd be good someday, or wouldn't care if I wasn't good, but would want me to play because he knew I wanted to play. Some things are more important than winning."

"I know that now. I wanted you to know that I realized that, how I feel."

"I don't care how you feel. Go away."

"But I'm your friend."

"I got no friends! First Dirk was killed—and now you may as well have died on me, too."

That hit home. I didn't have anything to say to that. I left. That night I walked a long time alone, feeling too sick to run.

The hills are always beautiful at dusk, and the river shines like thousands of quarters, bouncing and spinning, that somebody just dropped there. Guess that's inflation for you: pennies from heaven aren't enough anymore. Just before dark it started to drizzle. I walked up the hill to the cemetery, past Dirk Jenson's grave, to watch the river fade to black.

Over the rest of the summer I walked a lot, worked out a little, went to the swimming pool on sunny days to watch the girls in their bikinis, wondered how to get taller so baseball scouts would talk to me, too. I was growing some, but I'd never be as tall as Haynes from Northfield and have to bend over to talk to the scouts.

I read a couple of books, too, one that Ma said was her father's favorite, a book called *The Count of Monte Cristo*, about a guy whose friends betray him and he ends up in prison and the girl who loved him forgets him and he escapes and finds a huge treasure and gets even with the guys who betrayed him and falls in love with another girl at the end. Sometimes I pictured myself as the Count, but mostly I pictured him as Lenny.

I went to the library to get some more books, and the librarian recommended one called *Les Miserables*. I'd always wondered who that Les guy was, and why he was so miserable. It turned out to be a long story, not at all about a miserable guy named Les, but I read it anyway. It's about a guy who got thrown in prison for stealing a loaf of bread to feed his sister's starving children. He escapes, becomes mayor of a town, gets chased out, raises a little girl, rescues the guy who wants to marry the girl even though he knows the guy will take her away from him, and she's all he's got. And there's a policeman who follows the hero the whole time, wanting to take him back to prison, but at the end the policeman jumps in the river and later on the hero dies a free man. I pictured myself as the hero, Steve Presnick as the policeman (a stretch, I know), and Lenny as the kid the hero saves so the girl can marry him. I tried to find a place for Angelina or Lana or my mother in the book, but there wasn't any.

Ma told me *miserables* is French for "the miserable ones"; I guess that means poor people forgotten by the government and maybe by God. I wondered if it could mean short baseball players or people betrayed by their friends or people stuck in small towns or people who die in car crashes or people who raise children by themselves or people who are hungry or lonely or maybe just *people*, anybody.

That's the sort of thing that starts happening to you when you read books. You start to think, and that's not always so good.

What if I didn't get drafted at all? What if all the baseball scouts just ignored me?

It just struck me that I was soon going to be a senior, and I had no idea what I was going to do when I graduated. Where would I go if the scouts didn't want me?

I would have to grow up, to be a man, but how do you do that?

About a week before school started I got a call from Brian Schwartz. He and Jim Pavlich were going to the ocean, and he asked if I wanted to go along.

I had hardly ever been farther from Harmon Falls than you'd go for a baseball game. I had almost no money, just what I could get from painting jobs, cutting grass, and fixing a few picket fences. But I went anyway.

They waited an extra day for me so I could pick up some extra money: I even collected coke bottles from the side of the road for the return money they give you. I asked Lenny to go along to the beach, too, but he wouldn't go. Said he had to finish his car before school started because his uncle wanted him to work in his shop part-time during the school year.

Brian, Jim, and I drove all night in Brian's Camaro to get to Virginia Beach by morning. We spent three days swimming, watching girls, sitting in the sun. I didn't eat much, since I didn't have much money, but I ran on the beach every morning, anyway. I wondered what it would be like to be the Count of Monte Cristo, swimming for your life from the island prison, or one of the miserable people who scraped the streets of Paris for scraps of food, or a baseball player with nowhere to go and no place to play.

I love the hills and the green and gold glow of Harmon Falls on a sunny summer day, but if you've never seen the sun rise over the ocean and stretch its bronzed fingers to warm the sand beneath your toes, you've missed something.

I listened to see if the ocean would say anything to be, but it didn't. Guess it didn't know me as well as the river does. I could have used advice from either one.

14 Lana's Story

One thing I know for sure: all boys think they're men already, and all men are still, at least a bit, little boys.

I'm not really sure yet what women are.

Oh, I know we're not angels, and neither are they—not by a long shot. Some of us are more vegetable or mineral than animal, even: vines, pumpkins, pomegranates, crystals, gems, melons, ores, stars. At least that's how men think of us, and sometimes how we think of ourselves. But we're mostly more realistic than men. Boys and men live in fantasy land.

Another thing I know for sure: I want to get out of Harmon Falls.

Oh, I know it's not so bad, as little towns go. But I feel choked, like the soot from the mills and the coal furnaces has caked my lungs and my brains so thick that I may never be able to breathe or think straight.

It's not all sunny summer baseball days, you know.

And one thing I'd like to do, at least once in my life, is think straight. Call it my goal in life. Two things: breathe clean air and think straight.

By the way, I'm Lana. Willie's told you a little about me, but not much. If you want to listen, I'll tell you a little more, but not much.

Willie thinks he's in charge of this story, but he isn't, any more than I am or Lenny or his Coach or Stud or his mother or anyone else. To some extent, you are, but not entirely, either. We have to give you something to start with, and what happens to us is as much chance and whim as what happens to you. And we need you to be willing to go along with us.

But at least for a little while you'll hear part of the story from my point of view. Not that Willie isn't an honest guy: sometimes too much even, if you ask me. But if you want to look at a sculpture and really understand it, do you take one look, photograph it, and only look at the photograph after that? If you're like me, you look all the way around it several times, sides, back, and front, above and below, and then maybe you take some pictures from several angles, but you always go back and look at the real thing again as many times as you can.

They took us to The City once for a museum trip for Civics class, the high school teachers did.

What does a little girl like me from a podunk town know about art? you may ask. Not much, but I'm learning. I may study it in college, if I ever save enough money to get there. Or I may study psychology. Or literature. Or history. I'd study music if I had any talent. I want to study everything. If my uncle has his way, if I get to college at all, I'll study business, accounting, and come back to Harmon Falls to keep the books for his business.

Don't bet on it.

As for Willie, right now I'd like to punch him so hard his brains would rattle. You heard what he did to Lenny? Fine way to treat a friend, talk your coach out of letting him in a game. It's just a baseball game. I don't understand why guys take it so seriously. Like I said: all little boys. Not that my brother's much better. Just try to get him away from his car or his science fiction books. And lately he just gets weirder and weirder, more and more distant. You'd think that *I'd* kept him out of a baseball game, or that Willie had done something really bad, like steal his girlfriend or kick his dog. I figure Lenny will come around eventually, but till then, he's a real pain. He won't even go on walks with me. Maybe I'll throw out his *Playboy* magazines to shake him up a little. Anyway, he should know that women are more than just pictures.

I tried once to sort of fix him up with one of my girlfriends, Gloria Pennings, but she's not what he'd call really pretty, though I think she's a really nice girl, and Lenny just laughed at me. What can you do? Every boy thinks he should get the prettiest girl in town.

Willie and I haven't been walking all summer. Last winter, seemed like we walked all the time, tromping through the snow, sniffing the evergreens, watching the ice make leafy crystals on the spidery limbs of the deciduous trees. I don't know why or how we started, but we did. But as we all know, in the spring a boy's thoughts turn to baseball (not love, as some wise old fool once said), and he stopped coming by. I think partly he felt bad about Lenny ignoring him, but he looked like there was something else bothering him, too. When I asked him about it, he wouldn't say anything. He didn't seem to mind if he had me all in knots not knowing what he was thinking. So now I mostly just walk by myself or with Gloria or my other friend Jainie. We talk more, but it's not quite the same as walking with Willie. I always got the feeling he was just about to say something really startling, really different or interesting. He never did, so I don't know why I thought that, but I did, and sometimes I still do.

To be fair, Harmon Falls in the months of May and June is amazing. It can be cruel in March or April, snow and ice still or rain, rain, rain just when you think the sun is about to burst through and flood the whole valley with gold. But in May the hills wear a green velvet gown that sweeps all the way down to the river, and streaks of silver over the water look like you could catch them and spend them in heaven for anything you wanted. There are more apple trees around here than anyone knows what to do with, and the air is humid enough that by June tomatoes are starting to sprout in gardens and people are eating their own lettuce and onions and peppers and the sweet corn is just beginning to poke its ears up to find out if anyone else is listening to the sunshine.

I love my little garden in our back yard. This year I got some herbs from Jainie's mom, basil and parsley and coriander and dill, and when you squeeze them with a fingernail, they smell better than rain or your hair when a summer wind blows through it or clean skin or lilacs on Saturday evening. Mom laughed at me when I asked her if I could plant a garden, said I wouldn't take care of it. She laughed at me when I asked if I could get a puppy, even a free one from somebody who was just going to have to get rid of them anyway, because she said I wouldn't take care of it and it would just make a mess and she would end up cleaning up after it. She let me have the garden, but not the puppy. I think I could have managed both. Don't you just love puppies?

Girls aren't supposed to be smart and savvy—have you ever noticed that? Oh, it's all right if we get good grades in school, as long as we don't do better than the boys in math and science, but grades are just grades: we're not really supposed to *learn* anything or *do* anything. The way this town thinks, the best thing that could happen to a girl is for her to become a high school cheerleader and marry the captain of the football team, settle into a little house that he and his father built, and have a couple kids. That may be o.k. for some girls, but everybody? I'm hoping for a little more than that, thank you.

Though I don't know why. Why should I hope for anything? When I get good grades, Mom just tells me not to be so proud of myself, cause I'm just a girl. Her biggest fear is that I'll get pregnant before I graduate, even though there hasn't been any chance of that happening, or that I'll never ever get pregnant and she won't get to be a grandmother.

I dated Harry Kuschner for a little while. His band plays some pretty cool music, not as good as Pervis Easly's, but he got me out of the house and away from Mom when I went to hear them play. Mom didn't talk to me for three weeks after I went to the Homecoming Dance with him. She said she knew what was on his mind, and mine. After a while she eased up a bit, but all she did was snipe at me until I stopped dating him.

And yet she wants me to stay here, get married, and give her those grandchildren. What does she want me to do, marry Willie? Fat lot of good a baseball player will do me—how will he make a living, and what will I do if he's traveling all over the place? And I'll still be stuck here trying to get more hours to work in the library or maybe getting a full-time job managing the Dairy Queen, whoop-dee-doo.

Actually, I don't think Mom likes Willie much, anyway, though I don't know why not, unless Lenny actually talked to her. Oh well.

I do think about marriage sometimes, even though I'm still really young. Don't all girls, even if they don't really like boys? But what no one tells you is that boys do, too, though they'd never admit it. They look at girls and think, not only, "gee, I'd like to get her, uh, uh, uh," but also, "I wonder if she'll get fat?" or "I wonder if she'll grow up to look like her mother?" or "bet she'd have lots of boys if you could marry her." Except for Willie; I don't know if he's ever thought about marriage. I think he's still stuck in the Baseball Stage.

Mostly what I think about marriage is this: avoid it, run from it, spray it with Lysol or Raid, ignore it and maybe it'll go away, treat it with antibiotics and maybe it won't kill you. I hope I don't get married for a long, long time.

I want to travel. And get a job. And go to college. Or go to college so I can get a job and make enough money to travel. I want to go to places where people haven't heard of Harmon Falls—not too hard, right?—where they have huge castles and mysterious ruins and temples that reach to the sky, where people still sing and tell stories and eat something other than burgers and fries and where they have huge gardens. Does that sound like too much to ask? Mom says I should be glad to have food and a roof over my head. She's right, I guess. If I had been born in times past I'd probably have been a slave or a farm girl or a poor city woman working in a sweatshop or just a girl who got raped and killed in a war. Lots of fun, huh? I wonder how people have survived this long.

One cool thing about being with Harry Kuschner: at least I felt like somebody for a little while. I'm no Deb Dorian: everyone knows she'll succeed at whatever she wants—she's so smart, beautiful, cool—and coming from a rich family doesn't hurt. I'm no Angelina Zamboni, either, though Harry did take me out, and Rob Riddell asked me out but I told him no, and I've seen Willie look at me a time or two with more than just friendship in his eyes, if I'm right, though he's never tried to do anything about it. I wonder what I'd do, like, if he did? I'd rather listen to Pat Benatar or Stevie Nicks.

You should have seen Willie at the Homecoming dance my sophomore year. He doesn't go to many dances, and he looked like a lost puppy. How he squirmed when Angelina was dancing and making out with Pervis Easly: he kept almost getting up, then sitting down, almost getting up, then sitting down. And when Harry left me to dance with her, too, Willie wasn't the only one who wanted to punch *him*. I was so mad at Harry I almost cried, but I didn't want him to see that, so I played it cool, like somebody who knows how it is to go out with a prowler but knows how to bring him back when he starts to stray. Not that I know those things, but you can pull off a lot just by *looking* right—you don't necessarily have to *do* anything at all. And Harry eventually came back to me, his little sophomore girl, the one he took because the others were taken. Not that I'm so bad: I know how to talk to boys and, to tell you the truth, I don't look so bad in a swimsuit, either, even if I don't have bazooms like Angelina Zamboni's. I think it took a little horsepower out of Harry's engine when he saw Willie dancing with Angelina and not looking stupid, in fact, looking pretty good. Then he turned his attentions to me, maybe more out of frustration than anything else, but he was all I could handle for the rest of the evening, and I probably led him on more than I should have, because I wasn't too happy with Willie for really taking Angelina to the dance to begin with. He didn't owe me anything, but you'd think the clod would know better than letting That Girl just use him to get even with Pervis. Funny thing about boys: they don't seem to mind being used by girls with big eyes and bouncy boobs. Maybe it's hormones, but they should learn how to control them. I guess I should talk, huh? Ever since I started getting periods, part of the month I want to purr and part I just want to scratch somebody's eyes out. It's hard to be cool when half the month you're revving or raving, but when I brush my hair I practice this look in the mirror that says, don't mess with me, chump, or I'll cut your tree down to a stump. I saw some woman do this look in an old movie once; like, you just look at them like you know their every thought, and you know that their every thought is stupid. She was tiny, but she had big, round, glaring eyes, that movie actress. It worked there in the movie, and if you use it on the right kind of boy, especially the ones who don't have too much experience with girls, you can send them running with their tail between their legs. It doesn't work on the ones with really big egos, though: they think they're too good for any girl to turn them down. With that kind you'd better either stay away or carry a knife and be ready to use it— trust me on that.

One time I told Jainie about "the look." She asked me to show her, so I did, and we laughed and laughed. We laughed so hard that she tried it over and over again, but couldn't do it, because she couldn't stop laughing. Now I'm not sure I can do it anymore, because every time I think about it, I think about Jainie, and I start laughing and can't stop. Did you ever do that, you're just walking down the hallway, shopping at the corner store, or talking to somebody, and all of a sudden you think of something funny, and you laugh and laugh and can't stop?

I tried to tell Gloria about it, too, but she didn't quite understand. She thought it sounded cruel. That's when I thought she might be good to fix up with my brother Lenny, but you already know that idea flew about as far as a dead sparrow.

One thing I have found out about dealing with boys: you have to be cool every minute, let them know you're in charge and that you know more than they know, keep them wondering, because if you give up or give in for a minute, you're done for. Once they're off the defensive and they think you're vulnerable anywhere, they attack like they're starving to death and you're nothing but a hot pepperoni pizza to be eaten bite by huge bite.

Good thing for me I have Jainie and Gloria. If I ever tried to talk to Mom about this stuff, she'd call me a tramp and probably make me convert to Catholicism and become a nun and flog myself for the rest of my life while she watched and gloated and told me how trashy I was. I better not give her any ideas; do Lutherans have convents?

I got a few old tubes of oil paint and some beat-up brushes from the art teacher at school, and Gloria's mom got me a couple of canvas boards from the art store across the river where she works, so lately in

the evenings after I finish the dishes and the laundry and my homework I've been going down in the basement, opening all the windows,
and pushing around blobs of paint. There's something about the feel
of the brush in paint when it's thick and mushy, acrylic paint without
mineral spirits in it, and what you leave on the canvas has thickness and
dimension and texture as well as color and form. I can't paint really
nice pictures like Gloria does; she does horses and barns and seashores
and places where you'd like to go and lie down and sniff the grass and
take a nap. They're really cool. But I don't want to do that. I just make
a mess: figures and pools of color and light and ideas about how I feel
turned into sharp swirls or tight lattices or gooey curves or bony lines.
I float away sometimes for hours while I paint.

I also took Lenny's old guitar that Mom gave him that he hasn't
picked up in years down to Henry's Music and had it restrung, just
with cheap steel strings, and I dug up a twenty-five cent library throw-
away-table paperback on how to play guitar, and some nights I pick at
the strings instead of painting. Don't worry: I asked Lenny first before
I did it. He didn't care at all. I learned a few chords from the book
before it fell apart entirely in my lap, but now I'm mostly just teaching myself to pick simple melodies that come into my head or fiddling
with weird chord sequences that sound like something you might hear
on the soundtrack from bad Saturday night horror flicks.

I like to try different things. Willie likes to run so much that I
thought I'd try that, too, but not when anyone else was around to
watch me go slow and hoot at me. At first it hurt, like, I thought my
lungs would burn up, but after a while I got so I could just run and float
away in my mind to wherever I felt like going or imagining. I like to
run by myself, but I'm afraid to go at night or out in the country alone,
so usually I go in the morning before school or on Saturday down past
the grade school, up the hill, north a few blocks along the ridge of the
hill through a richer neighborhood—I like to imagine what it would
be like to live in one of those houses some day and have a cat and a dog
and a Camaro—then I weave street by street back home; then I do it
all again as many times as I feel like. Maybe I'll join the cross-country
team next year.

I almost tried to get Willie to ask me to the Homecoming this year.
You know what he did instead of going? Jainie told me she saw him
out running. The day after, I got up early while the sky was still orange
and went out for a run, and guess who I saw at it again? I called to him,

and he stopped, and when I caught up, we ran down to the football stadium. I'd never go there by myself, either, cause it's in a kind of bad neighborhood, but it was kind of fun for a change with Willie. Then we ran laps together and talked about the people in Harmon Falls, how we hate school, what books we read from the library, and what we want to do when we graduate. I asked him if he ran there often, and he said, no, usually down by the river and up the hill. I asked him why he likes to run by the river, doesn't it stink of dead fish, and he said not in some places, and that the river would sometimes say things to him. I was surprised that he would say that, because some people would think he was crazy, but I kind of understood. But I didn't want to let on that I understood. "So what does it say?" I asked. "If it would tell you how to get a job, I wish it would talk to me, too." He looked kind of hurt when I said that, so I didn't tease him anymore, but then it was hard to get him to say any more about it.

Finally, he said, "It doesn't really *talk* to me, that is, it doesn't say anything specific. It's as though it had some kind of general message about how to think or how to live, that it has seen thousands of people go by and live and die and that it had learned one thing by watching them, one thing that it believed really to be true, and that it would tell me if I listened closely enough. It has a voice that sounds old and deeper than words."

"So what is it trying to say?"

"I haven't quite figured it out for sure yet."

"Tell me when you do?"

"Maybe. O.k."

I ran along with him stride for stride, which made me feel pretty good. He might have slowed down a little for me so we could go together, but that made me feel good, too.

We turned out the gate and moved toward home. There wasn't much traffic yet, and the streets were quiet, lawns shiny with dew, trees still in the breezeless morning.

"So, JES, what *are* you going to do when you graduate?"

"I got a lot to think about between now and then, LAS. Baseball to play—we may do pretty well this year—some odd jobs to do to make some money, classes not to screw up. I don't know. I don't know. I don't know what to do."

We ran in silence for a while.

"See that house there?" I said. I really like that one. I'd like to live in one like that someday, but not here in Harmon Falls. Something kind of different, not boxy, with some gables and a garden and lots of old trees to make it look mysterious, but in some really neat place."

Willie gave me that funny look that he does sometimes, when I think he's about to say something amazing, but then he doesn't quite say it. "Where would you like to live?" I asked. I guess it was a kind of test.

"I don't know. I say that a lot, don't I? But I don't know. Somewhere where I can play baseball. If some major league team drafts me, I'll go wherever they tell me to go. You can play in the minor leagues for years, moving here and there, getting traded, making no money, wondering where you'll end up, never really living anywhere."

"Sounds kind of like slavery."

Then he looked almost angry at me. "Far from it. Exactly the opposite. What could be better, freer, than to be playing baseball, moving from town to town, seeing places, doing what you love to do, no responsibilities? And to make it to the Majors, even for a year, a month, you'd have something to remember all your life."

I didn't say anything for a long time. Then: "So that's what you want to be, a major league baseball player?"

"Be? That's what I want to *do*, at least for a while. Doesn't everyone who ever put on a glove or ever felt what it's like to hit a ball so square that it doesn't even feel like you hit anything, the ball just flies off faster than a thought, want to be a major leaguer? As for *being* something, at least for long, you gotta *be* really good to be a ballplayer and *stay* one."

He thought for a minute. I could see the wheels turning behind his eyes, slowly.

"That seems to be my problem right now. What do I want to *be*? Big problem, right? Like surviving an accident or cancer or poverty or war. Geez, did you ever realize that if Lenny and I had been born a few years earlier, we could have been killed in a war half a world away? But still, big deal or not, I have to choose to be something, but something that I can be, not something that I wish I could be. I don't know. I don't know. I guess I have to decide what I want to be before I can decide where I want to live. Your house, I mean the one you described, sounded kind of nice, though, wherever you find it."

He blushed visibly. A good sign.

We were coming near my house, so I had to talk fast, but I couldn't think of anything. So finally he asks me a question.

"Lana, what do you want to be?"

Now that question really surprised me, just because he asked it.

"Everything."

"What?"

"Everything. I want to be a painter, a composer, a musician, a writer, a business owner, a mother, a kid, an adult, a celebrity, a hermit, a gardener, I want to know everything about everything, I want to travel everywhere and see how people live and die and hear what they have to say about what they love and what they hate. I want somebody to love me so bad it hurts and I want to be able to say yes or no just as I please. I want to be the person who always knows what to do, who's so cool that nobody ever says "fool" or "tramp" or "slut" or "garbage" or "stupid." I want to be able to find my house and buy it and live in it for as long as I want."

"Oh."

"Yeah."

"Guess that means you don't want to work in the library or take bookkeeping and come back and keep your uncle's accounts," he said.

"You asshole."

We sprinted home.

I think in the summer I'll see if I've saved enough money from working at the library to take a college course at the Branch campus. Gloria says they'll let you do that if you're a good student in high school and your school will write a letter of recommendation. I wonder what I should take. Maybe I should ask the river to tell me.

It won't be bookkeeping, though.

15 The Last of the Last

So I'm in the on-deck circle, rubbing the handle of my Louisville Slugger with a pine-tar rag and stretching my legs. Then I dust some rosin on top of the pine tar and squeeze it in till my hands almost won't come off the bat, and some rosin gets in my nose and it's dry as smoke off the quarries and it makes me sneeze. I tap the barrel on my spikes to knock off the dirt and then on my head to make me mad and ready to hit, which does not now seem as good an idea as when I thought of it.

Harmon Falls, Willie White Shoes, senior year. We've made it to the state semifinals, single elimination, and now every game may be the last game of my baseball career.

I had a good senior year, not a great year, a hit just at .400. Nobody drafted me.

Like a Neanderthal man I am ready for the hunt with my club and my face paint, lampblack slick as birdshit striped under my eyes. I am a Lion. I am the Taurus primeval, or something like that—I think I read it in English class. But I am ready to hit, and there is no better thing to be ready for in this world, or at least not much that I know of. I say to myself a couple of times "Om," which my buddy Stud taught me to say to stay calm and get ready to hit. I don't know what it means, but it's part of my ritual now, so I say it every time, and I haven't had a really bad slump since I started saying it, and as everybody knows that's reason enough.

The semifinals are in the State Capital: big deal, and I mean it. Long way from little Harmon Falls. I bat fourth, which is silly, since I'm a leadoff hitter, but we got no big rbi men these days, so I do the best I can since Coach shifted me there after our first few games. I led the league in rbi's because our guys got on base. Now Ropes is on with a single after Samula flied out to left. Krick fans on four, so now I step into the box. As I said, I'm a senior now, so I'm serious, trying to set a good example.

As I step in, an announcer says, "Now batting for Harmon Falls High School: Willie Smith." You would think he at least would use my real name, or maybe "Will," but someone musta told him to call me Willie.

And to show you how serious I am, I take a pitch, a ball outside. And even better, I swing through one so Ropes can steal second, which he does. I close my eyes when I swing, because my eye has gotten good, and if I can see the ball at all I can't help but hit it. I haven't swung and missed in about twenty games.

I don't like Newcomb's pitcher—Newcomb, that's the team we're playing. You can't hit if you like the pitcher. He has long hair and a mustache and slumped shoulders and doesn't look like an athlete. He looks old, like about thirty. Short wind-up, quick delivery, but the ball jumps out of his hand, moves a lot, usually down and away or up and in.

So with Ropes on second I take another ball, then foul one down way down the left field line. Their pitcher is faster than he looks, but I will pull inside pitches. His ball is like a sprinter: it keeps getting faster all the way and gets by you before you know it's there. If I strike out, I'll die, so I dig in and move closer to the plate. Let him hit me if he wants to.

But now I concentrate, and everything disappears except me, the bat, and the ball, even the smell of the breeze over the grass.

Then with two and two I get an outside-corner knee-high fastball and I swing and the ball hits bat and then dirt and it's squirting between first and second and it squirms through quick as a snake in the grass and Ropes is around third and heading for home and I take my turn and I'm happy and we're up 1-0.

The wind blows straight in from center through the trees, and the song of the locusts rushes down like a waterfall.

I steal second, and I'm tempted to try third, but Pud, Bud's other brother, grounds out on the next pitch and the inning's over. Ropes brings my glove, and I want to do a handspring on my way to center, but since I'm a senior, I restrain myself and trot out more dignified.

Tree is pitching. His real nickname is Treetops, because he's about six-three, and some of the guys just call him Tops, cause he pitches pretty well, but I call him Tree, because that sounds more like a bat. I don't like him that much. He's a junior, and he always says how good the team is going to be *next year*—which means when I'm gone. But I hit .400 this year and drove in forty runs in not even thirty games, and we'll just see how Falls will do without me next year.

Tree is one of those guys who's always comparing himself to everyone. "How good are your grades?" he asks one guy, like anyone cared. "Your girlfriend isn't as pretty as Tiny's," he says to another. "Your batting average is only ten points higher than Krick's," he says to me. You know the kind: pitchers. I have never liked pitchers in general, as you know. And my average is at least twenty points higher than Krick's.

So Tree gives up a single and a walk, but we get them out before they score. I head for the dugout and go through the gate to the water fountain. As I go I step on the empty shells of dead locusts that crackle under my feet. You can't help it—they're thick as grass on a well-kept outfield at this time of year.

I go back to the dugout and sit by Samula. Lenny doesn't keep score anymore; he sits at the other end of the bench, and he does play an inning or two now and then, now that he's a senior. Yes, I'm glad, but still a little scared, when he plays. But I will say nothing except "Go, get 'em, Len."

Len looks at me for a minute before I notice he's doing it. "What?" I say.

"If we lose today, we're out of the tournament, and the season's over," he says. "If we win today, we play tomorrow in the finals. Either today's your last game, or tomorrow's your last game."

"Thanks for telling me. What would I do without you."

"What *are* you gonna do?"

I'm a little surprised, since Lenny hasn't said this much to me in quite a while.

"I'm gonna win today, and I'm gonna win tomorrow, and I'm gonna walk out of here a state champion, same as you and everybody else on this team."

"And then what?" Lenny is nothing if not persistent. Maybe he's both nothing and persistent. Maybe I am, too.

"Who cares."

"You gotta do something with your life." Lenny is still at it. He's got work at his uncle's car shop and college at the Branch if he can make enough money. Maybe he doesn't mind after all that I spent the winter walking with Lana. I thought maybe that had made him mad, too, like you-know-what.

So I give it a try. But I don't want to think about that now. It's depressing. "Right now, I'm thinking about winning this game, and you should do the same."

"I'm serious. What're you gonna *do*? Go to school? Get a job in the mines? What?"

"I dunno. Play ball and see what happens, I guess."

"You didn't get drafted."

"Thanks again. I never would have known that if you hadn't told me."

"I'm just trying to help. Maybe you could go to college and play there. Or you could work in the mines and play in the miners' league. Lots of good players do that. Or go to Big League tryout camps this summer. The Miners' or the Minors, huh?"

"Very funny."

We go down in order, and I'm half glad, so I can get away from Lenny. We haven't been as tight as we used to be, but just now he is making me tighten up. I want to think about nothing but baseball.

I run out to center. In the trees beyond the fence the locusts are buzzing like a chain saw. The trees are so thick with them that I'm surprised they don't fall out by the dozens, dropping like rain drops, dead from fighting over the leaves.

So before I know it I drop into a soft song, and I'm singing. I've been humming Elvis as well as Sinatra and Bennet lately, so guess what comes to mind? "My Way," and I don't want to sing that one, so I stop. Tony Bennett: "Because of You"—that's not the one, either. "Dang Me": that one fits.

You can hear the drone of the crowd as Tree runs another count to three and two. A radio blares classic rock off somewhere down the left field line, but the sough of the breeze blowing in from center at about fifteen knots cuts it into long, slow notes that fall like misty raindrops. The infielders chatter, some sparrows riff as they try to make fast food of the locusts, and I try to think of another song, but for some reason I can't get "Dang Me" outta my head, probably because of talking with Lenny.

The third out pops to me in center, and on my way in I notice a rough spot, a little ridge following a trough in shallow center straight out from second base. The ground crew always drags the infield, but they don't often do anything about the outfield besides cut the grass occasionally. Fact is, nobody cares much about the outfield, even here in the center of state, where somebody is supposed to take care of this stuff. We're just out there, and we're supposed to catch everything, and most of the time we do.

I head for the dugout and sit on the far end from Lenny. I don't want to talk any more. The wind picks up a cloud of orange dust, spins it in a banana shape, then drops it like a waterfall. Behind me I can hear Tree walking on the cement, his spikes clacking, as he goes for water. Empty locust shells crackle under his steps.

In the fourth inning I bat again, leading off. I take two and two, but he won't give me anything to hit, and on the next pitch I fly out to center. Hit it good, all the way to the fence, but not good enough. That's better than striking out, but it still leaves you with a sinking feeling that you didn't get your job done, that everybody knows it and they never will quite forgive you for it.

We don't score again, so I pigeon-toe my way out to center, ready to catch anything they hit, eager as the great Mays himself, my white shoes, old but fresh-polished, gleaming in the sun.

I wonder what he was like when he played high school baseball, the real Willie, Willie Mays. Did people know he was great then? Did he know he was? If he saw me, would he remember what he was like then, or would he laugh at some dumb kid wanting to play like him?

I want to play like him. I want somebody to say someday, "Yeah, Willie Mays was great, but have you seen Willie *Smith*? I also know that won't happen, but I want it to, anyway.

I want to win this game, and I want to play baseball for the rest of my life and then I want to die, when I can't play no more. Then I want to go someplace where they play baseball into eternity. No harps for me, though a little Sinatra wouldn't be bad, and some Ella Fitzgerald. I wonder if God likes Sinatra, and I bet he likes Ella. I know he likes Mays. And when I get there, Mays will be in centerfield, and I'll jog out with my gear on, and my shoes clean and white, and Mays will wave and move over to left, and he'll say, "Center's yours, man—we been waiting for you." And every day the wind will be blowing out and we'll play a doubleheader, and people will be there to cheer even when we lose, and when we do lose, we won't feel bad, because we'll always be back tomorrow, and we'll know that we've already won the big one, and we'll have baseball from there on out, and never a game lost to rain.

The only bad thing will be that we have to have pitchers, who otherwise would be shoveling coal down below, if you know what I mean, but we will put up with them because we'll all bat .400 and they won't be shitheads, because I can't believe otherwise they could get into heaven, and heaven wouldn't be heaven without baseball.

So I get back to the dugout, and who gets up and comes over and plunks down next to me but Lenny, and he picks up right where he won't leave off, and he says, "So what are you gonna *do?*"

"I'm gonna get a hit my next time up. Fact, I'm gonna hit one over that leftfield fence."

"Don't dodge the question. You know what I mean."

"I'm gonna hit the first fastball he puts in the vicinity of the plate."

"Look, Willie, when you get out, what are you gonna do?"

"I just told you, he's not gonna get me out. I'm gonna hit the first good fastball over the leftfield fence."

"When you get out of school in about two weeks."

"Look, Lenny, give him a break," Samula says. "He's gotta be thinking about baseball now. There's plenty of time for that later."

"But there isn't, Samula," Lenny says. "School's almost out, baseball season's almost over, and he's got no job, and no major league contract, and he's not going to school. What's he gonna do?"

"I don't know what he's gonna do, but I know if you don't shut up, I'm gonna kick your ass all the way out to second base," Turbin says. Samula was thinking it, but he's too nice a guy to say it.

"It's all right, Turb," I say. "Let him go. He means well. The inning's over anyway." And I manage to get out of it again.

"Look alive. Get your head in the damn game," Coach says as I run by him toward center, and he spits on my shoe. Wherever I go next, after this life, I hope they don't spit on my shoe.

Well there is no joy in Treeville, and not much in Willieville, either, as Newcomb gets a hit to left to lead off their half. The next guy fans, but the runner steals second. The next one lays down a bunt. Tree stumbles off the mound, bobbles the ball, and both runners are safe— the proverbial pregnant giraffe on the pitcher's mound. With runners on the corners, their guy on first steals second, but the batter grounds to third, so they got second and third with two out.

I'm thinking, get ready to fire the ball home on a hit. I hear "The Wreck of the Edmund Fitzgerald" pouring out of somebody's boombox down the leftfield line.

And what happens on two-and-two but the batter grounds one past Tree, 'tween Split and Whip, and into center for a hit.

I'm already coming in hard on the ball and—remember the little trough-and-ridge I told you about? Well the ball rolls up and my glove is down and the ball pops up and my glove's still down and I pull up but the ball knocks right off my forehead and the first runner's scoring and I'm bobbling and I've got it and the second runner's rounding third and we can't give them a lead and I'm throwing with all I got and the ball flies straight as a clothesline for home and the runner's sliding and the ball's whistling and they both get there and he's down and it's down and Samula's blocking the plate but the runner takes his leg out and Samula goes down and he's got the ball but I can't believe it the runner's safe and damn a lumpy outfield and dammit they're ahead and damn me for not coming up with the ball clean and how am I going to live with that?

There went my ticket to heaven, and Mays in centerfield is shaking his head.

The locusts are sawing away out beyond the fence, and thank God, cause they muffle the cheering from Newcomb's stands. Honestly that batter was lucky as a squirrel with big nuts to get that ball through. We're down 2-1, and Tree stares out at me like I gave up the hit. Coach spits, and I know he's sorry that my shoe's not there for him to spit on: some things never change, and sometimes maybe they shouldn't.

They say the locusts only get bad like this every seventeen years.

The next batter bloops to center, and I call everyone off and take it myself and run to the dugout to think about hitting. I go out for a drink at the fountain first, and I step on as many locust shells as I can, some with the locusts still in them.

"Good throw," Turbin says.

"Tough bounce," Lenny says.

"Shit on shinola," Pud says.

"Shitty outfielders," Tree says.

"Let's get us some runs," Tiny says.

I sit in the corner of the dugout and try not to think, just let the anger settle in, and to get ready to hit. Like I said, you can't think. Thinking only ties you up in knots.

"What are *you* gonna do, Turb?" Lenny says.

"Give him a break, Turb," Samula says. "Don't kill Lenny till after the game so at least he'll know how it comes out."

Turb stares at me and then Samula and then Lenny, and then he says something like this: "I wanna work on cars. I got this car at home. My dad got this old Volkswagen engine left over. The body gave out, but the engine's still good, even though it's got about 200,000 miles on it. And I worked last summer at the grocery, you know, and made enough money that I went to the junk yard and got like this '67 Corvette body, you know, and I spent last summer pounding out the dents and painting it and messing with that engine. And when the season's over, after we win state, you know, I'm fixin' to put that body on that engine, and I'm gonna supe it up, and I'm gonna drive it 100,000 miles anywhere I feel like goin'. It may not be fast, but it will look really cool. And when I get back I'm gonna open me up a repair shop and make some money and drink some beer."

Old Turbin knows what he's all about.

"Willie's seen my 'Vet," Turbin says. "Ain't she a beauty?"

"Yeah, she's a beauty," I say, though just now she's no more than an empty body collecting rain. Not an engine in the thing, not one cylinder. But the body looks good.

Well, we don't get a run, but neither do they, and before I know it, it's the last of the seventh, and no time for any more songs, even Sinatra. It's our last chance to catch up, and if I don't get a hit, it's the last of the last, and we're out, and I don't know what to do next.

So I'm leading off the seventh, and I've played four years to get here, and I've played with guys who wanted to win and with guys who didn't give a shit and didn't deserve to be on the diamond, and I put my helmet on tight and clear my nose and tap my spikes clean and dust my hands with rosin and spit on them and rub the pine tar tight and step into the box and take a deep breath of air and the lime and the dust and the wind is no longer blowing and I feel like my whole life comes down to this one minute and maybe one pitch and if I get a homer I don't care if I die a minute after, God, as long as I get around the bases and touch home plate first.

So I step into the box and dig in and everything disappears but the bat and the ball and I don't even think of the pitcher but maybe just a little about how I want to hit that home run and he winds up and lets go and the ball is coming shoulder high right down the middle and I'm swinging and I'm gonna someday Alice straight to the moon and I'm ready for the home-run trot and I swing so hard my air is gone and I almost fall and I didn't feel the ball and I can't believe it dammit dammit dammit I missed.

I swear.

I haven't missed except on purpose in twenty games.

I wipe the sweat from my eyes with my knuckle and dig my feet in. I windmill the bat slowly. The windup. The pitch.

Fastball high and outside. I swing hard and smooth.

Foul back.

I step out to collect myself. Down 0-2. Don't think. *Om.*

Just hit now. Watch for the waste pitch. The sun is beating down hot. I can't hear the locusts in the trees, but I know they're there. I find myself thinking about Turbin's empty Corvette and the Volkswagen engine. The pitch: curveball swooping like a bird of prey. Outside. I barely let it go.

The sharp smell of pine tar rises to my nose as I squeeze the bat handle tight. I think of abandoned railroad tracks and scrub trees and the shell of the old telegraph office along the river in Warrenton. I think of the streets of Harmon Falls, like black rivers in the night. I think of the river itself and wish it had a word for me now.

The pitch: curve again, it swings low, inside, just past my elbow. I don't swing.

The crowd oos and boos, but they are wrong. Two and two.

And now I dig in a little more, and I don't know how I do it, but I let a fastball go high for three and two. I look at Coach down at third. He stares back, expressionless as an overfed bird. Then he spits. I look at Coach Luke at first. He claps his hands and shouts something, God knows what.

I feel every at-bat, every throw, every catch, every pitch, every hit, every error, every game-winning rbi, every strike, every cheer, every boo, every dust-cloud slide, every cold bus ride, every practical joke, every extra-inning game in the rain, every joy and every pain of my baseball life funnel into this second and rush through me like a chill, and the ball is coming and its down and in and I'm on it and the meat of the bat goes straight into the meat of the ball and it feels smooth as butter and the ball jumps off down the leftfield line and its high enough and I know it's long enough and I've done it! but it's hooking and it turns foul and flies way over the fence and disappears 400 feet into nowhere.

Damn. Foul ball. That close.

The crowd, both sides, everybody there, utters a sigh you could hear a mile away.

I can't even look at the guys in the dugout. The pitcher looks as if nothing just happened, and in a way he's right. A foul ball is like nothing at all. The ump tosses him a new ball, and he's already ready for the next pitch. You gotta give him credit for that. He works quick.

No time to think and the next one's coming but it's chest-high out-side corner and I'm swinging again and everything seems slow so slow like I was watching from a hundred miles and a hundred years away with the last breath of my life and it was long and slow like an August breeze and I feel the ball and it's good but not too good cause I'm too far away and I look for the ball and it's in the air and it's right down the right field line this time and the rightfielder is running and I think Shit! and I think he's going to catch it and I start for first and I hear Coach Luke yelling Go, go! and I'm running now and the rightfielder is diving and the ball is falling and he hits the grass and it hits the grass and he's down and I'm rounding first and Coach Luke is yelling All the way, turn 'em, turn 'em! and the ball is leaping like a jackrabbit toward the rightfield corner and the fielder is up and that's all I see cause I'm turning second and heading for third and I'm looking for a signal from Coach and he's just standing there at third with his mouth open and I never noticed before but he's missing a tooth or two in the front and I'm rounding third barely touching the ground and heading for home and I hear Hold up! and I pull up so fast I fall and I skid and I slide and I scramble back for third and I look up and the ball is just to the cut-off man in back of second and I think, God Almighty, I could have made it home, but I'm glad I didn't say that and I'm standing at third and there's nobody out and we're down only a run and life is looking pretty good again. A gust has kicked up, and the flag beyond the center field fence is dancing with approval, and I brush the orange dust from the seat of my pants and from my shirt. I pulled up so fast I damn near left my teeth running on toward the plate without me.

It isn't a homer, but it's a triple, and that ain't bad, especially when you got three guys hitting .280 or better coming up behind you.

Coach comes up behind me and whispers, "Should we try him?" And I think he means steal home, but he probably means squeeze bunt, and I can't believe he's asking me anyway, which he never does, and I say, No, they'll hit me in, they deserve the chance to hit. Because that's the way the world should be: everybody deserves a chance to hit, a chance to be great, even if it's only for a minute or in a small thing or in a great thing like baseball, but I don't tell Coach that part, and you know what, I think he already knows it, and Lenny comes to mind, and I'm glad I didn't say it.

So Pud steps into the box and Coach gives him the hit sign. He goes two and two, then slaps a one-hopper to the pitcher. Coach whispers again to me, "We could still bunt you in." I don't know what to say, so I just look. Coach calls time, then waddles toward home to talk to the next hitter.

I'm standing on third when the third-base ump tugs on my elbow. "What you hitting now? Must be over .400?"

"I guess. But I'd give up every point of it for this run. Well, almost every point."

"Heard you ain't been drafted."

"Word sure gets around." How did he know that? Coach returns and flashes "hit away" to Split, our second baseman. He goes one and two. He can really dig in and get serious at the plate. Then he laces a liner foul down the rightfield line—you should have heard the fans catch their breath—and then he pops out to second.

Two down and I'm still on third, and I'm getting nervous.

Whip, our shortstop, steps in, another lefty. He takes a ball, then a strike, then fouls off two, then takes a ball in the dirt. The wind kicks up a dust devil, and we all pause and bow our heads to keep the dust out of our eyes. The Newcomb fans are on their feet cheering. So are ours, but not quite as many or quite as loudly. But even that doesn't matter now, cause we're down to our last strike, and we need a hit, and there's nothing I can do—it's up to Whip now, and I can only think that I wish I'd run through Coach's hold-up at third.

The stretch. The pitch.

Well wouldn't you know Whip fouls it off, and then two more, then takes a curveball in the dirt, then fouls off two more fastballs. Baseball is great, but this is ridiculous, even to me.

And now wouldn't you know the pitcher doesn't stretch—he winds up, and I'm off for home, and the ball is down the middle and Whip swings and makes contact and the ball shoots into the infield between first and second and the secondbaseman stretches and grabs it on a short hop and wheels and throws to first and my heart is pounding and the white shoes are flying and I see the ump's hand go up at firsts just as I cross the plate and I can't believe it, it's really over.

He's out at first. It's over.

Newcomb's players mob each other and the fans mob them.

Their pitcher pitched a helluva game, and they didn't hit much, but they hit enough, but I can't help thinking they didn't deserve to win any more than we did. But that's baseball games for you, and that's the world for you. They will be beautiful, and they will be cruel, and that's the truth of it. I walk back to the dugout to get my gear, and we are all careful not to say a word to one another. My mother is here, but she knows too not to say anything, and she doesn't come to the dugout. She will wait till I am ready to talk. Thanks for that, I think.

I breathe in the smell of the dust rising from the Newcomb celebration and rub pools of sweat from around my eyes. But the sweat keeps coming.

Even though I am a senior, I heft the bat bag to carry it to the bus so that I will have something to do. The stands have cleared quickly, and I'm almost out the gate when I see Ropes with his father, who has his arm around his son's shoulder. Ropes is only a freshman, and he reminds me of me, and he will be back for three more years of baseball, and maybe more after, because he's good. And Ropes' father comes over to me and puts his arm around my shoulder, and then I can't believe it, he says, "You boys got nothing to be ashamed of. You should be proud. You got to the state semifinals. You played great." You'd think he'd know you're not supposed to say anything. And I don't. I put my knuckle in my eye and walk on for the empty bus, carrying the bats, listening to the crunch of the gravel and the locust shells, trying not to think. It's still better not to think.

I am not ashamed, exactly. The papers will say we gave them a game and that I ended my career with two hits and an rbi and that I batted over .400 and that I made All-League and All-Valley and maybe, we'll see, All-State, and that nobody drafted me and that jobs are hard to get, even in the mines.

I could have made this story better by telling you we that we won or that we lost in the state finals, but that's not what happened. I told you what happened.

And whatever you are thinking I am not crying, because I have played a lot of baseball, and I will play more, somehow. I am a part of baseball, all the guys on the team are, as sure as Ruth and Gehrig and Mantle and Koufax and Paige and Clemente and Mays, between foul lines, where we all live. Baseball is the people who love it and play it whether in a Big League park or on the sandlots or in their own back yards. I will play it, and I will love it.

And you will read about me in the sports page of the newspaper. I swear.

16 Graduation

After the season ended the way it did, the rest of the school year descended quietly into anticlimax. What good is school if you can't play baseball anymore? All I had to think about was graduation and summer ball and the hope that something would come up. I wasn't sure what.

Nobody drafted me. You know that already, and everyone I knew kept telling me.

You'd think one major league team, or at least one of their minor league teams, could use a centerfielder who can hit for average, run bases like a demon, and put the ball directly on the center of the plate from three hundred feet away.

Have bat, have glove, will travel.

I certainly had the will to play, but where, and for what team? How do you call them when they don't call you?

I could hunt around and try to find tryout camps. Someone told me that the Pittsburgh Pirates have one every year not too far from here, though I don't know where.

No colleges had called me about playing, either. I had got some academic information from schools here and there. I could go to State like everybody else: at least that would be the big time, but I'd have to try out as a walk-on, and who wants to be one of fifty thousand students? I did get a letter from Northern saying their academics are good and the coach wanted to talk with me, but that they don't give athletic scholarships. It costs too much to go there. Central was a possibility: smaller pool of athletes, lower tuition, campus jobs available—though I imagined myself having to carry towels for some overweight, under-brained football jock and figured I'd rather join the Army than that. Mrs. Brickhouse had written to her old school, a nice small college down south, and told them about me. Imagine her doing that! They wrote me a note saying they could use a good English major and that everyone was welcome to try out for sports. But nice gesture or not, do you know what small, private colleges cost for a guy like me? Your body, your soul, somebody else's soul, somebody else's body, and the next twenty years of life making loan payments, that's what they cost. And imagine me an English major. I thanked her and them, but told them "no thanks," unless they could come up with a full ride, but they weren't well-off enough themselves for that. Good thing: what does an English major do, anyway? Speaking of the army: the week before graduation I ran into Stud at the basketball court. He hadn't got drafted out of school by any team either, but he had talked to the Air Force and the Army, and though the Air Force seemed like a better deal and a better chance to fly, which was what he thought he might like to do. He went to college for a year, ran short of money, and had joined the Army, because they let him play baseball. Imagine that! They had leagues and everything. He said a pro scout had actually talked with him there, but if that didn't work out, he was going to save enough money to go back and finish college, get an engineering degree, and go back for officer training and flight school! I thought about that, but sitting higher than the third row in the bleachers makes me air sick. And, to be honest, can you imagine me in the Army? I can't even deal with Coach telling me what to do, let alone some shark-mouthed sergeant chewing my heels through boot camp.

And speaking of Coach: the son of a bean *retired*! Can you believe that? He waits till I graduate and *then* retires. He said he bought himself that boat he always talked about and a little cabin on Lake Satchel up north so he can retire and fish. The way he chews and spits, I give him a year till he's killed off all the fish in that lake.

Funny thing: I went back to my locker after our last game to clean out my things, and Coach was sitting in his office going over our statistics for the year. I felt like I should say something to him after four years and at the end of his baseball career, and maybe mine. He just looked up at me, took off his cap, scratched his old bald head, and said, "Don't say nothin', Will. I'm gonna fish, and you're gonna play baseball. Damn scouts will spot you yet. You got the tools, and you got a attitude to win. Somebody's gonna find you, y'unnerstan? I swear." Who'd a' believed four years ago that he'd say something like that to me?

After the last day of regular classes, I stopped at Lenny's house on my way home. He was in the garage, and a tape was blaring from his player, an Alice Cooper song, the words echoing out into the road: "School's out for summer. School's out for ever!" I walked up and tapped him on the shoulder, and he turned the sound down just enough so we could hear each other speak, barely.

"What's happenin', Len."

"What's happenin', Will.

"You going to any parties this weekend?"

"No, I'm just gonna mess around here."

"Fixed up your summer plans yet?"

"Like I said, I'll work in my uncle's garage some, but he doesn't have much business lately. I got a couple little repair jobs to do for guys who are going to college and want their cars ready early. Not much else."

"Me neither." Lenny seemed to have magically acquired Dirk Jenson's ability and reputation with cars. I had always thought he would go to college, cause he always got good grades until our senior year, but now as far as I knew he was just going to hang around Harmon Falls and hope for work. At least he could work at something. It looked like I was going to have to apply at the mills and mines up and down the river and stand in the unemployment line, because nobody was hiring. I had summer baseball ahead, but that was it, and they don't pay you to play legion or miners' leagues.

And believe it or not, after that last game I felt a little tired of baseball.

Never thought I'd hear me say that.

Not for long, mind you. But talking with Lana a couple months back, I had begun to wonder what I would do after baseball, which has to come sometime for everybody, even the pros, and I began to look at other sides of myself. Time to get my A.B., maybe.

A.B.: life After Baseball. Lenny was right.

Would I end up one of those thick-wristed pot-bellied softball players for Drift Inn, or at least maybe an all-star centerfielder for one of the local miners' sandlot teams? Would I go to the Branch and learn bookkeeping—yech—or go to the Tech and learn to repair TV's and ride around in some guy's powder-blue van that said on the side "Ponzo's TV and Radio Repair: Call 24 Hours"?

Geez, nobody had prepared me for what to do next, least of all me.

To be fair, I have to say that Lenny had tried to say something. And tried.

I got my enthusiasm back when the manager of the Brookfield team in the miners' league called me and asked me to play for him over the summer. These days they let the teams have a few players who aren't miners, since the mines have cut back on hiring. The thought of sandlot ball against guys in their twenties and thirties brought me back to reality in a hurry: whatever else happened in my life, good or bad, as long as I could get out of my chair and move I had baseball. And there's a lot more comfort in that thought than you might guess.

During exam week I took things pretty slowly. I passed my tests and tried not to kill myself, since I already had an idea what that's like. There was only Senior Assembly to go, a big shindig where the seniors do sentimental speeches and bad comic skits and sing the class song and cry all over each other in front of the whole school like they're sorry to leave. I suppose some of them are. I wouldn't have been, if I'd only known what to do.

The morning of the assembly Deb Dorian came up to me and asked me a favor. I don't think she'd ever said anything to me other than "hello" in four years, though she had always said it sweetly. She asked me if I could bail out the class and do a small part in the skit where they lampooned teachers and all the popular students at Harmon Falls High School.

Now, I hate those things. Frankly, I had intended to sit in the back of the auditorium and slip out early when no one was looking. That weepy, croony, nostalgia stuff makes me queezy. But you don't say no to Deb Dorian. That would be like saying, "No thanks, I don't want the million dollars I just won in your sweepstakes—please give it to someone else," or "Look, God, I'd rather part the Red Sea for myself, thank you." It was especially hard to do what she asked, because the joke she wanted me to tell was about Tiny, a member of the baseball team. That was a betrayal that didn't sit quite right with me, but she explained that the joke was really flattering, and that they were poking fun of him because all the girls thought he was cute and were secretly in love with him. Now that, I thought, was a good enough reason to make fun of anybody, because he had nothing to lose: he had everything a boy could want already. Except maybe a contract to play baseball.

That joke got me to Senior Assembly, which turned out to be a good thing. I delivered my joke, got a laugh, apologized to Tiny, and was hanging around backstage trying to figure out a way to sneak out while the principal was announcing senior awards, when all of a sudden I heard my name called.

"Willie Smith," Mr. Sanders, the principal, said, "has just been named small-school all-state in baseball, as well as all-league and all-valley." The whole assembly cheered. And they went on cheering. I damn near cried, I was so lost for what to do. I didn't know whether to go out on stage or just sink into the backstage dust around my feet. They cheered and cheered. And I didn't even know they knew who I was.

After all the awards were announced, Mr. Sanders came backstage. He shook several hands and passed out some plaques and certificates, then he spotted me and smiled. He walked over and without saying a word, just smiling, pushed an envelope into my hand. Then he turned and walked away.

Confused? You bet. I looked at the envelope. Thick, substantial. Typed. Hmmm. My name on the front: Joseph Smith, Harmon Falls High School. Yes. Return address: Maldon College. Maldon College? What do they want with me at this time of year? I thought. And what the heck is Maldon College, anyway, I thought. And where is it? Guppy Goldberg, who graduated second in our class, told me they're small-college, somewhere in the midwest, won some games, good academics, and that a few years ago a guy from their baseball team made the Big Leagues. She was actually excited.

Hmmm.

Frankly, I was trembling as I opened the envelope. It contained two letters. The first one read:

"Dear Joe:"

I wondered if they could have meant the other Joe Smith.

What do you say to someone who knows your name better than your own mother does?

"Maldon College is a small, liberal arts"... what does that mean?... "college with a strong history of scholastic achievement and athletic excellence." Blah, blah, so on and so on, yes. "Your credentials in both academics and athletics suggest to us that you might thrive as a member of our college community. Therefore, in light of your accomplishments and potentials, we would like to offer you a half-tuition scholarship to attend Maldon College in the fall." Signed by Dean of Attritions or Admissions or something like that.

Numbers: somebody get me some numbers here, and some smelling salts. What does half-tuition mean in real dollars to a poor boy from a mining town?

Flipping the first page, I found the second letter, headed "Athletic

Department."

"Dear Willie:"

A little more promising: So I'm Joe to business people, but still Willie to baseball people.

"A couple of years ago I saw you play ball for Harmon Falls in a game at Bellview High School. I was impressed with your ability, but even more with your attitude and obvious love of baseball. Maldon is a small school, moderately expensive, and we can't offer full-ride athletic scholarships like the big schools I'm sure you've heard from."

Glad he's sure of that.

"But we can give you an excellent education and a chance to play baseball with a team that has won a Division III championship and sent players to the major leagues."

Players, plural? I like that.

"Should I reserve a spot on our roster for you for the upcoming year? Lots of boys want to play baseball, and many talented students want to come to Maldon, so please let me know as soon as you can. "Better yet, come and visit. I think you'll fall in love with our beautiful campus the same way I did twenty years ago."

"Best wishes, Dr. Nat Frigg, Baseball Coach and Professor of Phys. Ed."

You could've knocked me over with a change-up.

By now several people were reading over my shoulder and whooping and patting me on the back.

But I didn't know whether to be happy or not. Maldon College? What will Ma say to that? How much does it cost? Will half-tuition be enough? Can they give more? But a letter from the baseball coach *himself.* What about the first letter? What's a "Dean of Admissions"? I don't remember applying there—does that mean I'm already accepted and can just waltz in? How did they find out about me? Ah: the baseball coach. Good.

I slipped out the back door of the auditorium and went to the counseling office. It smelled of greasy food. Mr. Pugwurst was hiding in his office, shuffling through letters from colleges and companies, brochures for student-exchange programs, and food coupons from the newspaper. I knocked on his door, and he emerged from a pile of papers and french fries.

"Will. Come on in. I see you've got an important letter in your hand."

"Mr. Pugwurst, where the heck is Maldon College, and can I afford to go there?"

He laughed. "Here's a map. I had a feeling you'd be coming in, so I looked it up for you."

How did he know? I looked at the map.

"Out there, huh?"

"That's right. Yeah, not much around. Good school, though, from what I hear."

"How did you hear about them?"

"I've talked to them on the phone a couple of times."

"Good source."

"You probably can't."

"Can't what?"

"Your second question. Afford to go there. You probably can't afford it. But here's a catalogue they sent me. Let's look at the figures and see what you think."

We looked. Not good, but not impossible if I robbed a bank or two.

"They're not one of the really elite private schools, so they try to stay affordable to people like you, though there's no accounting for taste," Mr. Pugwurst said. Their brochure looked slick: lots of pictures of trees, fields, old buildings lit up at night, happy students walking along carrying books.

"An hour ago I wasn't even sure I wanted to go to college, and now I may be going to a college I've barely heard of. And I can't afford it."

"There are always loans."

"Easy for you to say. How do you pay them back on a minor league baseball salary, or if you can't get any job at all?"

"You get a job. Period."

"Have you looked at the unemployment lines lately?"

"A college education helps."

I looked at the college's figures again. "I certainly hope so."

"Good luck," Mr. Pugwurst said. "I don't think it's a bad choice if you can do it. Good academics. Baseball. Wish I could go." He smiled and submerged into his desk again.

I walked for a long time. It wasn't the majors, but it was baseball, and maybe it could lead to the majors. It had worked for guys before. What would staying at home get me? I could at least afford to go the Branch if I could get some kind of job. But you've gotta have your priorities: what good is life without baseball? But then even if I wanted to go, could I afford to pay for it? But.

I took the letter home and showed it to Ma.

"That's nice, Willie, but where will we get the money? I've saved a little bit, but not that much. Maybe you could work and go to the Branch for a year or two. Don't they have a baseball team? Not anymore? Well, you've got to have priorities"—my thoughts exactly—"and an education comes first. Not many people make a living with baseball. You need something you can count on, and that's education and a job, not baseball."

Heresy! Sacrilege! Slander! Disaster!

"We have to be realistic."

Worse and worse.

"We could go down to the bank and see about student loans, but loans have always scared me, because they can bind you for years to obligations you don't need when you're trying to start a career and a family."

Triple choke.

"Look, son, I know you want to go, but you don't come from a rich family. We'll manage what we can." Actually I didn't even know if I wanted to go.

The next Monday we went to the bank to check on student loans. After finding out how much and how long I would be paying on that, I didn't want to do it, either.

"Maybe they'll give you a better scholarship after your first year," the banker suggested.

Later that afternoon, Ma called Maldon College. Admissions told her they thought that was the best they could do, but they would try. I asked for the phone number of the baseball coach, and I made the first serious phone call of my life. He was friendly and hopeful.

"I for one would like to see you come here, Willie. What if we could turn up a part-time job for you, that is, until baseball season? Then we'd need you free, beyond your study time, that is, to practice."

Now there's a friggin' good idea. One step closer. I told Dr. Frigg that I'd call him back in no more than a week. In the meantime I'd cut some grass for money for stamps and paint a house or two so I could send in the official application and pay the application fee.

The only thing that would pay for the rest would be a really good summer job, and that would only give me enough to take care of my first semester. And what are the chances of getting a summer job in a town where full-time workers are getting laid off? And worst of all, working would mean, depending on my shift, maybe no time for baseball, just when I most needed to work on my game, when my future might depend on it, and when I was moving to a different level of competition. No sense in worrying till it happens, right?

Friday, the day before graduation, I walked to the county unemployment office in Bellview. They call it the "employment office," but nobody believes that for a minute. I talked to a man named Shaeffer.

"I knew your father when we were kids."

"What?"

"No kidding. He was a wild kid. Always doing two things at once, could never sit still. He loved baseball and football, hated school, loved chasing girls." Then he realized what he'd said and looked a little sheepish.

So he liked football? Good thing he left.

"He was a good kid, though," Mr. Shaeffer said.

"What happened to him?"

"Don't you know? Gee, I don't know. We lived just a few houses away when we were kids, but my parents moved to Bellview and I went to high school there. I didn't see your dad much after I moved."

He half-heartedly leafed through some papers. Lots of people do that, leaf through papers, especially when they don't know what to say. Then he said, "Don't you know somebody somewhere? That's how most kids get summer jobs, isn't it?"

Mr. Shaeffer was a nice man, but as much help with a job as he was with my father. Yes, everybody was looking for a job. He'd call me if anything turned up.

It was a long walk home. The world looked almost kaleidoscopic as the sun set gradually and my thoughts bounced around like a bagful of baseballs dropped from an airplane.

* * *

When I was turning up the road into Harmon Falls, a car rode by me, a white convertible VW bug with the top up—they were all the rage just then. The car stopped, then rolled back alongside me. The window rolled down. I looked inside: Angelina Zamboni.

We had spoken only three times since the Homecoming Dance

together: once for her to tell me what a good time she had and that she
hoped I had; once for her to ask me if I had good notes for a chemistry
test; once for her to tell me with a tear in her eye that she had got back
together with Pervis Easly and that they would probably get married
and move to Los Angeles where Pervis's band would make the Big Time
someday.

Now here she was again, and once again there was a tear tumbling
from the corner of her eye. She was wearing a dark blue dress and heels
and had her hair tied in back and falling in a great dark wave over her
right shoulder.

"Need a ride home?"

Need can mean a lot of different things, including *want*, so I got in.

"You're certainly dressed up," I said.

"Oh, I had to see this photographer in Bellview. He needed a girl
to pose for an ad, and he called my father and asked if I could do it."

"In the whole wide world they couldn't have found anyone better."

"You're always so sweet." Another tear fell. I was trying not to ask
about it. Sometimes it's better not to ask, just to listen and let people
talk when they're ready. "Where were you walking from?" she asked,
trying to keep composed.

"Bellview, too, the unemployment office. You know how it is."

"That's a long walk. Aren't you going to college in the fall?"

"I thought I might, till I got all the good news at the unemployment office and found out how hard it is to get a summer job to make
tuition money."

"Do you need a job for the summer?"

"Doesn't almost everybody?"

"You should have told me. I don't know if you'd want it, but my
brother is looking for someone evenings at the pizza shop. I'm sure you
can get it if you want it."

Angelina Zamboni, I could have kissed you. But then that was true
already, and you knew it.

"Well I'll just hop my butt down there and see him tonight. Do
you think that'd be all right?"

"I'll tell him to expect you."

One step closer to Maldon College. Too bad Angelina Zamboni
wasn't going there, too. But then she was probably headed to school in
Los Angeles so she could be near Pervis.

"So what's the story with you? You headed for L.A. soon?"

That did it. I really blew it that time.

Angelina didn't say another word to me. She drove me within a couple blocks of my house, stopped, and let me out without even looking at me. The tears were streaming down her cheeks, and when I got out and closed the door, she nearly choked from a sob. She drove off as fast as a VW can, which is to say I probably could have caught her if I'd run. I once beat a Chevy Vega in a forty-yard sprint.

I had a vague idea that I knew what was wrong.

That evening I walked late into the darkness kicking myself for not having better sense. And not just because I'd lost the summer job that could have got me to college by insulting the girl who would have got it for me. The only people I'd less like to see crying like that are Ma and Lana, and maybe Lenny. You might say I'll always have a hot spot in my heart for Angelina Zamboni.

I was walking down dark Oak Street, where the huge trees form a canopy over the still brick-topped road. If you catch it when the moon is crescent or new, it's almost like walking in a mausoleum: I saw one of those on a TV documentary once. Mix of awesome and pathetic.

I was so lost in thought that I almost didn't hear the familiar whirr and tick-tick-tick of a VW bug pulling up beside me.

Angelina again.

I was afraid to walk up to her window.

I looked in. She was wearing a soft, gray dress, tight-fitting to the waist, that buttoned down the front.

"Will, would you come talk to me?"

What would *you* say? I got in.

We drove for a while, faster than I thought a VW could go and faster than I would have liked, up and down streets, north of town where the streetlights end and the road is black as the river at night. We rolled down the convertible top so Angelina could feel the wind in her hair. I felt happy to sit there in the near-blackness and watch the wind toss her hair.

"You're not talking," she said. "I want you to talk to me."

"What about?"

"Anything you want. Say something nice."

I thought about that for a minute. Just how nice a thing should I say? Or should I just apologize and get it over with?

I decided on simple honesty. "I love the way the wind tosses your hair. It looks like midnight bound up for someone to keep as a keepsake."

She reached her hand over and put it on my wrist. I think I chose the right thing to say for once. Then I chose the wrong thing.

"I'm sorry about earlier. I didn't want to say anything to make you feel bad."

"You should have stopped when you were ahead." She drew her hand back to the wheel.

We sat in silence for a while. People do that a lot, don't they? Then Angelina said, "You're always honest, at least. Were you born like that, or did you learn it somewhere? It's really kind of scary sometimes."

I waited. Then tried again.

"So be honest with me and tell me what's bothering you," I said. "Maybe telling will make you feel better. Don't Catholics believe in that?"

"Confession. But that's to a priest, not to a baseball player."

"I can listen as well as he can."

"But you can't absolve me, and you're more dangerous than he is." She glanced at me for just an instant with something like longing in her eyes. Could I have read that right?

She sighed, took a deep breath. Here's the gist of what she said. She started crying halfway through, so that I was certain she was going to crash the car and kill us both—poor Dirk Jenson popped into my mind. "I just got a letter from Pervis. He's in Los Angeles with his band and is doing well. He wrote to tell me that he loved me very much, but that he has met a girl there who has done wonders for his creativity and his career, and he knows I would hate L.A., and he's sure that some nice guy will sweep me off my feet and take better care of me than he ever could and pay me the attention I deserve. He didn't even give me a chance to go there with him! What am I going to do now?"

What do you say to that one? Tragic? Horrible? Obvious? You're right: I didn't say anything. Fortunately, Angelina pulled over to the side of the road, and I just sat there with her while she cried and cried. For a while I held her hand. The sky was a scorecard full of clouds and stars. The night air felt good as the sky spread its black velvet. I thought of a hundred things to say, all of them stupid, and said none of them.

When she came back to herself, she leaned over and hugged her head to my chest. She sobbed. Her hair smelled better than lilacs, clean and rich and musky, like summer and love. We sat there for a while, then she touched me on the cheek, started up the car, and turned back toward town. She drove past the football field, past the downtown, past the high school, to the west side of town, this side of the little nine-hole golf course, nestled under the hill where a park disappears upward toward the back of the cemetery. The grass rolls up and down among the trees like elf-mounds, and in the summer, if we've had some rain, you can hear the creek trickle by to the south between the park and a wood that shelters the few country-club style houses in Harmon Falls. This park is quiet and lush, with lots of maples and evergreens, and in the dark it feels almost like soft hands hugging you gently to the hill that rises quickly and protectively to the west. Angelina pulled up and parked just as an edge of moon popped free of some clouds to light a path among the trees.

"Come and walk with me. This is my favorite place on earth."

She got out, her thin, summer dress trailing almost to the ground, took off her shoes, and disappeared among the trees before I could think of anything to say. I followed, slowly, not wanting to come on her too quickly and startle her if she wanted to be alone for a minute. The grass was thick and smooth as a carpet.

I strolled, licking in the breeze that carried just a hint of dew and just a hint of Angelina's perfume. It was late, and even the sky looked sleepy. My heart did all it could to betray me by beating faster than an outfielder's feet after a gap-shot.

I turned past a short row of spruces and looked ahead on the lawn to a maple tree just lit by a shred of starlight. From behind the tree, Angelina was looking back for me. I could just see her smiling in the darkness. I could hardly walk toward her, my legs felt so rubbery, but by now my body was acting without me, moved by something older and deeper than anything I had found in myself before, and then I was standing right in front of her and we were fumbling and I was kissing Angelina our tongues slipping and sliding and our bodies close and she unbuttoned her dress and it fell and her skin felt like milk or silk and she shimmered in the dark and my clothes came off and we were both shivering in the heat and she said don't worry I'm clean, are you? and I'd said I've never before and she said never? and I said no and she laughed and I said I don't know much about and she said I don't know much and I said nothing? and she said not nothing but not much and I said enough? and she said more than enough and I said here? and she said oh and then she and I said oh and I said oh shouldn't we do something about and she said it's already taken care of don't stop right there now do this oh and I said oh and we were in the grass and I couldn't believe what she was doing and then what I was doing but then I believed it and I wanted her so bad that I said my God we should stop and she said no and I said no? and she said no, yes, and I said oh and oh and she said no and I said no? should I stop and she said maybe so and I said oh o.k. but please I thought and then she said oh, no, no don't stop and I said yes? and she said yes oh really yes and I said oh and she said oh and I said safe? and she said yes, here, and she said oh and I said oh and then we stopped saying and I disappeared out of myself and she did too and then some time passed and we dressed.

"So you've never done anything before?" Angelina asked.

"No."

"Mmmm. But don't let it go to your head. You need practice."

"I'd love to," I said.

In a while we eased through the darkness back to her car, and she drove me home. What was there to say? When I got out, I walked around to her door and kissed her softly on the lips.

"Thank you for being with me tonight," she said. "I felt so alone."

"You can't thank me for that. You will be in my memory forever." I couldn't say what I wanted to say. There were no words. I smiled, and so did she.

It's funny how we both knew that we had no future together. But we had something, a present that would soon be a past that we would never lose as long as we lived.

At least I thought so.

We talked for a minute about nothing. Then she drove off and disappeared into the night. Just a hint of orange blinked in the eastern sky.

I went in to bed and slept long and hard.

I awoke feeling wonderful and terrible about what we had done.

I know I told you once before that I knew more than nothing about women. Truth: before that night with Angelina, I knew as close to nothing as you can get without its being absolutely nothing. I still didn't know much.

Poor Angelina. Should I not have? Or should I have? And a little voice in the back of my head was telling me it should have been Lana Simms, not Angelina Zamboni. It was my voice.

Another voice was telling me, you lucky shit. You dog of a dog.

That voice was Lenny's.

When I got up, I ate a quick breakfast and hurried to Mrs. Pasquale's house to do a few odd jobs I had promised to finish. I only charged her a couple of bucks, cause she's pretty old now and doesn't have much money, but she gave me lunch, too. That can make up for low pay unless you're saving for college and you need every dollar you can sock away, which by then I was.

That night was graduation. What a week, huh?

And graduation: what a way to waste a good Saturday.

Ma was there at the football field, where they always hold the ceremony when the weather is good. She always comes to these things when she can, though I don't know why. Surviving one graduation of your own is enough without having to sit through somebody else's and try to look interested. Lana was there, and Lenny, of course, and their mother had come to see graduation. The principal lined us up alphabetically, so when Lana waved, I couldn't tell whether she was waving just at Lenny, or at me, too. Her mother didn't wave. It didn't even look like she smiled. I spotted Angelina Zamboni almost at the end of the line of graduates, just before Dan Zelinski, Mary Zink, and Charlie Zwiback: how could we have so many Z's at such a small school? Angelina didn't look upset. In fact, she seemed her usual smiling, composed, bouncy self.

Whew.

All those blue robes! We looked like a great dark sea flooding into Harmon Falls, disappearing in the serpentine distance. Thank God I didn't have to say anything for the ceremony. A just sat among the blue masses, waiting to take the paper that, along with a baseball glove, was my ticket out of Harmon Falls. Or not. Graduation was hot and long—isn't it always, even at small schools? They bring in someone to make the same speech other kids are listening to at thousands of graduations all across the country, every city and every hill-and-dale little town, about how we are the future and they love us and are depending on us. That's why there are so many jobs waiting for us when we graduate, right? And students make speeches about how we accept the challenge of our future and how we'll miss our school and our cozy little town and how we'll do our best to make the world a better place for our children, as our parents have done for us. I wonder what Flap, or Mange, or Dirk would say about all that. Or what I'd say myself, if someone asked me. I guess that's why they didn't ask me to speak.

Deb Dorian, our valedictorian, gave a rousing speech—but then all Deb ever had to do was open her mouth to captivate anyone in hearing distance. I have no idea what she said. She could have read Dr. Seuss or the telephone book and it wouldn't have made any difference. Besides a fly that kept buzzing around my ear and the sweat trickling down under my clean, white collar, that's all I can remember of graduation, besides trying not to throb in a certain place from thinking about Angelina Zamboni.

After the ceremony and the cheering, as we swept toward the gate, people crying and hugging and patting each other on the back and yelling old cheers, I went to meet Ma. By the gate was Angelina Zamboni with her parents and her brother Alonzo. Alfonzo, the older brother, must have been at work already at his pizza shop. She left them and came running up to me.

"Oh Willie, congratulations! Alfonzo was wondering why you didn't stop by the pizza shop to see about your job. He says it's yours if you want it. Don't worry: go see him! I've got to run for now, but"— she whispered—"thanks for listening. You're a great guy."

"Thank you. See you." That was too much to process all at once. I didn't feel like I, the luckiest guy in the universe, deserved any thanks from anybody.

She nodded, dropped me a smile loaded with regret, and hurried back to her parents, who whisked her away to some fancy graduation party. They glanced at me strangely, as though I were some sort of exotic bird, but they didn't look angry. Who knows what they knew?

Ma took me to Rosie's Restaurant for dinner. We almost never ate out.

I remember what she said when she paid the check. "She looked me right in the eyes and said, "Be a good man, Willie. Be a *good* man." I didn't see Angelina for the rest of that summer, though I did see her VW driving in the distance a couple times. I did once run into Alberta Donally. She told me that Angelina had taken a month's vacation in Italy with her parents and was spending the rest of the summer at her grandparents' summer house up north, far from Harmon Falls. Alberta had seen her once, said she looked thin and tired around the eyes, but was trying hard to get over Pervis Easly, who clearly was gone forever, and that she had said she missed me, too.

I would have liked to help her get over Pervis, rather than simply being missed.

On Sunday I went to see Alfonzo Zamboni at Mama Sicily's Pizza. He teased me a bit, called me his sister's "little friend," but gave me a job, as many evening hours as I wanted to work tossing pizzas, cleaning, and helping in the kitchen: no tips, but enough wages to put me over the top on tuition money if I worked six days a week.

I think if Alfonzo had known more than he must have known, I would have ended up pizza dough or part of the old family concrete business.

The bad news: I'd probably have to dump sandlot baseball after a couple games, because the miners' teams play all their games in the evening, and I worked evenings and couldn't get off.

But I begged Mr. Socco to keep me on the Legion team even though I could only play weekends and the occasional early game of a twilight doubleheader. Without some baseball I wouldn't be ready for college in the fall. I'd run when I got home from work, after midnight, and lift weights when I got up in the morning, and play ball on Saturdays and Sundays. I wasn't going to get any taller, but I could stay strong and fast and maybe add some bulk, especially working at a pizza shop, and keep my batting stroke out of mothballs with a few at-bats.

The good news: on Monday I called Dr. Frigg and told him I'd go to Maldon College.

I shook like a loose sleeve in a high wind, and my stomach felt like it was full of knuckleballs, but I did it.

Relief and fear. Mostly fear. Some joy: I felt more real than I had ever felt before, and for the first time I realized down deep that I had absolutely no idea what the future would be like.

I did a couple extra sets of curls, ran some short sprints, swung the bat for half an hour, took a shower, and pressed a crisp, white shirt for work. Oh, did I tell you? Uncle Fred had a friend of his put in a shower in our old bathtub. Way better. Way better.

The strange news: when I got to work my first night who should be sitting there waiting for a pizza but Steve Presnick.

At first I didn't recognize him. Then I thought I was dead.

Then I looked closer and thought he was dead.

Then I felt safe. But not good. Steve looked terrible: thin, worn, eyes bloodshot, alone.

"Willie White Shoes," he said in a low, tired voice. He didn't even get up. He looked like he almost couldn't stand. And nothing in his look or voice gave me any reason to fear.

"How ya' doin', Steve?"

"Aw, great, man." Right.

He told me that out of school he had entered the Navy, but had been discharged. Then he had got heavy into drugs and alcohol. His skin looked like it was stretched tight over his face, and his eyes had a gray haze.

Alfonzo appeared with a pizza. "Here ya' go, Stevie. Come back again, now. And you, Mr. Baseball, get to work. You're on my clock now."

When Steve stood up, he looked barely taller than I was, he seemed so bent. He could have passed for forty years old, or older, and he couldn't have been more than twenty-two. I told Steve so long and good luck, and we actually shook hands. He wobbled out the door.

I washed my hands—twice—and got to work.

That was one weird summer.

I already said too much.

17 Memory

Funny how as you look back on things through the lens of years, you can't always be absolutely sure that what you think you know absolutely happened did in fact absolutely happen.

Absolutely.

Here I am, long after the time of the story you're reading, interrupting my narrative as I re-type it, looking back, wondering if any of it is true, if I ever really made love to Angelina Zamboni, if I ever did play almost for a state championship. A yellowed newspaper clipping attests to the game; nothing can document the other: no newspaper clipping, prom photos, or high school Annual. Not even the sudden experience of a strange fragrance wafting from lilacs or summer trees—or a pizza shop—will bring back a rush of fumbling, of beautiful, young, impossible, momentary passion in a way to make it seem unequivocally real.

I wonder how much of my memory isn't really memory, but fantasy, things I wanted or thought I wanted or things I feared or thought I feared, or things I dreamed, or things that make a story.

Document. The trace of things written nowhere but here in these pages and in the brain, circuits that will one day fall to molecules of alcohol or to Altzheimer's disease or to nothing more dramatic than the natural call of time and death—or simply to forgetting—that trace is all we have. When Angelina is dust and I am dust and our memories are dust, will any of that night, if it ever really happened, ever have happened? It never was *history* in any proper sense. But it drifts back to memory as a river follows the course it cut for itself. It drifts back to mind as something of my essence or what I want to have been my essence.

Or maybe not.

People like to use that turn of phrase: "and the rest is history." How do they know? For an event to be history, mustn't someone else care enough to remember it and write it down? Otherwise, it's autobiography, or lies, and therefore suspect, or nothing at all.

Is everything we write or say of ourselves merely hopeful autobiography, and therefore suspect?

I could merely have dreamed of Angelina on an early summer night, cleaned up after, faded back to sleep, wakened in the morning with a vague feeling that the dream was more real than any real memory and have recorded it among my memories or the notes that serve to embellish my memories. Since I have written the story, has it acquired a validity of its own, regardless of what happened? If only stories had reliability, in the statistical sense, what a youth I would have had, because of what stories I could tell! Or maybe not: maybe I would, having gained assurances that certain things were *true*, have lost something dearer. Maybe if I had done things I've dreamed about, I'd have got v.d., or played football, or died.

Can one perfect memory validate a lifetime?

Can one dubious dream?

Maybe if I could rewrite my memories to make each one turn out the way I want, if enough people read them, they would become in some way true, citable fact: "Where did you get such difficult stuff?" Humpty Dumpty asks Alice; "I read it in a book," she replies.

What does Angelina Zamboni remember? I haven't seen her and hadn't thought about her for years. When my memories, anyone's memories, everyone's memories, of Lana, beloved Lana, fade, when her memories of me fade, will she be gone from the world I know? That would be something worse than sad. If I had lost Lana, if there were no Lana or I had no Lana fixed in my memory, by now in every cell of my experience, then I would have, perhaps, no dearest beloved, no daughter, no adult life such as I have now. Who knows what course things will take as each little choice blows every other choice that might have been to immemorial dust? I wanted to say *smithereens* there, but I'm not sure what that means. Are *smith*ereens all the thousands of tiny children I might have fathered had I married an impossibly fertile girl or many girls, one by one, or all together? *Smithereens* sounds like an Irish word. Who was that Irish girl who would have patiently born thousands of smithereens who looked just like her or me? Should I feel sad that I never met her? I don't, at least not for long—that again would mean no Lana, or at least not Lana as I know her now, and she may never have appeared in this story, except perhaps in place of Angelina Zamboni. No, Lana wasn't like that, though in retrospect I find no fault with Angelina, either, and I hope she finds none with me. I find plenty of faults with me.

I don't know what might have been. But sometimes I feel ecstatic happiness that I know Lana and that she knows me.

Know, in the Biblical sense, as they say, an accident of Jacobean
English: that's not what I mean here. *Know* in the many senses, in
the greatest sense a person ever can, not sexually alone, but in the daily
course of living, of espousing and spousing, of learning what someone
else thinks, feels, until—except for PMS and menstruation and giving
birth, she tells me—you almost feel things with her, for her, think or
feel them exactly as or even before she does, because you live every now
and then almost inside her skin, because you love and want to love that
much.

Growing up, becoming a man, means trying to live at least for a bit
outside your own head.

It means not being a selfish shithead.

A friend of mine, a guy I met in college, told me he used to belong
to the *Passionists*. At the time I was afraid to ask exactly what that
meant, because when he told me a little bit about his religious life in
a Catholic order, my imagination, far from the truth, would drift to
strange, bloody rituals in which hermetic priests recreated the suffer-
ings of Jesus on the cross in their own flesh or fled their monasteries in
the deep dark of night to strange orgiastic encounters. I wasn't ready
to learn whether such things happen or they don't. If he'd told me
too much, I might have lost all the romantic/spiritual imaginings that
murmur the undertones of the word: *Passionists*. Passionists, plural,
people who do or have passions, people who feel mystical religious
experience passionately, people who focus their meditations on the
Passion of Jesus: why would people choose to call themselves that? I
wanted to believe and want to believe that someone may feel about religious experience the way I feel about Lana or even about baseball, or
at least something akin to it: layers of loving, layers of understanding,
layers of commitment to one's love, to God, to friends, to sport.

One of the saddest things in life is to have had too few friends. I
heard on TV that Ty Cobb said before he died that: if he could live
over again, he'd have had more friends. How does he know that? Does
he assume that they would have liked him any better or that he would
have liked them? Would he have taught his friends' children how to
spike infielders when they'd steal a base? Would he have had any black
friends and so have chilled his racial hatred? Would his friends have
bought him too many drinks, softened his competitive spirit, and sent
his Hall-of-Fame career spiraling into oblivion? Why do things "spiral"

into oblivion? Why don't they just fall faster than a pigeon intercepted in flight by a flyball, faster than a Nolan Ryan fastball, faster than the skills of a retired home-run hitter deteriorate? Does *oblivion* have gravity? If so, is that where all the socks go when they disappear from the dryer? Are the socks sitting there in a pile along with dead pigeons and dead baseball careers like mine? Is oblivion where dead dreams and memories go?

I would feel a little sad if I didn't really make love to Angelina Zamboni on that warm spring night, but the saddest thing of all to me, sadder than if there had been no world at all, is if I had not known Lana. Isn't that selfish of me? I hope Lana will forgive me if she thinks that I do hope I made love to Angelina—please don't tell her. The world is a better place if a boy, at least once, can have made love to Angelina Zamboni. And if a girl can have made love to whatever is the male version of Angelina Zamboni—that's not me, certainly. If only you could have seen her, you'd understand. As I think back, I can't really say for sure what happened, but I remember she was beautiful in a way that can make a person cry for everything in the world that isn't beautiful. I know we kissed for a long time under the stars. Beyond that I'm not certain.

Now, to me, Lana is even more beautiful. Much more beautiful.

That's as true as anything I can tell, you, I guess, and I've told pretty much the truth, as such things go, as Huck Finn says. So many things I could tell you about the future, about things like why we named our daughter _____: but where's the fun in that, when you haven't even heard the end of this story yet, let alone the beginning of her story?

I could tell you things that may happen to you or even will have happened to you, maybe things that you'll want to remember or that we could remember together. We could embellish them over drinks. You could tell me about what you did in high school, the place where you lived and the things you remember. *Remember*: what does that mean? Am I sticking things that are now dead back together again, re-membering something dis-membered by time and the course of life? Should I do that, or should I just be happy that I've lived, and so let things take their course? If I re-member the past, do I get it right, or do I build from its fragments some eight-legged, slant-bellied, wobble-eyed beast far from different from the instructions in my "Build-Your-Own-Memory Kit" that come in Japanese, then get translated into English by someone who's never spoken either language? Why would I choose the things I would choose to reassemble, since I certainly don't want to get back everything, all the parts missing from my life? I'd try to be more mature for my mother, to ease her mind, to understand people better, to speak less, but help more, to read more, to think more clearly, first never to do harm, as the Hippocratic Oath says—a pretty good idea even for those of us who aren't physicians, or politicians, or lawyers, or, God forbid, writers. What else would I do differently? Would I make love with Angelina Zamboni, if we didn't, or would I not, if we did? Look: nobody really chooses to have sex on wet grass, right?

One thing I'd do for sure, if I could get hold of some effective mosquito repellant: I'd sit at night up on the hill and watch the boats and barges go down the river, listen to their whistles and the faint sound of the water echoing, see the few lights of Harmon Falls mirror the sky with their blinking; I'd take Lana there and try to experience with her the passing of time, to feel what it means to live each second as it goes by, knowing that it's going by, but knowing that it has meaning and existence because I'd share it with her as it disappeared. In that rock song, the line "time keeps on slippin', slippin', slippin' into the future": what a silly thing to say. Time slips into the past; if it slipped into the future, we'd live forever, which some people seem to want, but seems to me a pretty bad idea. Then we'd always sit, watching the moments go by, never really living any of them for lack of appreciation of their value, assuming—knowing?—they'd go on, little changed, forever.

I'd want to sit with Lana on the hill, looking out into the light-blotched blackness, down the boat-spotted river, feeling each living moment as it passed. Something about the boats in my memory: they feel comforting, like someone dependable you know, but don't know well, who always says hello when you see him but who never stops to talk for long. Those boats must be going somewhere important, doing something important dependably, bringing people somewhere something they need. The last time we went home to Harmon Falls, while Lana was talking with her mother and letting her play with her granddaughter in the evening, I climbed the hill and looked out over the river. Most of the factories are closed, the sky was overcast, and I saw no boats on the river. I could hear one in the distance, I think. I wish they were still there for other kids to see. Do kids even climb the hill to look for boats and see the stars anymore, or are they too busy with computer games and cars and music lessons or school activities or the thousand other distractions businesses have invented for them or their parents to buy for their passing amusement?

An old neighbor, when I was small, before the story of this book begins, used to tell me stories about playing baseball when he was a kid. He'd come home from day shift at the mill, sit on his back porch, and drink beer and watch if the kids were playing catch or pepper in the alleys. He'd call me over and tell me about sandlot baseball, must have been back in the 1920s or before. Sandlot sports were big then, football as well as baseball—why we won WWI and II, he'd sometimes say, because all the kids used to play all day long nearly every day in all the different towns up and down the river, so they were better conditioned than kids from anywhere else in the world and could lob grenades farther than anyone else: sad use for sports, but true.

He had an old wife, too, a friendly, quiet, mousy lady who spent summer evenings reading bestsellers on their front porch while he'd listen to baseball on the radio on their back porch. Though I seldom saw them sitting together, I suppose they must have loved each other. They had one son, a poor fellow who was born with a deformed leg and walked with a limp. He visited occasionally, but never stayed with them long and never said a word to me. Maybe he didn't care for baseball, but I think it was more that between their generation and his, we lost something. We lost the simple, easy, natural friendliness we'd had before. Maybe the Great Wars did that.

I'm not quite sure why, but I can feel that fact sometimes now when I greet my neighbors over our lawnmowers or passing on the way to the mailbox. "Hayhowahya?" we say, but we don't really mean anything by it, and they certainly don't want to know how I am. Sometimes I *do* want to know how they are. I want to know if they're happy or sad, healthy or ill. I'd actually be willing to listen if they told me, because I think back to my neighbors, the man and woman, not as old as they looked, and how he'd spend an hour re-creating before my imagination, with his voice, baseball games he'd played forty or fifty years before, in the minutest, most compelling detail, and then he'd ask about my games, and we'd talk the technical details of hitting and fielding and throwing till darkness and whirr of cicadas filled the maple trees that drooped out over the streets and alleyways, and the occasional streetlight uncovered the shadow of a raccoon bent on an evening of sifting garbage cans neighborhood by neighborhood.

As he and his wife turned yet older and grayer and finally mixed with the shades of even darker alleys, so will I, so will Lana, so will you. That's most why I miss that friendliness, the time before anybody was *cool*, when nearly everyone was poor or nearly so, when we'd actually look each other in the eye and mean "good morning" when we said it. "I really hope you do have a good morning," that meant, "and a good day and evening, a good life, and a gentle death. And when you're old and gray, may you have someone young and eager with whom to talk baseball."

All that's wrapped up in a "good morning," at least when I say it.

"When you are old and gray, and nodding by the fire, take down this book," says Yeats to the beloved who scorned him, "and dream of the soft look your eyes once had": that guy's clearly still hurt after all those years, feeling himself graying, feeling sorry for himself, wanting her to feel sorry for him and for herself so that she'll realize she erred in scorning him and feel even worse than he does. Fat chance. She moved on, buddy. No Angelina for you. Go find your Lana. You can really love her, and if you're really lucky, she'll love you, too.

When you are old and gray, reader, I hope you have good baseball to remember, and good love, and good friends, some of whom you don't have to remember because you can see them anytime you want and talk with them and find a way to let them know that they live not only in themselves, but in your memory. And may they do the same for you.

Maybe by the time we're old and gray medicine will have reached the point cosmetics have now, and we won't have to be gray, though we be old. We'll have interchangeable parts and injections to lubricate creaky joints, and we won't have to take as long to run to first base as we used to take. Any one of us can clear the bases with a gapshot, inside-the-park homer.

I guess we already got there. Damn the damned drugs, and your little asterisks, too.

If all our dreams of youth were to come true, and every ninety-year-old of us comes to look like a movie idol and feel like a Hall-of-Famer, will we even care about baseball anymore? Will we ever care about friends any more, or will we retire to computer-generated virtual cyber-heavens eternally powered by electricity from plutonium breeder reactors, farther away from our friends than if they lived on some distant planet we're daring to consider colonizing?

You know what Lenny does now? He gave up auto mechanics

except for fun, in his spare time, and went back to school, learned all he could about computers, and designs computer games. In one of his games, a baseball game, there's a batter that looks a lot like a tall, muscular version of him that can knock the seams off the ball and another that looks like a shorter, dumpy version of me that for comic relief takes a huge swing that winds him up like a corkscrew—and he strikes out every time.

That's reconstructing memory, and I only modestly resent it. Better things, real things, wipe away the failings of any cyberworld.

Nothing, no eternally young Angelina Zamboni, no neverending pure and sunny baseball day can replace late-night cuddling on the couch with Lana, our legs intertwined like warm and breathing ivy. When we drink lemonade, watch an old movie, and trace invisible notes to each other with our fingers on the backs of our hands, snicker as we try to figure out what they say, in the darkness filtered only by the silver, noirish glow of TV light, I am for that time perfectly happy. I hope Lana is, too.

And get this: to stay limber Lana's been taking yoga classes from a master-teacher named Jeev Behra. Hard to believe how odd the world is. Lana is actually studying with Yogi Behra. How weird is that?

* * *

Warning: this chapter has been an announcement from my future and yours. You need not take it seriously, though. The publisher and I now return you to the normal course of the narrative. Please remain horizontal or vertical or however you were or would like to be. I hope I meet you some time, and we can have a beer and talk about your memories and those we've lived together in this story and those between this story and whatever *now* we're living in then. Maybe I will have written something good by then, or maybe you will have, and we can talk about it.

We can talk about baseball and about stories, how we make them and what they mean, how many voices join and shape them, and how, as Hamlet probably should have said, for a brief time they break the silence before it becomes unbreakable.

18 The Longest Summer

Now where was I before I so rudely interrupted myself?

Oh, yes: summer, work, and what happened next.

For one thing, working is, truly, a drag, man. Y'unnerstand what I mean?

Imagine me a working man, like a used-car salesman or employment agent or a baseball coach (an especially funny one, don't you think?). I spent almost all of the summer after my senior year of high school tossing pizzas at Mama Sicily's Pizzeria in Harmon Falls under the watchful eye of Alfonzo Zamboni. He doesn't look as good as his sister, but I must admit he taught me a lot about how to run a business, how to make a pizza, and how to treat people.

Alfonzo teased me a lot, but then he teased everybody who worked for him and anyone else who'd listen. "Hey, Baseball (he always called me that), why can't you toss a pizza as well as you toss a baseball? Nobody's gonna believe you're Italian; you're gonna ruin my business. I don't know why I keep you here. Hey, you gonna be a college boy and you can't remember the olive oil goes before the sauce on the *Delux*? You even know what *delux* means? Look, we're talkin' meatballs here, not your balls, so don't squeeze 'em so tight: be gentle." But during all this talk he was either counting receipts, or washing counters, or cutting vegetables, or making change for someone, or checking inventory. The man was good at what he did, and he did it even though his family had money, and if you don't think making good pizza is a service to humanity, you've never eaten at Mama Sicily's Pizzeria in Harmon Falls. It may be the one establishment in this town that you couldn't duplicate anywhere else—and yes, I know the world has millions of pizzerias.

Alfonzo kept us hopping. He worked hard himself, and he held the opinion that while we were at work on his clock, we'd better use every minute to make a better pizza or a happier customer. He knew everyone in town by name and knew their voices on the phone when they'd call in orders. He knew what they'd order, or he'd tell them the night's special and talk them into it. He'd tell them jokes, just the right kind for each customer, dirty jokes for the high school boys, gentle humor for the old folks—or was it the other way around? When people came in that he didn't know, he'd introduce himself, and if they were visiting town, he'd welcome them and tell them to come again. He kept his place spotless, and he used the freshest food he could get: he wanted everyone to know that at Mama Sicily's place, they would get the best food they could get anywhere and that he would never let them down. And he'd wash his hands right in front of them and always say "God bless" when they left, to reassure them that he held cleanliness second only to godliness.

And on our breaks, he'd let us eat—up to a point. He knew how high school kids can eat, so he kept us to a half pizza each. But it was the same great stuff the customers got. He knew that one day we wouldn't be employees, but customers like everyone else.

But he knew his business, too. Not too many products, all products that sold regularly, and absolutely no credit: cash on the line, no credit, checks from folks he knew only. No lost stock, no unaccounted-for receipts, no discrepancies in the books, or heads rolled, and I don't mean lettuce.

Though in later years he gave in to credit cards like everyone else.

I had to run every night after work so I didn't end up the summer as round and happy as Alfonzo Zamboni. And I saved money like a Scrooge.

But one night he just about scared me to death. I was spinning dough, pitching it high, catching it, pitching it again to perfect size and thickness, just as he'd taught me, and Alfonzo was sitting next to me with a three-inch high vegetable knife turning green peppers into tablets, when all of a sudden he asked me:

"Hey Baseball, you ever screw my sister?"

I swear I nearly fainted.

I thought, say your prayers, JES, cause you're a dead man for sure.

"Would I do that to you, boss, after all you've taught me? And she's too nice a girl for that."

"That's what I thought," he said. "But just watch yourself. I know she liked you, and you're a good kid, you work hard, but I love my sister and I want her to be happy, know what I mean?"

"Yes, I do."

He smiled and wiped his knife clean.

I ran an extra three miles that night, even though that didn't get me home till nearly two in the morning.

But working wears you down when you've got baseball and love on your mind. Two games a week makes a bum, not a ballplayer, and I was pining for Angelina—maybe not so much Angelina as what she meant to my imagination. My body was fully awake now, and if I let up on work or workout for a minute, a tree grew in Brooklyn.

All I could do was spend afternoons at the pool, hide behind mirror sunglasses, watch the girls, and keep myself covered with a towel. But I was getting too old for that, and most of the kids at the pool were starting to look awfully young.

Sometimes you're better off staying a kid.

And even worse, I was missing my old walks with Lana. I was dying just to talk with her. I never knew what she was going to say, and I liked that. But I didn't dare even go around. It had been a month since I'd talked with Lenny at all, and he never came by to see me anymore, even though in the old days we'd see each other almost every day. He didn't even come to Mama Sicily's since I'd been working there, though he called in an order sometimes. And the last time I had gone to their house, their mother had stared at me like I was a dangerous space alien come to steal her children for dastardly experiments.

By the way, I had also been watching trashy sci-fi flicks on late-late night TV

Summer rolls by like the endless cycle of an old rock song you can't quite remember, playing over and over in the back of your mind. By mid-July I had saved some money, but I hadn't told anyone but Ma that I was for sure going to Maldon. I was getting in a few baseball games, playing for one of the old coal-mine teams, but my mind wasn't in them, so I was hitting worse than I had since my freshman year. Even my legs felt tired, so I wasn't stealing bases our scoring a lot of runs. Mr. Socco, my coach, didn't seem happy with my play, and he was usually pretty forgiving. He dropped me to sixth in the batting order. Fortunately, we did have a good team and were winning despite me. After good service the white shoes were losing their luster. They weren't even white anymore, more brown and gray with a few off-ivory spots here and there, tearing at the edges.

You can't be old at eighteen, can you?

I kept working six nights a week, as many hours as I could. I had been running at night because cars were few, the air felt cleaner and cooler, and no one was around to ask me about my future—or my present. I loved running the empty streets, jumping parking meters, scaling the hills, dodging trees, watching the barges wander downriver in their streaks of light. I hardly saw my mother even because she worked days and went to bed early. Now that Mutch Humbugh had gone off the air in a flood of disdain and she didn't have anyone on late-night TV to grump at anymore, she'd fall asleep watching Johnny Carson. I was spending my whole summer alone.

Yeah, there were the guys at the pizza shop and the customers, but I mostly worked alone in the kitchen. I had weekend baseball games, but it was a hot summer and few people were coming to the games, and the other players, mostly much older than I was, didn't talk to me much. And when I wasn't hitting, even Stud's "Om" didn't help. After one game I even heard some fans mumbling, "So he's supposed to be an all-stater?" Afternoons at the pool I'd swim some, when the little kids weren't there, but that only made me feel more tired yet. I wasn't a good swimmer: I've always sunk like a brick.

At first being lonely was kind of comforting. I had a life to put behind me. But after a while every day got to be a grind, because my new life hadn't kicked into place yet. One Friday night after work we had a light rain, so I decided to go to bed right after work and get up early in the morning to run. When the alarm went off, gray light crept in between the blinds, and I thought of what a stupid idea it was to get up early for this. When I sloughed out of the sheets, my body felt dull and heavy and begged me to squeeze back into the old skin of my bed, but I needed to do something to shake up my schedule just to feel alive again.

Outside, morning was just turning yellow and bees were bobbing softly from flower to flower. I felt like I was stretching rusty cables instead of tendons, so I just gave in and started at a slow jog. After a few easy blocks, my brain and muscles started to unclog a bit, and I looked around. Fat robins were pulling at dewy grass, boys on bikes were delivering morning papers, and eighteen wheelers were beginning to rumble by on the distant highway. At least someone was feeling younger than I was.

How do people work at a job for forty years?

I turned the corner of Pine Street, and there, a block ahead of me, was Lana, out for her morning run. Of course she was. I don't know why I didn't think of that before. I'll just catch up and run with her for a while, I thought.

But catching up wasn't that easy.

Lana had been running pretty hard for months, and her long legs fell into a naturally easy stride. I short-cut one corner, picked up the pace, crossed a lawn, and diagonalled up to her in about a quarter mile.

"Morning. Want some company?"

"Why not? When did you become a morning runner?"

"When I heard some unidentified girl was out burning up the streets at seven a.m."

"So you've been working at Mama Sicily's all summer. Do you like it?"

"It's money. Hasn't done much for my batting average. I've seen you afternoons at the library."

"Yeah, same old thing. At least it's air-conditioned. I don't get to swim much anymore, though, so I've been pretty faithful with my running."

"So I see. How can you run this fast in the morning? My body isn't even awake yet."

"Too quick for you, huh? That's because you work till midnight. I'm usually done by six or seven even when I work ten-hour days, and if I run early I don't have to sit through breakfast with Mom and Lenny. "

"That bad, huh?"

She didn't answer. We ran in silence, other than my puffing, for a while. A change of schedule can really foul up your pace.

"You been lifting a lot? You look bigger."

"A little, mostly when I get up in the morning or the afternoon. I've been running when I get home at night. Gosh: hope it's not the pizza."

"You run after midnight?"

"Sometimes till one or two in the morning."

"I've never tried that. Maybe we could do it together sometime."

The sun was angling down on us now, the air growing ripe with humidity.

"So what are you going to do in the fall? Have you decided yet? Full-time pizza man, maybe?" She sped up a little.

I didn't say anything for a long time. Now we were puffing together in unison, fighting the rising summer heat. I took a chance. "I signed up to go to Maldon College."

She almost stopped but not quite, and didn't quite look at me.

"Maldon College, huh? Big baseball place?"

"Little baseball place."

"I guess Harmon Falls will just have to live on without you, difficult though that may be."

"How about you?"

"What do you mean?"

"What will you do in the fall?"

"Oh, you know, same old thing. What else? Gloria and I might take an evening class at the Branch when I'm not working at the library. Try to get a better job and save money for school."

We stopped at a water fountain in the park by the little league baseball field. Kids were beginning to bounce around the playground like bees. "I suppose somebody in Harmon Falls will miss you when you're gone," Lana said.

"Who's that?" I asked.

"I don't know."

Did you ever get the feeling that people almost never say what they really mean?

"So have you seen the beautiful Angelina this summer?" Lana asked.

"No, not once all summer. I heard from Alberta that she's doing all right, though, vacationing and that kind of stuff."

"Alberta still going with Brian?"

"Yeah, I think so. Actually, I'm not sure."

"But not you and Angelina?"

"We never were going together. We just went out once—a couple of times."

"And I thought you two were an item. Didn't you meet her after graduation? I thought I saw you two together. And she got you a job in her brother's pizza shop. I'm surprised you're not bopping around wearing an Italian flag."

"She was always nice to me, but I don't think she liked me all that much. And I don't think she really *got* me the job: she let me know that her brother needed somebody. Though who knows. I don't really think about her much."

"That's not what your eyes said at the Homecoming Dance."

"That was a long time ago. Besides, you looked pretty busy at that Homecoming Dance yourself."

"Hmph. So just how nice was Angelina to you?"

"What does that mean?"

All during this conversation we were sitting under some trees, the big ones that lined the baseball field, inching closer to each other, even though we were sweating like pigs. I had the sudden feeling that however cool she always was, Lana might feel just as lonely as I did. We stretched out on the grass.

"So you and the lovely A. Z.: did you make it with her?"

By now I am lying on my back in the grass, Lana's face poised over top of mine. I knew what she wanted me to say. But when she looked straight into me, those honest blue eyes bending into mine intense and probing, then I especially hated to lie.

"Maybe."

"What! You did!" She rolled over on her back and laughed.

I sat up and turned toward her. She rolled up on her knees, and then she hit me in the face. Then she got up and started running across the park.

I almost let her go. Then I got up and raced full speed after her.

I am not slow. But I had to burn, because Lana wasn't slow anymore, either, and I'm no morning runner.

I passed her and turned, stopped directly in front of her, face to face, my shoes squealing in the grass. She took another swing at me, but this time I ducked. She kept running.

Fast on her heels, I caught up to her again, and she fell in the grass gasping and laughing as hard as she could. I dropped down next to her, convinced we were both crazy. The way her hair was bobbing, I couldn't tell whether she was laughing or crying.

"I'm sorry," I said.

"Oh, you are? Why?"

"Not sorry about Angelina. Sorry if what I said hurt you."

"Why should it hurt me?"

"Good question. Why did you run away?"

"Because you told me."

"I didn't tell you anything. You asked."

A few weeks back I had found a silly little rhyme scribbled in pencil in my great-uncle's old college literature book. It was from sixty years ago, probably. Just then it popped into my head:

Praise to the angels of heaven,

E'en praise to the furies of hell,

But damned is the guy who will spoon with a girl

And then go around and tell.

I wondered what spooning was, exactly, and if I was damned.

"You shouldn't have told me." She sighed and lay back in the grass. "When did you do it? Come on: details."

So now was I supposed to tell or not? Yeah, it's definitely easier to remain a kid: you can always get away with telling the truth, and most of the time even if you don't. But a kid wouldn't have made it with Angelina Zamboni and wouldn't be lying in the grass now trying to make sense of life with Lana Simms, trying to come to grips with why it mattered so much to me what Lana thought.

"The night before graduation. She was trying to get over Pervis Easly, and I happened to be handy."

"So you're saying she's a slut and would have made it with anybody she happened to find."

"No, I would never say that. I think she just needed somebody to hang out with."

"And you just happened to be there. Just like for the Homecoming Dance: you just happened to be there. How nice of you."

I wondered why she kept bringing up the Homecoming Dance.

"You think it's that simple, Mr. Fast Willie White Shoes. Like you're just a cucumber she picked up at the grocery. Do you love her?"

"Well, I don't know. Who wouldn't."

"He's in love with Angelina Zamboni," she said, exasperated, and fell back on the grass with her hands over her face.

"I didn't say that."

"You just did!"

"I didn't. I didn't say I was *in love with her*. I might as well be in love with the moon as with Angelina Zamboni, because she will never be in love with me."

"That's not a good reason."

"I kind of love her because she's nice to me, and beautiful, and because she's herself, and because: you know. But I love other people, too. I love..."

"Who? Who else have you done it with, you shithead?"

"Lana, that's not fair."

"Who else?"

"I didn't do it with anyone else. Maybe I didn't even do it with her."

"Yeah, right."

"Well don't expect everybody to be like you, miss perfect and virginal. I didn't seduce her. Sometimes things just happen, like a breeze blowing in your window."

"What makes you think I'm a virgin?"

At that I damn near fell over.

"That's right, old Fast Willie Bonehead."

"Will you stop that with the names? Look: so you've... done it?"

"That's right. You're not the only one to give in."

"Who...?" I started, and then felt like I shouldn't ask.

She looked me straight in the eye. With anger. "Harry Kuschner. After the Homecoming Dance. In his car. It was wonderful." She got up to leave.

"I can't believe you did it with Harry Kuschner." I said that to myself rather than to Lana. I remembered the way he almost ignored her at the dance. And then she went out and did it with him.

"Believe it or not, I don't care, as if it's your business."

"Lana, don't go yet."

"I have to. I'll be late for work."

"Lana, wait. I'm sorry I asked. I had no right."

"I'm not sorry. At least now I've said it to somebody."

Harry Kuschner of all people. Why couldn't it have been someone else? What did she see in him? Music? Romance? I hoped not drugs.

She started to run home. I fell in beside her, stride for stride. I noticed a wet spot on her cheek that wasn't from sweat.

"I lied," she said.

"About Harry?"

"No, not about Harry. It wasn't wonderful. It was terrible." She started crying, harder and harder, but she kept running. "I don't know why I did it. Maybe I figured you were doing it with Angelina Zamboni, so why not. I wanted to know what it was like, and everybody said Harry knew what he was doing. He didn't do anything for me. I'm not even sure that he cared it was me, or even that he knew, he had drunk so much by then. Oh, shit."

We ran home by the loneliest streets we could find, but we couldn't help bringing stares from people as we passed. We ran like mad people, but stride for stride.

When we got near Lana's house, I said, "Please, wait: come with me for a minute."

"What do you want?"

I took her by the hand and led her to a small wood just beyond her street.

"I'm not going in there with you."

"Just for a minute. I want to tell you something where people won't watch us and listen. Come on. Listen. Here's what I want to say: don't feel bad about it, about what happened."

She tried to wrench away from me and almost fell down. We sat down on the ground together.

"Listen: we all do things, but you don't have anything to feel bad about. I want you not to feel bad about it."

"Easy for you to say. I feel like shit. Oh, I'm not as mad at you as I am sick of myself. But I'm mad at you, too."

"So we've both maybe done it. It's just too bad we didn't do it together and then we could feel bad about it together instead of on our own."

That really caught her by surprise. She couldn't say anything. We just sat together for a while. Only sitting there looking into her sad, uncovered eyes did I bring to conscious thought how beautiful Lana was and that I really did love her, too.

Was I *in love* with her, or did I just *love her*?

"If you felt that way, why didn't you ask me to the dance?"

"How could I have explained that to Lenny?"

"Oh, come on! Are you afraid of Lenny?"

"Lenny is my friend. I didn't want to betray him. You don't hit on your friend's sister. It's part of the code."

"You can do better than that."

"It's hard to explain. I always got the feeling that you were off limits, like, you were smarter and better than me."

"I saw you looking at me. More than once."

"Sorry."

"I have to get to work."

"I know. Let's go. I just had to tell you. I know you feel bad, and I just want you to know I feel the same about you as I always did."

"It's o.k. for guys to do it, but a girl does it and she becomes a tramp. It's not fair. But that's the way people take it."

"Lana: it's o.k. We have our secret. And Harry probably doesn't even remember."

"Thanks a lot."

"I didn't mean it that way." Sometimes I'm such a bonehead.

As we stumbled out into the street, before I knew what I was doing,

I had taken Lana's hand again, and when she turned around, I kissed her. She didn't say anything. I couldn't say anything. We jogged back to her house part smiling, almost crying, silent as two apples growing next to each other on a tree.

It wasn't a great kiss: too fast, sweaty, not quite on target. But I felt an enormous relief.

I left Lana at her house, then went home and lifted weights for two hours. My head was spinning, and not just from the workout.

I worked at Mama Sicily's into the first week of August. One night Brian Schwartz and Phil Johnson stopped in for a pizza and told me there were going to take that weekend and drive to the beach. Jim couldn't go, but I could still go with them if I wanted. I said maybe. Thursday night before the weekend they'd set, it started to rain, and the weather report said it would rain all weekend. That meant no baseball games. I told Alfonzo that something had come up: I had to quit a week early. He didn't look happy, but he said, "Well, you've been a good worker, but I'll replace you." By Friday afternoon we were on our way to the beach, two rich kids (as rich as they get in Harmon Falls) and one hanger-on with two weeks to figure himself out before leaving his home town for the first significant adventure of his life.

Before we left, I had Brian stop his Camaro in front of the library. I ran through the rain in to see Lana. I found her reshelving books.

"Lana."

"Willie."

"I just wanted to tell you. I'm going to the beach for a couple of days with Brian Schwartz and Phil Johnson. I'll be back. And I'll be thinking of you."

"Me and about a thousand beach bunnies."

"You. Trust me."

"Sure. I need some time to think, anyway."

"See you."

"See you."

We drove for three hours before we cleared the clouds and pushed blue skies in front of us. When we got there, to save money, we got a hotel room with two beds: Brian and Phil took one each, and I slept on some couch cushions on the floor. They didn't ask me to pay much. And, even if only for a very short time, the beach would be mine. We had got there in pitch dark just in time to follow the one bright light near our hotel to an open-late ice cream shop and have a cold drink under a cabana. There were three girls at the counter sipping drinks from straws, and the six of us spent about a half an hour smiling and nodding and waving back and forth. When they left, Brian and Phil insisted we follow them, and we did: straight back to our hotel. They beat us to the elevator and had disappeared before we could climb the steps into their hallway. Brian said we should file them away for the morning, since we were too tired from traveling to do any sleuthing that late. I didn't ask either one of them about their steady girlfriends.

In the morning we slept later than we had hoped, but went right for the beach without breakfast. You can eat anytime. You can body-surf only at the ocean. Brian and Phil looked for the three girls from the night before. Frankly, I was thinking about Lana and couldn't wait to get away from other people.

I walked and ran on the beach all afternoon. The breakers crowded in like fans flooding a stadium. Gulls cried and guffawed above the surf. There's nothing like a long run on the beach to clear your head.

When I got back, Brian and Phil were sitting on the beach in front of our hotel with the three girls from the night before: the statuesque blond with Phil, the trim brunette with Brian, and the spunky but cerebral looking redhead apparently waiting for me.

Now I'm not good at this sort of thing, chatting up girls I don't know and partying on the beach, but the others had things well in hand before I got there, so I just sort of hung out and listened to their banter slick as a grounder in a shortstop's glove.

"And here's number three," Phil said.

"No, I'm number ten. That's my number."

"So you think you're a ten, huh?" the readhead asked.

"Better than being number one or number two." I'm usually not that quick.

"Numbers one and two look pretty happy right now. How about you?"

"I'm sure I'll get by, and then some."

"Will's a baseball player, all-state," Brian said.

"Oh, into leather, huh?" The redhead was much quicker than I am.

You get the idea. Those things go on until somebody can't think of something brilliant to say, and you just hope that you're not the last one to get nailed with a joke, cause then you spend the rest of the day feeling like a dope and acting kinda surly. Eventually we got tired of talking, and we all went for a swim.

That evening the six of us ate supper at a taco stand and went dancing at a disco. As I've told you, I'm an outstanding dancer, Fred Astaire and Michael Jackson rolled into one, but luckily I got by without too much dancing, because Janine, that was the redhead, mostly just wanted to sit and drink beer and talk. Fortunately, for me that meant drinking water and listening and not needing to talk. No more beer for this boy.

I've learned how to be brilliant when I listen. I peer into the speaker's eyes and nod wisely, make sympathetic sounds. It's only when I have to say much that I get into trouble.

But Janine went on and on. I heard Lisa, that was the blond, mumble to Phil that Janine had been droning for the whole trip about the boyfriend she'd just split up with. And Brian and Julie were dancing away and having a good old time. I guess Brian and Alberta had split, figuring they were going off to different colleges and different futures. Nobody entirely survives graduation, even the rich kids.

Pretty soon Phil and Lisa disappeared, and in a little while Brian leaned over and told me that he and Julie were going for a walk. I listened to Janine for a little while longer and suggested that we also get out of the heat of the disco and walk on the beach.

Nothing feels quite like wet sand squishing between your toes, and if you want to get an idea of what nothing looks like, gaze out into the darkness that gloves the beach on a starless night. It looks like, if you stepped out into the water, you'd sink into something deeper than earth, deeper than the sky, deeper than sleep, and you might yell and yell but no one would ever hear you again. You might swim off the edge of the earth and tumble someplace where not even dreams come from.

Janine and I walked far north, beyond the public beach, where no boardwalk lights broke the darkness. Blowing clouds blanketed the sky like a tide. A few raindrops fell, but we kept walking. Awhile back she had begun to talk about her boyfriend again, or ex-boyfriend, I wasn't sure which. She still went on and on.

"What about you?" said Janine finally, and scared me near to death: she had actually asked me a question and might want an answer.

"What about me what?"

"Are you here to get over a love affair, too?"

"I wouldn't call it that, exactly."

"What would you call it, exactly."

I felt a little uncomfortably talking about love with someone I hardly new. "Well, I don't know what to call it exactly."

"You're not gay, are you?"

"No!—why would you ask that?"

"It's hard to tell these days, even with a macho type like you."

"Am I a macho type?"

"Yeah, I'd say so. A little rednecky, too, maybe."

"Compliments flow from your lips." She laughed at that. "So, was he, or are *you*?" I asked.

"What?"

"Gay. Is that what went wrong?"

She laughed at that, too. "No," she said, "but I might as well be, with the way my boyfriend has been treating me lately. Or had been, till we split up. He didn't want to talk, didn't want to, you know, touch. Didn't want to anything."

I could see how he might get tired of listening sometimes, but, frankly, Janine seemed like a nice enough girl, and she was kinda good looking, the kind that grows on you, and finally makes you grow up a little, because despite all the talk you actually like her. She had the kind of look in her eyes that said, "If you'd just say the right thing, and hear what I'm saying to you, I'd be yours mind and body." And neither looked to be an especially bad deal. Though funny thing: after I'd float away, every time I'd come back, I'd get this wishful startle that I was walking with Lana instead of Janine. And that was what I really wanted. I tried not to let on.

She had been talking again. "I get the feeling you got it bad for somebody. Is that right? What's her name?"

"I'm not sure if I do or not. She's the sister of the guy who's been my best friend since grade school."

"So what?"

"Well, it just doesn't seem right."

"You ever kiss her?"

"Once."

"Did that seem right?"

"I'm not sure. I need to try again. So what about you and Albert?"

"Allen!"

"Sorry."

"Sex was really good when we first met at college, but then we kind of lost our spark, and he started watching every girl that went by. I notice you don't do that. That's why I thought you might be gay."

College, huh. "I guess I'm just thinking about Lana."

"That's her name, Lana. Nice name. But you've never done it with her?"

"No!"

She laughed again. "What college do you guys go to?"

"None yet. We just graduated from high school."

"No kidding? Probably still a virgin. Well, kid, you've got a lot to learn."

The rain picked up, so we started back and slid under the first cabana we could find. Janine talked more about Albert for a while as we sat close together under the broad umbrella. The drops pattered on it like steady applause.

"But I do get really lonely, even though for some strange reason I still love him," she said. "Guess I just don't get over these things as easily as some people do."

She was quiet for a minute and looked at my eyes with a little smile crossing her lips. "So, you want to do the deed, or what?"

"What deed?"

She laughed. She had a pleasant, musical laugh. "You know, silly, *that*." She rubbed her bare foot along my calf.

I wasn't expecting that. Lightning rolled up my spine and down again, and despite myself I felt my shorts tightening. Here I was on the beach in the dark, all alone, rain falling and the surf thundering, with a girl who was suddenly sexier than I had realized, probably knew what she was doing, and who was apparently willing. She looked right into my eyes.

Call me stupid. Call me a wimp. I couldn't do it.

I reached out and took her hand. She slid lithely toward me.

"I can't. I'm sorry."

"What's wrong? You sick? Old baseball injury?" She leaned closer so that I could feel her leg against mine, and I did the hardest thing I have ever done.

"No injury. Everything works as far as I know. But I just can't do it. It doesn't seem right. You're really beautiful, but I just met you, and whatever we did, I'd be thinking about Lana, and that's not fair. That's the absolute truth, though God knows I feel clogged up to my eyeballs."

She laughed, kept rubbing my leg with her foot.

"I'm sorry. I really am. It just doesn't feel like the right thing to do."

She laughed again: I was kinda getting used to hearing that laugh, and I liked it. She backed away, and told me it was all right. We talked for a long time, having a good time moaning to each other about lost loves without touching again at all.

The next day I met her outside the hotel and apologized.

"That's o.k., really," she said. "I understand. Actually, it's really sweet, just talking. I wish Allen had been like that sometimes. Something besides hormones and appetites."

We got iced teas and talked for a while.

We talked about all sorts of things: the world, life, books, even, yes, baseball. She actually listened. And so did I. When we got back to the hotel, she kissed me softly on the lips. My pants bulged instinctively. I must have blushed, too. "Ha. At least I'm not a total failure at arousing a man," she said.

"Far from it."

When I got to my room, the door was locked, and I didn't have I key. I knocked softly: no response. With my ear to the door, I could hear cooing noises coming from inside: either Brian or Phil and one of the girls. Nothing to do but go back to the lobby and wait, since it had begun to rain, too hard to walk outside. I sat and read hotel and local-attraction pamphlets and watched the rain.

About an hour later Brian came in with his new companion. They said good-bye at the elevator, but didn't kiss. Brian came over to me and sat down with a deep sigh. "Nice girl," he said. "College freshman. Goes to school far away, though. Got her phone number, but heck of a lot of good it will do me. Maybe I can transfer after a year, if Alberta and I don't get back together. Hey, why are you here in the lobby?"

I told him about the room.

"Oh. We'll, we'd have to root Phil out sooner or later, so it might as well be now."

Phil wasn't too happy to be interrupted. Lisa, hiding in a sheet, just giggled, got dressed, and disappeared quickly down the hall.

That night I dreamed that I was walking on the beach with Lana, and we sat down under a cabana, and a huge wave, a hundred feet high, rolled in and engulfed us. We were swimming for our lives. I woke up with my head spinning.

That morning all Phil could do was tell us over and over what a babe Lisa was. And I can't blame him. She looked great draped in a sheet, that's for sure. "Man, I think we must have done it three or four times."

"Any protection?" Brian asked.

"Don't spoil it," Phil answered.

"How about you guys?" Phil asked. "Get any?"

"I tried, but she's really got class. Said we should get to know each other better first," Brian replied. "I really like her." Then they both looked at me, so I had to say something.

"Naw, I kinda got someone else on my mind. We talked, though, and took a walk way up north past the lights. It was nice."

"Slow Willie White Shoes," said Phil, I couldn't tell whether out of disdain for me or disappointment for a good story lost.

We met the girls for breakfast. The rain continued, so the beach was off, but we sat and talked for a long time. Phil and Lisa were practically in each other's laps, Brian and Julie talked quietly, and Janine and I told each other all the jokes we knew. She knew more than I did. The girl had a great memory for jokes considering she was still suffering from a break-up.

"What did the musical mama cotton bug say to the baby cotton bug who couldn't learn his letters? You got to change your weevil A's, baby."

"What happened when *Newsweek* and *Playboy* merged? *U.S Nudes and World Report.*"

"Is a baby from Warsaw a tad-Pole?"

You get the idea. Pretty bad. Be glad you missed it. But I laughed anyway.

Before noon we said our good-byes. The rain had calmed just a bit, so I made one more stop on the shore, to get the sound of the waves planted in my brain like rows of corn. I couple of laughing gulls swung close hoping for food, but just got a laugh instead: "ha-ha-ha-ha-ha-ha." The waves tumbled and crushed. And then the waves spoke. One word: "Lana."

The ocean voice sounded like the voice of the river, but a little deeper and more hurried. More people to talk to, I suppose. No matter: I got what I'd came for, and a little more.

The same storm that had blown us to the beach had turned around to blow us home. Phil groaned the whole way home about feeling lonesome for Lisa, and Brian talked about how he'd like to find some way to move closer to Julie if he didn't get back with Alberta. I was thinking about what I was going to say to Lana. I didn't know what, but I badly wanted to say something, and I wanted it to be the right thing.

We got home late Sunday night. We had left the rain petering out about two hours behind. I slept late and dreamed hard.

Late Monday morning the ground was still wet, but the sun came up hot. The legion team was supposed to play at Bellview in the afternoon if the field was dry enough, so I loosened up, did some light lifting, and set off walking. I stopped at the library, but Lana had taken the afternoon off. I got to the ballpark about half an hour before game time, too late for batting practice but soon enough to get my arm loose. The field was still damp, with a puddle here and there, but when the season is almost over, you get in every game you can, and this was the last one before the postseason tournament.

Mr. Socco didn't look so happy to see me. "I'm not sure we can get you in, Will. Usually you're only here for weekend games, and the other guys have been faithful and are used to playing." That was partly a way of chiding me for not being more dedicated, partly a way of saying I hadn't been hitting that well, anyway. A baseball coach will play even a troublemaker as long as he hits.

"I don't know, coach," said Ropes. "My arm's a little sore to play center today. You could put me in right, since these guys all pull the ball, and put Johnny at third, since Tiny can't be here today. I have a feeling Willie's gonna blast one today." Either Ropes was becoming a young me or he had just done me a big favor. I really needed to play; I'm not sure I could have stood sitting on the bench and watching the other guys play baseball without me.

"Well, all right, but he better hit something," said Mr. Socco. A team is a team and should play together, college tuition or not."

"We do," said Ropes. I nodded my thanks. "Go rip one, Will. Show 'em you still got it," he whispered to me.

Imagine that: *still.*

Mr. Socco put me in centerfield, fifth in the batting order.

When you've played a baseball for a while, you can almost smell a tide turning. Baseball has, for all its permanence, its own particular currents, its own ebbs and floods. I felt mine changing, my hitting ready to flood.

Even after travel and no b.p., for some reason my legs felt strong and my arms felt fast.

But with two on and two out in the first, I ended the inning by flying out deep to center. I damn near got it, but hit just a little underneath it. In the fourth I made an over-the-shoulder catch in center to save I run, but flied out again at the plate. Mr. Socco wouldn't even talk to me. I think he would have pulled me out of the game if he had someone to substitute, but he had replaced our starting pitcher, who came up with a sore arm in the second, double-switched with Ropes, and his bench was empty. In the fifth we rallied. I came up with one out, two on, and a run already in. On a 2-2 pitch I got a ball I could hit, down and in, thigh-high inside corner, and I turned on it, hit it as cleanly as I had hit a ball in quite a while, right on the sweet spot. It didn't rise much, stayed low on a line, but it carried and carried down into left, hooking. It crossed the fence just inside the foul pole and kept flying on into the thick grass beyond. A three-run homer: not a long one, but one I needed very badly, just to convince me I could still hit a baseball. It should have come sooner.

The home run put us in the lead, and we won going away. I got a sacrifice fly in my last at-bat, just short of another homer, and we won 10-5. Ropes came up to me after the game: "I had a feeling about you today," he said. "I knew you had one in you. Welcome back."

My batting average still wasn't much for the summer, but I felt as though I'd found the key to a door that had been shut in my face for a long time. Mr. Socco and his son even gave me a ride home.

When I got home, Ma told me that Mrs. Pasquale had called about a painting job she needed done: her *whole house*. It was a small house, just small enough that I might have time to get it done, make a few bucks, and not miss any baseball games for the rest of the summer. It looked like my ticket to Maldon was finally paid, at least for one year.

I washed and ate, called Mrs. Pasquale and told her I'd start the next morning, and went for walk. I knew where I wanted to go, but I walked many blocks, circling and circling, before I got there. When I did it was pitch dark, and I didn't know what I was going to do or say anyway.

One thing made it easier.

Lana was sitting on the front steps of her house.

Just as though she was waiting for me.

"Welcome back," she said.

"Good to be back," I said.

"Have fun with your beach bunnies?"

"Not so much. I was thinking about you."

"Prove it."

"Want to go for a walk?"

She stood, and we set off up the street. Her hand slipped into mine. I held it tight.

We walked and talked until the stars had nearly fallen asleep in the sky.

When I walked her back home, I asked if she would come to our next game. It was at home, at our old high school field on top of the hill.

"I'd love to," she said.

I didn't quite believe that. The little smile said, *Aw, ok*, not *I'd love to*. "Six-thirty," I said anyway, quickly, before she changed her mind.

"If enough guys don't show up, can I play right field?"

"You bet."

"Will: hit a home run for me."

As I began to go, a thought stopped me and I turned: "Lana, you ever thought of going to Maldon College?"

She stepped toward me and kissed me, my first real kiss from someone I loved and to someone I loved. It felt like pillows and roses and muffins and the first day of spring sunshine, like for an instant the world was real and perfect, and I'll never forget it, and I mean *never*. And I don't know if I'll ever have a better one.

* * *

So now it's the next day. I've just scraped off layers of paint from my arms and legs, and I'm getting ready to go to the game. I feel a four-for-four day ahead. This morning I got up and practiced my swing for half an hour, and I can feel it returning, coming back with a smooth ease and power that I haven't felt all summer. Outside in the backyard I stretch and test the wind: it will be blowing out to straight-away center tonight. The sky is clear, and the ground is drying nicely. I resist an impulse to call Lana; I think of her and my heart beats fast as feet circling the bases. I feel more confident, more myself than I have ever felt, maybe. I stretch.

As I get my gear to go, Ma pokes her head out the window: "Good luck, Will. I have a feeling about this game tonight. A homer, I think."

"How about two?"

"Two is fine. Hit one for me."

"I will." And one for Lana. Or maybe she'll play right field and hit one for me.

Gear in hand, I set off at a jog for the hill and the ballpark. Lana will be there! The white shoes, torn and aging, will be flying, maybe for one last time.

Maybe I will get new ones. Finnegan is pitching for us today. I haven't told you about him—he's another story—but he gives up a lot of flyballs, which, with me in centerfield, is not a great problem for him but will keep me from singing too much. I think I will be batting lead-off.

Some things have changed since we first began to talk. I have grown up, at least a little, though I make no claim to be a man yet. We have both got older. I am in love. I hope you're in love. Baseball is still a great game, and it always will be, regardless of idiocies like steroids, which have nothing to do with you (I hope) or me. Life, when it isn't stupid or tragic, is still a silly game, or worse, and it always will be.

I'm on foot, light-hearted, and heading for the game. I still like to run up the hill before we play baseball. It doesn't do much for my hitting, but it gets my legs pumped up for the game. Hey, I think I see Lana up ahead, and she's waving.

End

OTHER
ANAPHORA LITERARY
PRESS TITLES

PLJ: Interviews with Gene Ambaum and Corban Addison: VII:3, Fall 2015
Editor: Anna Faktorovich

Architecture of Being
By: Bruce Colbert

The Encyclopedic Philosophy of Michel Serres
By: Keith Moser

Forever Gentleman
By: Roland Colton

Janet Yellen
By: Marie Bussing-Burks

Diseases, Disorders, and Diagnoses of Historical Individuals
By: William J. Maloney

Armageddon at Maidan
By: Vasyl Baziv

Vovochka
By: Alexander J. Motyl